A More
Perfect Union

What Reviewers Say About Carsen Taite's Work

It Should be a Crime

"Law professor Morgan Bradley and her student Parker Casey are potential love interests, but throw in a high-profile murder trial, and you've got an entertaining book that can be read in one sitting. Taite also practices criminal law and she weaves her insider knowledge of the criminal justice system into the love story seamlessly and with excellent timing. I find romances lacking when the characters change completely upon falling in love, but this was not the case here. I look forward to reading more from Taite."—*Curve Magazine*

"This [*It Should be a Crime*] is just Taite's second novel...but it's as if she has bookshelves full of bestsellers under her belt."—*Gay List Daily*

"Taite, a criminal defense attorney herself, has given her readers a behind the scenes look at what goes on during the days before a trial. Her descriptions of lawyer/client talks, investigations, police procedures, etc. are fascinating. Taite keeps the action moving, her characters clear, and never allows her story to get bogged down in paperwork. *It Should be a Crime* has a fast-moving plot and some extraordinarily hot sex."—*Just About Write*

Do Not Disturb

"Taite's tale of sexual tension is entertaining in itself, but a number of secondary characters...add substantial color to romantic inevitability"—Richard Labonte, *Book Marks*

Nothing but the Truth

"Author Taite is really a Dallas defense attorney herself, and it's obvious her viewpoint adds considerable realism to her story, making it especially riveting as a mystery. I give it four stars out of five."—Bob Lind, *Echo Magazine*

"As a criminal defense attorney in Dallas, Texas, Carsen Taite knows her way around the court house. This ability shows in her writing, as her legal dramas take the reader into backroom negotiations between the opposing lawyers, as well as into meetings with judges. Watching how Carsen Taite brings together all of the loose ends is enjoyable, as is her skillful building of the characters of Ryan and Brett. *Nothing But the Truth* is an enjoyable mystery with some hot romance thrown in."—*Just About Write*

"Taite has written an excellent courtroom drama with two interesting women leading the cast of characters. Taite herself is a practicing defense attorney, and her courtroom scenes are clearly based on real knowledge. This should be another winner for Taite."—*Lambda Literary*

The Best Defense

"Real life defense attorney Carsen Taite polishes her fifth work of lesbian fiction, *The Best Defense*, with the realism she daily encounters in the office and in the courts. And that polish is something that makes *The Best Defense* shine as an excellent read."—*Out & About Newspaper*

Slingshot

"The mean streets of lesbian literature finally have the hard boiled bounty hunter they deserve. It's a slingshot of a ride, bad guys and hot women rolled into one page turning package. I'm looking forward to Luca Bennett's next adventure."—J. M. Redmann, author of the Micky Knight mystery series

Beyond Innocence

"Taite keeps you guessing with delicious delay until the very last minute…Taite's time in the courtroom lends *Beyond Innocence* a terrific verisimilitude someone not in the profession couldn't impart. And damned if she doesn't make practicing law interesting."—*Out in Print*

"As you would expect, sparks and legal writs fly. What I liked about this book were the shades of grey (no, not the smutty Shades of Grey)—both in the relationship as well as the cases."—*C-spot Reviews*

Battle Axe

"This second book is satisfying, substantial, and slick. Plus, it has heart and love coupled with Luca's array of weapons and a badass verbal repertoire… I cannot imagine anyone not having a great time riding shotgun through all of Luca's escapades. I recommend hopping on Luca's band wagon and having a blast."—*Rainbow Book Reviews*

"Taite breathes life into her characters with elemental finesse… A great read, told in the vein of a good old detective-type novel filled with criminal elements, thugs, and mobsters that will entertain and amuse."—*Lambda Literary*

Rush

"A simply beautiful interplay of police procedural magic, murder, FBI presence, misguided protective cover-ups, and a superheated love affair...a Gold Star from me and major encouragement for all readers to dive right in and consume this story with gusto!"
—*Rainbow Book Reviews*

Switchblade

"I enjoyed the book and it was a fun read—mystery, action, humor, and a bit of romance. Who could ask for more? If you've read and enjoyed Taite's legal novels, you'll like this. If you've read and enjoyed the two other books in this series, this one will definitely satisfy your Luca fix and I highly recommend picking it up. Highly recommended."—*C-spot Reviews*

"Dallas's intrepid female bounty hunter, Luca Bennett, is back in another adventure. Fantastic! Between her many friends and lovers, her interesting family, her fly by the seat of her pants lifestyle, and a whole host of detractors there is rarely a dull moment."—*Rainbow Book Reviews*

Courtship

"The political drama is just top-notch. The emotional and sexual tensions are intertwined with great timing and flair. I truly adored this book from beginning to end. Fantabulous!"—*Rainbow Book Reviews*

"Carsen Taite throws the reader head on into the murky world of the political system where there are no rights or wrongs, just players attempting to broker the best deals regardless of who gets hurt in the process. The book is extremely well written and makes compelling reading. With twist and turns throughout, the reader doesn't know how the story will end."—*Lesbian Reading Room*

Taite keeps the stakes high as two beautiful and brilliant women fueled by professional ambitions face daunting emotional choices... As backroom politics, secrets, betrayals, and threats race to be resolved without political damage to the president, the cat-and-mouse relationship game between Addison and Julia has the reader rooting for them. Taite prolongs the fever-pitch tension to the final pages. This pleasant read with intelligent heroines, snappy dialogue, and political suspense will satisfy Taite's devoted fans and new readers alike."—*Publisher's Weekly*

Lay Down the Law

"Recognized for the pithy realism of her characters and settings drawn from a Texas legal milieu, Taite pays homage to the prime-time soap opera Dallas in pairing a cartel-busting U.S. attorney, Peyton Davis, with a charity-minded oil heiress, Lily Gantry."— *Publishers Weekly*

"Suspenseful, intriguingly tense, and with a great developing love story, this book is delightfully solid on all fronts. This gets my A-1 recommendation!"—*Rainbow Book Reviews*

Reasonable Doubt

"I was drawn into the mystery plot line and quickly became enthralled with the book. It was suspenseful without being too intense but there were some great twists to keep me guessing. It's a very good book. I cannot wait to read the next in line that Ms. Taite has to offer."— *Prism Book Alliance*

Above the Law

"…readers who enjoyed the first installment will find this a worthy second act."—*Publishers Weekly*

"Ms Taite delivered and then some, all the while adding more questions, Tease! I like the mystery and intrigue in this story. It has many "sit on the edge of your seat" scenes of excitement and dread (like watch out kind of thing) and drama…well done indeed!"— *Prism Book Alliance*

Without Justice

"Carsen Taite tells a great story. She is consistent in giving her readers a good if not great legal drama with characters who are insightful, well thought out and have good chemistry. You know when you pick up one of her books you are getting your money's worth time and time again. Consistency with a great legal drama is all but guaranteed."—*The Romantic Reader Blog*

"This is a great read, fast-paced, interesting and takes a slightly different tack from the normal crime/courtroom drama having a lawyer in the witness protection system whose case becomes the hidden centre of another crime."—*Lesbian Reading Room*

Letter of the Law

"Fiery clashes and lots of chemistry, you betcha!"—*The Romantic Reader Blog*

By the Author

Truelesbianlove.com
It Should Be a Crime
Do Not Disturb
Nothing but the Truth
The Best Defense
Beyond Innocence
Rush
Courtship
Reasonable Doubt
Without Justice
Sidebar
A More Perfect Union

The Luca Bennett Mystery Series:
Slingshot
Battle Axe
Switchblade
Bow and Arrow (novella in Girls with Guns)

Lone Star Law Series:
Lay Down the Law
Above the Law
Letter of the Law

A MORE PERFECT UNION

by

Carsen Taite

2017

A MORE PERFECT UNION
© 2017 BY CARSEN TAITE. ALL RIGHTS RESERVED.

ISBN 13: 978-1-62639-754-5

THIS TRADE PAPERBACK ORIGINAL IS PUBLISHED BY
BOLD STROKES BOOKS, INC.
P.O. BOX 249
VALLEY FALLS, NY 12185

FIRST EDITION: DECEMBER 2017

CREDITS
EDITOR: CINDY CRESAP
PRODUCTION DESIGN: SUSAN RAMUNDO
COVER DESIGN BY SHERI (GRAPHICARTIST2020@HOTMAIL.COM)

Acknowledgments

There are things I know a lot about: pizza, breakfast tacos, and the law top the list, but there are plenty of things about which I have very little direct knowledge, but wanted to incorporate into this, my second book set inside the Beltway and the Pentagon. Thank goodness I have lots of amazing friends willing to either serve as experts or hook me up with contacts I could go to for research. The non-exhaustive list includes:

Sgt. Roselle Graskey for all things Army.

Major Mary Buchanan, ANC; Colonel Julie Tizard, USAF; Corporal Jude Dinan, USMC; Staff Sergeant Susan Jacobsen, USA; and General Deborah Shea, USA, for insights into life inside the Pentagon.

Captain Golden Broughton, USAF, for her insights into present life inside the military (and Rachel Wise and my sis, Rachel Tyler, for the intro).

All of these folks generously loaned me their knowledge and expertise—any errors about any of these subjects are entirely my own. Thanks to each of them for their service.

When it comes to the finished product, a whole bunch of other folks make me look good. From Sheri's amazing cover design to the editorial wonder and magical production genius of Cindy Cresap.

A special shout-out to:

Len Barot and Sandy Lowe who make Bold Strokes Books a nurturing home where authors can thrive.

VK Powell for running around DC with me so I could get the logistics right and for her honest and thorough critiques of the manuscript.

Nikki Littles for her help picking out romance-y picnic spots in DC.

Ruth Sternglantz for the perfect title.

Kris Bryant for loaning me a name from her book of names.

Ashley Bartlett for Haiku, friendship, and an extra set of keen editorial eyes.

Once a month, I have the privilege of meeting up with the most amazing group of fiction-loving women. Thanks to the Women with Pride book club for the support you provide to readers and writers alike.

Thanks to my wife, Lainey, who takes care of all the things while I'm holed up in my office writing or traveling to literary events around the country. None of my success would be possible without her.

And to all of my readers—your support fuels my inspiration and daily word counts. Thanks for taking this journey with me.

Dedication

To Lainey and our perfect union.

Chapter One

The 747 pitched and rocked, sending several carry-on bags flying. Some of the passengers cried out while others clutched their armrests, but Zoey merely shook her head and methodically clipped her seat belt in place. The flight attendant in first class urged everyone to remain calm, but when she almost fell forward into the seat in front of her while delivering the admonition, her words did little to calm the passengers.

Zoey turned to her seatmate whose face had taken on a gray tinge. "It's just turbulence. We'll probably be through it soon." He grimaced his reply, and Zoey offered an encouraging smile.

The flight attendant clapped her on the shoulder. "Thanks for the assist, Major. If only everyone had your stomach for rough flying."

Zoey smiled. "This is nothing compared to hitching a ride in a C-17 into Kandahar."

"You're made of tougher stuff than most." She stuck out her hand. "Karen Birch. Thanks for your service."

"My pleasure." The words were rote, but she meant them. Zoey grasped Karen's hand, taking note she held on for a few seconds past casual. When Karen left to take her seat, Zoey relaxed into the cushioned first class seat, as much as possible in her stiff Army blues. It wasn't customary to dress out for commercial flights, but her orders had been clear, and now she was thankful her uniform had garnered the upgrade. The pallor of the guy in the window seat next to her finally returned to normal, and he pulled his laptop from a bag under the seat along with a stack of folders. When he bumped into her arm, he apologized.

"I have a meeting with Senator Barstow as soon as this flight lands," he said. "Better start preparing for it."

Zoey nodded, her thoughts already focused on her own meeting in the hours ahead. She'd been summoned from her base in Texas, but her orders said only to report to General Bloomfield at the Pentagon. She'd known better than to ask for details from her commanding officer. He'd been only too glad to be rid of her after the events of the last few months. Frankly, she'd been relieved to get away from the toxic atmosphere at her base, but feared she might be headed to stormier waters.

Deep in thought, she barely noticed when Mr. Window Seat tapped her shoulder. She turned toward him, and her gaze followed his finger, pointed at the screen of his laptop. "Hey, isn't that you?"

She stared at the official press photo, which reflected a younger looking, more naive version of the soldier she was now, and forced herself to remain calm as she read the caption. *Whistleblower Major Zoey Granger, USA, is scheduled to testify before Congress next week regarding pay to play scandal involving Nine Tech Inc.*

"Yes."

There was more, a lot more. The guy scrolled down the page, gulping in all the information—some fact, some fiction—but all of it life-altering, not only for her, but also for the dozen soldiers who'd been implicated in the scheme along with their civilian cohorts. They were all facing dishonorable discharge, prison, or both, while she'd simply been ostracized and forced to shoulder the weight of choosing between country and her fellow soldiers. The last few months had been hell. She'd been called back to Fort Hood to face her superiors and submit to endless interviews that felt more like interrogations, and now she was being summoned by both the Pentagon brass and the Senate Committee on Armed Services.

She shouldn't be surprised to be recognized, even here at forty thousand feet. Her CO had pointed out, in extremely colorful language, that as a result of her disloyalty, she could expect the spotlight of attention and scrutiny for the rest of her military career, however long that may be. His implication was far from subtle, but she had no intention of seeking a discharge, especially when she'd only been doing her job. The contractors who'd bribed her peers and the soldiers who'd compromised their mission were the ones who should pay, and if she went down with them, then it would have to be because she was forced out. She'd started her career with the end goal of retiring as one of a few female generals. If the Army wanted to kill her dreams, she'd fight them every step of the way.

The turbulence finally abated and the plane settled into a comfortable cruising altitude toward DC. The flight attendant, Karen, who'd been strapped in during the worst of it, walked back down the aisle encouraging passengers to keep their seat belts fastened should the winds kick up again. She stopped by Zoey's seat and bent down close. "Major, may I buy you a drink?"

Zoey recognized the subtle flirtation and shook her head. "Besides, I thought drinks in first class were on the house."

"They are, but I wasn't talking about right now." With the ease of a practiced flirt, Karen slipped a small folded piece of paper into Zoey's seat back pocket. "I'll be in town for a couple of days." She straightened. "I meant what I said earlier. Your service is much appreciated. And thanks for standing up for what's right."

Zoey nodded her response, noting several other passengers had perked up at the attendant's last words and wishing she could melt into the seat. She'd have plenty of attention focused on her over the next few weeks, but right now she craved the peace and solitude of this cross-country flight.

When Karen moved on to check on the remaining first class passengers, Zoey pulled a book from her small carry-on and pretended to read as a way of cutting off questions and conversation, but the attendant's words nagged at her. Standing up for what's right. That was exactly what she'd done, but nothing about the fallout had reinforced her expectation that honor was an act to be rewarded. As the words on the page blurred, her mind drifted to the paper Karen had tucked into the seat back pocket. In what she hoped was a subtle maneuver, Zoey retrieved the paper, and using it as a pseudo bookmark, read the message inviting her for "a drink or whatever." Signed simply Karen, followed by a phone number. She should crumple the paper and dispose of it discreetly, but instead she tucked it into her book. Maybe a drink and "whatever" would be the perfect remedy to the clusterfuck she was about to endure.

❖

Rook Daniels stood in the middle of Reagan National Airport and stared at the screen above her head, willing the information to change. Unfortunately, her superpowers weren't up to the task today. Her flight to New York was delayed, and the airlines hadn't posted a new time. The desk agent had ducked out within seconds of changing the flight status at the gate, and Rook had yet to find anyone who could answer her question about the reason for the delay. The limbo drove her crazy. If the wait was only an hour she'd be fine, but if it was more than that she might be better off abandoning the flight for another form of transportation. She pulled out her cell phone and speed-dialed her office.

"Daniels's Agency, how may I assist you?" The familiar, pleasant voice answered on the first ring.

"Lacy, it's Rook. I made the wrong call booking commercial. The flight's delayed and I can't get an update on the new schedule. Ask Ben to see what he can find out. I need to know ASAP if we need to delay the press conference."

"On it. Anything else?"

"I guess you better start looking for another way to get me to New York. And, Lacy?"

"Yes?"

"Delaying the press conference has to be the last resort. Understood?"

"Got it, boss. I'll be in touch soon."

Rook kept her phone in her hand and maintained her vigilant stalking of the gate, but after a few minutes, decided she needed a distraction or she'd come unhinged. She plowed her way through the milling crowds of passengers swarming the gates and took a seat at the bar where patrons were glued to several television sets broadcasting the NCAA basketball tournament. She wanted a drink but ordered a club soda and lime to keep her head clear, tipping the bartender generously to compensate for taking up a seat for a two-buck beverage. A few minutes in, she got a text from Lacy. *Engine trouble. Looking for another plane. Should know more soon.*

Encouraged by the fact she finally had some information, Rook settled back in her chair. The roar of the crowd in the bar pulled her out of her thoughts, and she looked around to check the source of the commotion and saw the team from UNC celebrating on the big screen. She joined in with the cheers and almost missed the buzz of her phone.

Not looking good. Will have another solution ASAP.

Rook started to type a reply, but another commotion distracted her. This time the noise was coming from outside the bar, and she spotted a small band of cameramen lunging toward a gate agent across the way with shouted questions. Instinct forced her out of her chair, but before she could take a step toward the scene playing out across the way, a hand on her arm stilled her progress.

"Please stay. If you move, they'll spot me for sure."

Rook turned at the sound of the strong, sure voice and locked eyes with a tall, slender woman in a dress blue uniform. She catalogued her findings: Army officer, commissioned. She took note of the gold leaf on her shoulder and added major to the list of things she could file away as knowns. Rook slid back onto the bar stool and motioned for the major to sit next to her. Rook pointed at the disturbance across the way. "Is that about you?"

The major nodded, but her face remained otherwise stoic. Rook took a moment to assess the situation which included running through the list of stories she'd read in the *Post* and *Times* earlier in the day. She didn't recall any news that would have the press barreling through the airport looking for a victim, but maybe this was breaking news. "Is it chase down the military day and I almost missed it?" She stuck out her hand. "Rook Daniels."

A hint of a grin showed in the woman's deep brown eyes, but her expression remained impassive. "Zoey Granger."

Rook made a mental note that Zoey wasn't loose with the pleasantries and took it as a challenge to get her to say more. *Granger, Granger.* She rolled the name over in her mind a few times until the slots fell into place. Major Zoey Granger. US Army. She'd exposed a massive fraud scheme between a group of soldiers and Nine Tech Inc., one of the nation's largest defense contractors. The story had dominated the news on and off for the past few months, and Rook recalled reading yesterday that Granger would be testifying before the Senate Armed Services Committee this week. She started to acknowledge Zoey's act of patriotism, but Zoey's guarded manner prompted her to decide against it. "Nice to meet you, Major," she said, opting for the subtle reference to Zoey's rank to convey her inside knowledge. She jerked her chin at the reporters across the way. "They're going to get restless eventually and start fanning out, especially if they're certain you were on that plane."

"How in the world did they even get past TSA?" Zoey murmured, as if talking to herself.

"Wouldn't be the first time the cable news outlets bought plane tickets to get a scoop. Small price to pay for first crack at a big story." Rook stood. "Come with me."

Zoey's eyes narrowed. "Excuse me?"

"You want to get out of here, right?" Rook reached out a hand. "Trust me. I got this." She cast a look over her shoulder at the gaggle of press who, as she predicted, had started to spread out in search of their prey. Zoey followed her gaze, sighed, and placed her hand in Rook's, following her to the ladies' room. Rook glanced under the stalls and then pulled off her suit jacket. "Here, put this on."

"I can't take your clothes."

Rook grinned. "Well, that's moving a little fast, even for me." She cleared her throat while Zoey glared. "I was only offering my jacket. The other stuff will have to wait until our second date."

"You're hilarious," Zoey said, her tone flat.

"I get that all the time. Now, put it on."

Rook checked her phone. Right on time, Lacy had texted her own escape route. *Get to private terminal. SkyLight Helo standing by. You'll be on time.*

She typed a quick response. *Thx.* She shoved her phone back in her pocket and shook her jacket in Zoey's direction. "Come on. We've got to get moving."

Zoey tugged on the jacket, and Rook admired the way it fit over her uniform. It wasn't a perfect disguise, but it might work. "Now, let down your hair. Literally. Shake it out and we'll be ready to go."

She watched while Zoey looked in the mirror, grimaced, pulled off her beret, and reached a hand up to loosen the pins holding her hair in place. When the auburn waves tumbled down onto Zoey's shoulder, Rook swallowed a gasp. The major was a stunning beauty despite the perpetual frown. "Much better. Now plaster a smile on your face and stay close."

She didn't wait for an answer. A quick peek out the door revealed the path was clear for the moment. She motioned for Zoey to follow her and dashed down the hall, away from the churning crowds arriving and departing at the cluster of gates.

"Where are we going?"

Rook placed a finger against her lips and kept moving. A turn to the right and then left and then they were standing in front of a door that blared Airport Security in big red letters. Rook rapped a hand on the glass, but Zoey started edging away.

"What are you doing?"

Rook ignored the question and waved at the short man who appeared on the other side of the door. He shook his head as if resigned and cracked the door. "Daniels, you're killing me."

"Sorry, Gary. I'd say it's the last time, but..." She raised her shoulders. "If it makes you feel any better, you'd be serving your country with this one." She pointed back toward Zoey. "The major here has an important meeting at the Capitol, but there's a crowd that won't let her through. If you can get us both to the private terminal, I'd owe you big time." While she waited for his answer, she typed a quick text to Lacy.

"I have a big box of your IOUs." He wagged a finger at her. "Watch out. Someday I'm going to cash in. Come on."

He motioned them forward, and Rook glanced back at Zoey who still looked hesitant about forging ahead. Rook could hardly blame her since essentially they were strangers. She'd gotten used to clients following her instructions over the years, especially since she made strict adherence to her directives a condition of employment. She couldn't help but wonder if Zoey's decision to obey her instructions was because she followed orders for a living, but her thoughts quickly devolved into how sexy Zoey looked in her uniform. The reporters at the gate would've had a field day with her.

Not if I can help it. She started to grab Zoey's hand again, but opted to be more discreet, nodding for Zoey to go with Gary through the network of halls off limits to the general public, until they reached a door leading outside. Gary held it open. "I've got to get back, but you can find your way from here," he said, pointing at a hangar about a hundred yards away. "Good luck."

Rook thanked him as the door closed and checked her phone while Zoey looked at the closed door and then back at her. "What's the plan now?" she asked.

"We hike over to the hangar and catch a ride."

"I'm not getting back on a plane." Zoey placed her hands on her hips as if to emphasize her defiance.

"Who said anything about a plane? You'll have a car and a driver who will take you anywhere in the city you need to go. No questions asked."

"And you?"

"As much as I wish I could accompany you on this little adventure, I have a meeting I need to get to." She looked into Zoey's eyes and thought she spotted the tiniest tinge of regret. Rook wanted to act on it, but there wasn't time. "Come on."

A few minutes later, they were in the hangar reserved for charter flights. Rook gave her name at the desk, and the woman pointed outside to the helicopter on the pad. Before she could ask about the car, she spotted the familiar vehicle. She told the woman she'd board in just a second and walked back to Zoey.

"Your car is ready."

Zoey followed her gaze. "Are you going back to the main terminal?"

"Nope. That's my ride." Rook pointed at the helicopter as she escorted Zoey to the car. "It's been fun tearing through the airport with you." They were steps away from the car, and now that it was time to part ways, Rook wished she hadn't had to rush. She started to ask for Zoey's number, but the driver's side window lowered and her driver, George, peered out. She resigned herself to handing Zoey's care over to him. "Major Zoey Granger, meet George Olson. George will take good care of you."

Zoey looked between them and then, apparently satisfied there was no danger in accepting the favor, shrugged out of Rook's jacket, handed it over, and stepped into the car while Rook held the door. She wanted to say more, ask how long Zoey would be in town, ask if she could see her again under different circumstances, but her strict rule about not getting involved with clients stopped her despite the fact Zoey wasn't an official client, but more of a pro bono on the fly rescue case. Still, she had a press conference to get to, and the sooner Zoey cleared the airport, the better off she'd be. She squeezed Zoey's hand, stepped back, and shut the door on this fun little chapter. Time to go to New York and straighten out someone else's mess.

Zoey watched through the car window as Rook climbed aboard the helicopter. Rook was rakish, dashing, and devilishly handsome, and Zoey shook her head at her good fortune at running into her. But now that Rook was gone and Zoey was in a car with a stranger, she questioned her lack of discretion. For all she knew, Rook Daniels was an opportunist, exactly like the reporters who'd been chasing her through the airport in an attempt to turn her life into a front-page story.

"Where to, ma'am?"

She looked at the driver, George, surprised at the soft, quiet tone of his voice. She made a split-second decision that he seemed harmless enough despite his hulking frame. "The Pentagon."

"Excellent." He took a moment to consult his phone. "Traffic is light. We should arrive in about thirty minutes." He pulled out of the parking lot, and Zoey watched the helicopter carry Rook into the sky as they drove away. Resigned to her decision to let this scenario play out, she leaned back into the cushioned leather seat and tried to relax.

The summons from General Bloomfield had come with very little information, which wasn't in itself unusual, but the timing—so close to her testimony before Congress—was suspect. She'd been trained not to question orders, but now that she was within a half hour of obtaining more detail, she couldn't help but wonder if the summons was a not-so-subtle means of dismissal.

Whistleblower laws were designed to keep people in her position safe, but that was the law, not the reality. She'd heard anecdotes of people in her position leaving quietly, choosing to resign their commissions rather than fight the system and potentially lose the benefits they'd worked so hard to guarantee. She didn't want to fight, but she'd already decided she would if it came down to it. Maybe the hearings would buy her a little time since she doubted the brass wanted her appearing in front of Congress with a discharge fresh on the books.

She pulled out her phone and glanced at the screen, just then realizing she'd forgotten to take it off airplane mode in the flurry back at the terminal. When she switched it back on, the screen blew up with alerts. She skimmed the texts from General Bloomfield's assistant, and her apprehension grew.

Corporal Stine will pick you up. He'll meet you at baggage claim. Text him when you land. A number followed. The next text read: *All bags claimed and you're nowhere in sight. Report.*

Twenty minutes later: *Flight manifest says you were on board. Is disappearing one of your special skills?*

She punched the number for Stine. "Stine, it's Granger. Stand down. I didn't get the message you'd be picking me up until just now, and I had to duck a gaggle of reporters at the airport. I'm en route to the Pentagon. I'll call and let the office know I'm on the way."

"Better let me call, Major. No need in you taking more of a beating than you have been."

Zoey breathed a sigh of relief at the friendly overture. "Thanks. Much appreciated. Sorry you had to make a wasted trip."

"Not a problem. Drive safe."

If George's calculations were correct, they'd arrive at the Pentagon in twenty minutes and she could do with a dose of non-military conversation before being submersed again. Fact was, her mind kept wandering back to Rook, and curiosity won out over duty.

"George, how well do you know Rook Daniels?"

He flicked a glance at her in the rearview mirror, and Zoey sensed she was being sized up. "I've known Ms. Daniels ever since she came to DC. I used to drive for her father."

Cagey answer since Zoey would need a few extra pieces of information for his comment to make sense. She wanted to know more, but sensed George either wasn't able or willing to indulge her curiosity, so she just nodded and moved on. "I'll be here for about a week. Anything special I should do or see?"

"First time in the capital?"

"Yes."

"Do a nighttime tour of the monuments. Weather's perfect for it this time of year. Bus will take you around to most of them over about three hours and stop long enough for you to walk around and check them out. When they're all lit up, there's nothing else like it."

"Sounds perfect. Thanks for the tip."

"My pleasure."

Zoey settled in for the rest of the ride, and for just a few minutes, let herself imagine being dressed in plainclothes, riding around the city with Rook Daniels at her side. Completely improbable on so many levels, but that's what fantasies were supposed to be, right?

CHAPTER TWO

Zoey took pride in her ability to walk fast, but the Marine escorting her through the Pentagon was next level. Of course, he wasn't wearing heels and a skirt, so there was that. "Where exactly are we going and will we still be in country when we get there?" she asked.

The sergeant laughed. "First time at the Puzzle Palace?"

"You're quick."

"It's a little overwhelming until you get used to it. End to end, the building will hold the Statue of Liberty, but you can move between any two places within ten minutes. We don't have time today, but grab one of the honor guards and get the nickel tour when you have a chance."

Zoey nodded but figured that wouldn't be happening. Once she got her in-person scolding for violating code and testified before the Senate, she'd probably be shipped off to serve out the rest of her career in some remote outpost. In the meantime, she drank in every detail she could about the enormous building. They'd passed a row of shops that carried goods ranging from fancy candy to jewelry and a food court with every unhealthy fast food option imaginable, and she was beginning to feel like she was at a shopping mall instead of a military complex.

"Here's your stop, Major."

Zoey glanced at the door and back to the Marine waiting to be dismissed. She nodded, squared her shoulders, and pushed through. "Major Granger, reporting to see General Bloomfield," she announced to the soldier manning the desk.

"Good afternoon, Major." He pointed at the door behind him. "Go on in, the generals are expecting you."

Generals. Zoey wondered if she'd misheard the plural, but didn't bother asking since she'd find out soon enough. She rapped on the door to signal her entry and the door swung wide. "General Sharp!"

She immediately regretted the exclamation, but it had been years since she'd seen her first CO and she didn't expect him to be here. David Sharp had been her champion from the moment she'd graduated from boot camp, and she took some measure of comfort at the sight of a familiar face.

"Major, good to see you," he said. "Come on in." He swept an arm toward a couple of chairs in the center of the room, and she did a quick recon to see if there were any other surprises waiting, but there was only one other person in the room who she assumed was Bloomfield. After Sharp sat, she followed suit.

"Major Granger, I'm General Bloomfield. I appreciate you getting here so quickly. The Armed Services Committee is about to chew their own arms off if they don't get a uniform in the hot seat on this Nine Tech crap. I'm afraid you'll be raw meat to the hungry beast, but it can't be helped. The first hearing is tomorrow afternoon, and you'll meet with counsel's office to prepare. Tell the truth, nothing more, nothing less. Sharp has volunteered to make sure you're situated and to escort you to the Capitol. Understood?"

"Yes, sir." Zoey hesitated for just a second as she spoke the words. She was relieved to know she'd have a friendly face with her at the hearing tomorrow, but she'd expected a little more of a dressing down about dragging half a platoon through this ordeal.

"I heard a but, Major. You have something to get off your chest?"

Zoey resisted the urge to glance at Sharp for guidance. For the first half of her career, he'd been a careful mentor, guiding her in and around bureaucratic minefields as she escalated up the ranks to achieve her own command. Much of the way she exerted authority was based on the lessons she'd learned from him. Relying on everything she'd learned under his command, she took a page from his book and asked what she really wanted to know. "Permission to speak freely?"

"Say what's on your mind."

"I fully expected a chewing out and a little more 'here's what we want you to say...'" She paused. "I understand the issue with Nine Tech is likely to cause a lot of problems with the Senate, especially with regard to budget."

"Are you asking for a script, Major?"

Bloomfield's tone was gruff, but his eyes were kind, urging her to get it all out. "No, sir. Just letting you know I understand how difficult this situation has become. I assure you I didn't have a choice."

"You always have a choice, soldier, but in this case, you made the right one." He jabbed a finger in Sharp's direction. "I've known that man since he was a ninety-day wonder, still wet behind the ears," he said, referring to Sharp's stint in Officer Candidate School. "If Sharp says you're a good soldier, I trust him. Don't get me wrong, you created a shit storm, but you're going to help us find our way out of it. Understood?"

She nodded even though she knew he expected a verbal reply. He was out of his seat and the implication was clear—she was dismissed. Sharp motioned for her to follow him, and a few minutes later, they were walking back through the building on a different concourse than the one the Marine had led her in on.

"Are you hungry?" Sharp asked as they passed by a Pizza Hut.

The idea of a greasy slice of pizza twisted her stomach in knots. "A little, but after airplane food, I could use something with at least the appearance of green. I can wait if there are meetings scheduled this afternoon."

"One this afternoon with staff counsel, and one in the morning with some stiffs from the White House. Lawyers," he said with disdain, "even when they aren't billing by the hour, they're looking for an angle. If you want to push through today, I'll get you out of here in time for dinner. We've got you set up at a hotel in Alexandria. There's a decent restaurant there."

"I can wait."

"There's that 'but' again."

She considered her next words carefully. "I'm just wondering why they have you escorting me around. Seems a little beneath your rank."

"It is," he said, "but I volunteered." He slowed his brisk walk and turned to face her. "We all got the reports, and I know you've been taking a lot of flack out there for blowing the lid off this thing. Least I can do is make sure you scoot through this part of the process unscathed."

She should be grateful Sharp was still taking a personal interest in her career, but a small part of her was offended at the idea she needed protection from the fallout of her decision to report members of her platoon when she learned of the scheme they were running under her command. "I expected pushback at the base, but even here?"

He nodded. "Bloomfield's the exception. There are a few of the top brass who wish you'd gone through back channels to report what you found."

"And you?" She asked the question before she thought it through, and once the words were out, she braced for his answer. If her mentor said she should have kept quiet, she wasn't sure she could ever recover her respect for him.

"You did the right thing, no question. But you had to know there would be fallout."

"What did you teach me? It's a bureaucracy. There's always fallout."

"Fair enough." He started walking again, double time. "Come on, soldier. The lawyers are waiting."

Later that evening, Zoey emerged from a steaming shower, slipped into the courtesy robe, and contemplated the room service menu. After a grueling afternoon answering dozens of practice questions, all she wanted was some real food, a stiff drink, and solitude. She placed her order and turned on the TV, hoping to escape into a mindless comedy or a thrilling adventure movie. She clicked quickly past the local channels and the Home Shopping Network, but when she landed on MSNBC, she froze. The screen filled with the image of her savior from the airport, Rook Daniels, standing next to a handsome couple at a podium, fielding questions from reporters. Based on the time, Zoey figured the news conference had taken place a few hours ago. New York City. So, that's where Rook had been headed when she'd boarded the helo in the private terminal at National. Zoey turned up the volume.

"Well-known DC fixer Rook Daniels appeared with her client, US Representative Buster Jenkins and his wife, Farah Hamil, to answer questions about the breaking news that lewd photos of Jenkins showed up in an online chat room. We have a panel assembled to discuss the fallout, but first let's go to our New York affiliate for the highlights of the press conference."

The screen changed to show a tall blond reporter standing outside the St. Regis in downtown New York. Zoey had never been there, but she recognized the iconic building from movies.

"Good evening, Chris," the reporter said. *"The press conference was what we've come to expect from Daniels. She put her clients front and center for the camera at a distinguished locale and let them speak directly to the press, but there was no doubt they'd been well-prepped to field any questions lobbed their way. Jenkins denied the charges. Hamil stood by her man. No surprises here."*

"There's been speculation that Farah Hamil has been planning to launch her own campaign for mayor of New York. Any word on that and whether her husband's troubles will have an impact on her political future?"

"The question definitely came up, and I have a clip to show how it went down."

Zoey turned the volume up, her gaze riveted on Rook who leaned into the microphone at the podium and called on a reporter from the *New York Times*.

"What impact will the pending charges have on Councilwoman Hamil's expected announcement for the mayoral run?"

"Clever, Charlie," Rook said with an engaging smile. "First of all, there are no pending charges, merely an investigation. Second, the only expectation Farah Hamil has right now is that you will report fairly and objectively about her husband's case and give their family the space to deal with these troubling accusations. One more question," Rook said, turning her attention to the other reporters in the crowd.

Zoey smiled at the screen, both charmed and annoyed by Rook's evasive, yet telling doublespeak. If she were inclined to gamble, she'd lay odds that Farah Hamil would be divorced and running for mayor of New York within the year. But what really captured her attention about the coverage on TV was Rook. If possible, she looked even more handsome than she had at the airport. Clearly comfortable in front of the cameras, she assumed her role of "fixer" with ease. While normally Zoey would find the moniker abhorrent, Rook had certainly fixed things for her when she'd needed help, so she really couldn't judge. Besides, even if she didn't care for Rook's chosen profession, she couldn't deny Rook looked good doing it, and she certainly couldn't deny she enjoyed watching the show.

❖

Rook stood at the podium, well practiced at not blinking at the prolonged burst of shutter flashes or the onslaught of prurient questions about the naked photos of the congressman. Eyes focused on the press crowded in front of her, Rook still felt the palpable discomfort of her client, US Representative Buster Jenkins who was posed ramrod straight next to his steely-eyed wife. Rook had coached them well in the time they'd had since her helicopter had landed, but she still would have preferred better casting for this press conference. Unfortunately, while she was very selective about whom she chose to represent, her clients rarely came from central casting.

She'd first met Buster years ago, before he'd started his political career, when he married noted lawyer Farah Hamil. Farah was a long time acquaintance from law school, but the wedding invitation was the first time Rook had heard from her since their graduation.

Rook attended the wedding, more for the opportunity to see other friends from their class than because she was invested in the couple's future happiness, and she'd sensed from the beginning Buster and Farah were a typical power couple, destined to either promote or implode each other's success. Like similar couples before them, they appeared to have entered a tacit agreement to escalate Buster's political ambitions first, but the political gossip mill was already churning about Farah's expected announcement to run for mayor of New York.

Until this week, when the pictures were splashed on the front page of the *Enquirer*, showing Buster in a compromising position with another woman, a much younger woman. Panicked about her own political future, Farah had contacted Rook's office and implored her to do her magic to make it all go away as quickly as possible. After an in-depth conversation with Farah about the potential options and an intensive video conference with the couple last night, they'd agreed to a press conference to get in front of the story.

So far the questions had been probing, but Rook handled them with ease, deflecting where necessary and hitting the issue of privacy hard, but it was time to wrap this circus up. "One more question," Rook said, pointing to the political reporter from *Vanity Fair*. "Diane?"

"Is there any evidence the photos have been tampered with in any way, so they are not what they appear to be?"

Rook nodded. "I'm not at liberty to share any such evidence with you at this time, but it's clear someone is trying to impugn Congressman Jenkins's excellent reputation for good character. I will say this." She paused and met several key sets of eyes in the crowd of reporters. "Anyone can make anything look real on the Internet." She glanced back at the troubled couple. "On behalf of Congressman Jenkins and his wife, I'd like to thank you all for being here. They are both anxious to put this nightmare behind them and return to serving the citizens of New York. You may contact my office for updates." Rook ignored the continued chorus of shouted questions and walked away from the cameras. She placed an arm around Buster and escorted him and Farah through the private exit at the back of the hotel ballroom that had been designated for their use. The getaway plan brought up memories of rushing through the back halls of the airport with Zoey Granger at her side, and she wished she were with Zoey pursuing that chase instead of this one.

When Rook was certain they were alone, she motioned for the couple to stop.

"That was brilliant," Buster said, "Ending with the assertion the photos are fake. That's going to be the lead."

"Except for one thing," Rook said. She turned to Farah and fixed her with a stare. "Do you want to tell him or should I?"

"What?" Buster asked, looking furtively between the two of them.

Farah cleared her throat. "The photos aren't fake and anyone with half a brain can figure that out."

"Well," Buster stretched out the word. "At least the assertion buys us some time to come up with a new defense." He play-punched Rook on the shoulder. "Isn't that why we're paying you the big bucks?"

Rook shook her head. "There's not enough money in the world to create fact out of fiction. Delay is all you get, but you're right, I tossed out the idea to give Farah time to decide what she wants to do, and I think there's something she wants to tell you." She watched as Buster's expression spun through a list of emotions, from surprise to shock, finally landing on denial.

"You can't leave me," he said to Farah. "Not now. Hell, you're about to announce."

"Rook thinks I'll make a much more sympathetic candidate as the spurned, but strong wife who chose not to stand by her man, especially if it means I lose the baggage of an adulterer."

Rook winced at the attribution. She'd merely pointed out the options and let Farah choose her future. She wholeheartedly agreed with the choice, but she'd have found a way to make other options work if Farah decided to salvage her marriage. She might choose her clients, but she was being paid to get the outcome of their choice, and no one was better at arguing both sides.

An hour later, Rook was back in her room at the Peninsula Hotel, lying back on the bed, contemplating the room service menu. Farah had invited her to dinner at Gramercy Tavern, but Rook knew no matter how well intentioned, downtime would quickly turn into more conversation about Farah's marital woes and political prospects. Rook had had enough rescuing damsels in distress for the day, although she hardly considered Major Zoey Granger a damsel in distress. No, Zoey had been more like a soldier out of her battle zone. Rook closed her eyes and played back portions of the afternoon at the airport, running slow motion past the part where Zoey tugged her hair out of the tight bun and her auburn waves cascaded onto the shoulders of her crisp uniform. Uniforms were usually a no-go for Rook, but the sharp contrast of Zoey's vulnerability with the hard edge of her insignias intrigued her, and she was in no hurry to brush Zoey Granger to the back of her mind.

Her phone rang and she glanced at the caller ID, instantly recognizing the White House exchange. She answered with a mock stern tone. "Tell the president I'm not interested," Rook said.

"That's what I used to say, but look at me now."

Rook laughed at the sound of her old friend Julia Scott's voice. They'd had a running joke since Julia had accepted the president's offer to become his chief of staff. Julia had tried, on many occasions, to get Rook to join the administration as an advisor on strategy, but Rook had made it clear she wasn't interested. "You whisper into the ear of the most powerful man in the free world," Rook said. "Of course you had to say yes to the job. I, on the other hand, like being my own boss."

"Keep telling yourself that. Pretty sure whoever pays you owns you."

"Ouch."

"The truth hurts."

"Maybe so, but I'm still not coming to work for you or your guy."

"'My guy,' she says. Whatever. I didn't call to pressure you this time. I called to invite you to a party."

"What? Are you finally making an honest woman out of Addison? Beltway rumors say you've been essentially shacking up for the last six months."

"Between you and me, the rumors are true, but it's been a little complicated trying to balance our jobs and our love life."

Rook had no doubt it was true. The mix of president's chief of staff with the chief justice of the United States resulted in a relationship fraught with trip lines. "I can see the headlines now. DC power couple tipping the balance of power. Couldn't you find a nice nobody to fall in love with?"

"When *you* find someone and settle down, then you can tease *me* about my love life. Until then, button it up."

"Fair enough. So what's the occasion if not a wedding?"

"It's Addison's birthday. I'm having a thing. It's kind of gotten out of hand, and now there are going to be way too many people coming, half of whom I barely know. Promise you'll show up and keep me sane?"

"You know you can count on me even if I won't be your White House lackey."

"Someday, Daniels, someday. By the way, nice job with the press conference tonight. When is Farah going to divorce the creep?"

"No comment, even for you. You'll have to hear about any fallout in the gossip columns just like everyone else." Rook decided to fish for a little gossip of her own. "Hey, what do you know about the Senate hearing on Nine Tech?"

"Plenty. Why? Something specific you're after?"

Rook started to tell Julia about meeting Zoey at the airport but hesitated. It had been a chance meeting and she'd done a good deed, but it was nothing more than that. Telling Julia felt like she was making more out of it. "Nothing. I saw an article in the paper this morning. Just curious."

"I think it's all in the dustup phase now. The hearings are just a way for the senators to show their constituents they're guarding the coffers. They'll grill the girl, shake a stick at the Joint Chiefs, and move onto the next drama du jour."

"Woman."

"What?"

"You were talking about the major who exposed the corruption and you said girl. Besides, shouldn't you be calling her *soldier* or some other military thing? The patriarchy you're part of is rubbing off on you."

"Look who's talking. Pretty sure you just stuck up for a man-creep of the highest order while making his wife stand at his side for the camera. If you want me to turn in my feminist card, you're going to have to go first, my friend."

"Touché." Rook heard a knock at the door. "As fun as this little catch-up has been, my dinner just showed up and I'm starving. Count me in for Addison's party and I'll see you soon." She hung up and answered the door to usher in the room service waiter impatiently waiting while he arranged the table with a T-bone, loaded baked potato, and a salad with more toppings than greens. When he started fiddling with the bottle of Cabernet, she shoved a twenty in his hand and told him to leave the bottle opener. Solitude, food, and the better part of a bottle of very expensive wine were the only things she wanted right now. As she settled in to enjoy them all, she wondered if Zoey was tucked away in a DC hotel room doing the same thing.

CHAPTER THREE

Zoey reached for the pitcher and filled her water glass with deliberate slowness. She was on her fifth day of Senate hearings with no end in sight. She'd repeated, numerous times, the full details of how she'd discovered that managers at Nine Tech were bribing soldiers under her command to requisition munitions and other equipment in exchange for kickbacks, including how she'd uncovered that the soldier who ran the scheme on the Army end was also selling the excess equipment on the black market and double dipping from the already profitable enterprise.

She'd taken no glory from her findings. These men and women had been under her command, and their crimes reflected on her abilities. Her superiors had suggested to her more than once that she keep the disciplinary action in-house to save face, but she'd ignored the well-intentioned advice. If Nine Tech was bribing soldiers in her unit, chances were good they were making similar deals with other military bases as well. Not coming forward simply wasn't an option. Not one she could live with anyway.

"Major, please describe for us again how you were able to detect the discrepancies?" the senior senator from Texas, Connie Armstrong, asked. Before Zoey could answer, the senator added, "I'm interested because I think your methods should probably be implemented system-wide if we want to prevent this kind of large-scale looting of our limited military coffers in the future."

Zoey cleared her throat, pushing down her first response that questioned if it was a good use of taxpayer dollars to keep her away from her command to answer the same questions, over and over. But Senator Armstrong had lobbed her a softball, designed to help her look like a hero instead of a failed commander, so she set aside her frustration and repeated the information she'd relayed no less than a dozen times in the past few days.

Two hours later, the committee chair thanked her for her time and service, excused her from her subpoena, and adjourned the committee for the day. Zoey turned to the Pentagon lawyer beside her. "Is it over?"

"For now, for you, yes," he said as he packed up his briefcase. "They'll start on the not so friendly witnesses next. Are you headed back to your base? I'll need to be able to get in touch with you in case the committee has any follow-up questions about the documents we provided."

Zoey had wondered several times over the past week what her future would hold, but she hadn't let herself dwell on it. But now that he'd asked, she realized she didn't have a clue. She fudged. "I'm supposed to check in with General Sharp as soon as we're done here to get my orders. I'll get you my updated contact info as soon as I know."

She tucked away his card, hoping she never saw him again, and left the building. It was just after three on Friday afternoon and the mass exodus of legislators was in full swing. She should probably head back to the Pentagon right away, but it was a gorgeous spring day and she hadn't had an opportunity to experience anything in the city so she lingered for a moment. The hearings had taken place in the Hart Building, a couple of blocks from the Capitol, and she started out in that direction, determined to at least capture a couple of pictures to send to her mother back home. As she walked onto Constitution Avenue, she was surrounded by history with the Supreme Court and the Library of Congress to her right and the Capitol building to her left. She walked by a group of tourists posing for pictures with the statues in front of the Library of Congress and wished she were here under different circumstances, dressed in jeans, T-shirt, and sandals with no agenda other than to soak up some history.

The buzz of her phone rousted her out of her daydreams. "Granger," she answered the unknown caller.

"Major, I hear it went well."

She recognized David Sharp's voice and seized on the lifeline since he was likely to have answers about her future within the service. "Glad that's what you heard, although that's a little spooky since we just finished up. I guess it went okay, but it's kind of hard to tell when you're being chewed up and spit out over and over again."

Sharp laughed. "Been there. Trust me, it doesn't get any easier. Happy you survived."

She waited, wondering if he'd called just to check in or if he had something definitive to tell her about her future. He rambled a bit longer about his own experience testifying before Congress, and when he paused to draw a breath, she seized the opportunity. "When should I report back to base?"

"We should talk about that. In fact, that's one of the reasons I called. Take the rest of the afternoon off but plan on sticking around for a few days. There's a function tomorrow night and I'd like you to go with me. Service dress. I'll pick you up at your hotel at seven sharp. Let me know if you need anything between now and then."

His conclusory tone didn't invite any questions, but she had plenty. Why was she sticking around? What was this function? Did she still have a future with the Army or was he taking a little extra time to let her down easy? "Will do," she said, but he'd already clicked off the call. Resigned to waiting until the next day to learn her fate, she focused on the right now. If she hurried, maybe she could fit in a tour or two before they shut down for the day. Her mind drifted to Rook Daniels and the way she'd effortlessly guided her through the airport. No doubt as a DC insider, she'd know exactly where to go and what to do in the capital. But Rook wasn't here now and she was on her own. Zoey pulled up the camera on her phone and snapped a few photos of the buildings lining Constitution Avenue, and then made her way to the tall columns of the Supreme Court building. She might not be from a big city and she definitely wasn't an insider, but she'd do just fine on her own.

❖

Rook swung through the door to her office suite and waved at Ben, the receptionist.

"Jenkins's office has phoned exactly seven times in the last fifteen minutes," he called out cheerfully as she walked briskly down the hall.

"On it." She stopped in front of her assistant's desk and waited impatiently for her to finish her call.

"That's right," Lacy said into the phone. "We'll have a full statement within the hour." She shook her head. "No advance copies, for anyone. Thanks for—" she stopped abruptly and then muttered "asshole" as she hung up. "That little jerk from Fox thinks he's entitled to the inside scoop. He'll get his copy of the press release exactly five minutes after everyone else."

Rook waved a hand in front of her face. "Earth to Lacy."

"Hey, Rook. About time you got here. Everyone's in the conference room. They should have a draft ready for you."

"Maybe you could lead with that next time. Any messages not about this case?"

"Several, but they can all wait." Lacy flicked her hands at Rook. "Go, now."

"Trying to remember why I hired the bossiest assistant in the history of assistants," Rook said as she walked toward her firm's conference room.

"Ignoring you," Lacy yelled back.

Rook pushed through the conference room door and took a second to watch her team at work. Images projected onto a light box on the wall captured the most important aspects of the Buster Jenkins case including the bombshell that had interrupted her afternoon meeting with a high level executive from Diamond Credit who wanted advice about dealing with a recent hacking scandal that had resulted in the exposure of their clients' private information.

Buster's case had taken a wicked turn. What had started as an embarrassing case of infidelity had turned criminal this afternoon when FBI agents showed up at his DC office with a search warrant.

Rook's phone had started blowing up during her Diamond Credit meeting and hadn't stopped since. Lacy had George on standby to drive her back to the office, and on the way Rook had contacted one of her sources at the US Attorney's office to see what she could find out. What she'd learned had been shocking, and her first call was to Farah to see if she was still hired to work the case. To her surprise, Farah had told her to fix it and money was no object. With her full team assembled, she planned to do just that.

"Talk to me," she said to the room, before turning to her senior associate, Blake Wyatt. "What do we have so far?"

"The FBI showed up at three o'clock," Blake said, reading from the notes in her right hand, while she ran her other hand through her short blond hair. "They had the Capitol Police with them and carted out a couple of boxes and four computers from Jenkins's office. As of right now, Jenkins has not been arrested."

"Is he going to be?" Rook asked.

"Too soon to tell," Harry Etheridge, her other associate, said. "We have a copy of the warrant but not the underlying affidavit, so nobody knows what the allegations are yet."

Rook's phone pinged and she glanced at the screen. "Well, we know now." She tossed her phone at the man seated to her right, Eric Pryor, their resident computer expert. "The affidavit is attached to that email. It'll be encrypted."

"Gimme just a sec," Eric said as he typed on her phone, and then his computer. A moment later, he pointed at the front of the room. "There you go."

Rook digested the words on the screen and waited for the rest of her team to catch up. The affidavit to the search warrant accused Buster of texting nude photos of himself to an underage girl he'd met in an online chat room. Suddenly, his marital infidelity and reelection prospects were the least of his worries since he was looking at possible prison time and sex offender registration.

"Holy shit," said Harry. "Did anyone else see this coming?"

"Sure," Blake, the always skeptical former CIA agent, said. "I always thought he was a little skeevy, but I figured if Farah was married to him, then he must have some redeeming quality. Guess I was wrong."

"We need to get out in front of this. Harry, get Paul Hanson on the phone," she said, referring to the managing partner at one of the top law firms in DC. "Tell him we want a female partner assigned to the case. Get whoever it is a copy of this affidavit and tell her all statements need to be vetted by us before they go public." She turned to Eric. "You cloned Buster's computer, didn't you?"

"I did, but only his personal one and the one he uses at his office. From what we can tell, the feds seized several others."

"Those probably belonged to his staff. Someone needs to talk to them as soon as possible. Blake?"

"On it. I've got their names and addresses, and I'll head out as soon as we craft the statement."

"Go now." Rook pointed at her head. "I already know what we're going to say. Senator Jenkins is fully cooperating with law enforcement, and he trusts in the criminal justice system to ensure justice is done. No press conference, just issue the statement through the usual channels."

"Doesn't sound like a very vigorous defense to me," Harry said. "You sure we want to be that blasé about these allegations?"

"I'm certain we don't want to overstate our case. I don't expect we're going to be on this one much longer, and I don't want to put Hanson's firm in a box by promising something no one's going to be able to deliver. Farah's exact words were 'do no harm.' She's telling us she's ready to move on from the not-so-honorable Buster Jenkins. We're here for triage and that's it."

"Such a shame," Harry said. "I love a good kiddie porn case, said no one ever."

"Once the statement's out, let's go full tilt on opposition research for Farah," Rook said. "I want to know every little, itty, bitty thing anyone has on her. We've got one month before she has to file and our job is to clear a path. Understood?"

The three of them nodded, and she knew she could count on them to make miracles happen. "Eric, can I see you in my office in five?"

"Sure, boss."

She left the group to their work and walked back to her office, waving off Lacy who tried to waylay her at the door. "I need a few minutes alone. Let Eric in in five."

Lacy looked at her watch and nodded.

Rook shut the door and paced in front of the windows that looked out over the courtyard in the center of her building. The offices of the Daniels's Agency occupied the entire three floors of the historic New Orleans style brownstone, choice real estate she'd purchased several years ago. She and her team didn't need an entire building, but she'd steadfastly refused to parcel out the spacious offices despite the enormous financial benefit she could reap from renting out the extra space. Her clients expected privacy, and being the only occupant of the building afforded them that. Besides, she was a firm believer that the appearance of success attracted more of it. Since they'd relocated from their smaller offices in Arlington, the caliber of their clientele had grown exponentially.

Farah had been one of her first clients, and her needs had been simple back then. Opposition research to help Farah's young, handsome, but not the brightest guy, husband get elected to the House of Representatives. Rook had found a few murmurs of office flings, but nothing anyone was willing to substantiate at the time. She'd given all the information to Farah and let her and Buster make the call about whether to risk the rumors turning into prime time news stories. One woman came forward and told her local news affiliate she'd slept with Buster in exchange for promises of career advancement, but she quickly retracted her story when Rook visited her to discuss her frequent use of cocaine at campaign parties, a tale her associates had been only too happy to tell. Rook hadn't threatened or bribed. She'd merely pointed out that if Jenkins really was a philanderer, the news outlets would find out as easily as she had been able to find out about the woman's drug use. She wasn't particularly proud of the method, but in the end she figured she saved the woman from an embarrassing public ordeal.

"Eric's at the door," Lacy's voice boomed through the intercom. "You ready?"

"Yes, send him in."

Eric, dressed in skinny jeans, a tweed vest, and a vintage tie with a full Windsor, was not your typical Mountain Dew sipping, basement dwelling hacker, but no one was better at busting through secure systems than he was.

"Diamond Credit," Rook said without preamble. "I met with their president today."

"Last I heard, almost a quarter of a million accounts compromised."

"They think it might be twice that. The FDIC is all over them, and they need some cover. Only thing I can think of is to find out who did the hacking so we can start pointing fingers in their direction. Maybe even file a lawsuit."

"I'm no lawyer, but I don't think you're going to get anywhere with that. Whoever did it is probably sipping ice cold shots of vodka and posting videos of a shirtless Putin on the dark net."

"Exactly. We don't want or need a real lawsuit. That'll just drag things out forever and the only people who'll win are the thousand-dollar-an-hour lawyers. We just need someone to blame who isn't our guy." She handed him a jump drive. "Here's your front door access to their system. Get in the back door and see whose trail you're following. Can you do that?"

He laughed. "You're kidding, right? I'll get right on it. Anything else?"

"Not right now, but stay close. I don't know what else might blow up on this Jenkins thing."

"Can I just say how much I hate these cases? We need a juicy political scandal, not more of these 'who cheated on who' deals."

Rook laughed. "When the guy who cheats is a congressman, it is a political scandal."

"You know what I mean."

"I do and I totally agree, but these things are our bread and butter. I promise I'll do some networking and see if I can drum up something more to your liking."

"That's why you're the boss." Eric started toward the door. "I'll call you when I find something."

Rook sank into her desk chair. She hated domestics as much as Eric, but when you specialized in the people business, they couldn't be helped. The Diamond Credit thing was more up her alley—much easier to advise a corporate entity devoid of emotion than two individuals watching their relationship destruct, especially when one of them turns out to be a sex offender.

But working with people sometimes had its benefits. Her mind wandered back to earlier in the week when she'd helped Zoey Granger escape the clutches of the press. The brass at the Pentagon should have taken better care of their star witness—at the very minimum making sure she got off the plane without being mobbed—and if she'd been advising them she would've told them so. Rook had caught some of the coverage of the hearings, and although Zoey was generally unflappable, it was clear from her occasional expressions of shock when asked a probing personal question that had nothing to do with the investigation, this was her first time being caught in the cross fire between the military might and the elected officials that funded them. The paper said her testimony was wrapping up today, and Rook wondered if she was headed back to her base. Images of Zoey's long, sculpted legs appeared in her head, and Rook knew her musings were about more than Zoey's case.

Lacy's voice buzzed through the intercom. "Lyra's school play is tonight so I'm headed out for the day. I bought that crazy expensive bottle of Scotch for you to take to Addison Riley's birthday party and it's on your bar along with the invite. You need anything else?"

"No, I'm good. Tell Lyra to break a leg."

Rook looked over at the Scotch. She hadn't talked to Julia all week and she'd already forgotten about the party. After a week in the public eye, she'd rather spend the weekend in the office, catching up on work, but maybe a little socializing would be good for business. An image of Zoey Granger's legs popped into her head again. Maybe good for some relaxation too.

Chapter Four

Zoey stood in front of the hotel, waiting for General Sharp and enjoying the cool night air. The hotel valet had offered to come get her when her ride arrived, but she preferred the outside. Back in Texas, even the evening temperatures were already in the seventies, and she was happy to have at least a few days in the cooler climate.

She'd spent the day being a tourist. Her impromptu trip to the Library of Congress had made her too late to book a nighttime tour of the monuments last night, but she'd already purchased a ticket for Sunday. Today's adventures had taken her to the Smithsonian Air and Space Museum and the White House where she'd stood along with huge crowds of tourists, along the fence that lined the ellipse, and snapped photos through the bars. She'd enjoyed the day, but thoughts about her future distracted her. She only hoped Sharp would have some answers tonight.

As if summoned, a black sedan pulled up and the rear window rolled down to reveal Sharp in the backseat. She walked toward the car, and he got out and motioned her in. She was surprised to see a civilian driver in the front seat.

"Major, meet Carl. Carl is the only reason I stay sane. If I had to drive around DC on my own, I might be tempted to declare war."

Zoey waved at Carl who nodded before he pulled out of the hotel drive and onto the roadway. "Makes sense. I'm completely turned around and I've only been here a week."

"And a rough week too. How are you holding up?"

"Good. I managed to get in a little sightseeing today. Figured I'd take advantage. Who knows when I'll be back."

"About that. General Bloomfield would like to meet with you Monday morning."

"I expect he wants a report on the hearings?"

"That and other things." Sharp drummed his fingers on the armrest. "This is not public yet, so it's imperative that what I'm about to tell you not go any further than this car."

Zoey resisted glancing at Carl who she was certain could hear every word they were saying. If David trusted him, who was she to question? "Understood."

"The president is nominating Bloomfield for Chairman of the Joint Chiefs. If he gets the spot, I'm his pick to replace him as Army Chief of Staff."

"Sounds like congratulations are in order." Zoey appreciated the intel, but wondered why he was sharing it with her. She had a feeling there was something more he wanted to say.

"Thanks, but congratulations are a bit premature, since all of this has to be approved by the same contentious group of people you testified before all week. Speaking of confirmations, Bloomfield submitted your 0-5 and you're being reassigned to the Pentagon, effective immediately."

Zoey took a moment to digest the information. She was being recommended for promotion to lieutenant colonel a full year ahead of when she'd normally be eligible. This wouldn't be the first time she'd received a below the zone promotion, but after the Nine Tech fiasco, the news was definitely a surprise. The promotion would be subject to Senate confirmation, and she wasn't entirely sure, in light of last week's performance, if that was a good or a bad thing.

"Are you going to say something?"

"Frankly, I'm not sure what to say. The promotion is one thing, but reassignment?"

"Wondering if you're being praised on one hand and punished with the other?"

"Something like that." Zoey wasn't sure how to feel. She'd taken pride in her command, but now that she was back stateside, she'd had a hard time reintegrating to regular base life, especially in light of her role in the Nine Tech scandal. She'd heard work at the Pentagon was mired in bureaucracy, but with over twenty thousand fellow employees, she'd have a better chance at blending in and getting her career back on track.

"Bloomfield likes you. He got good feedback from counsel's office." Sharp shrugged. "And no, I didn't make this happen, although when he asked I told him I thought you deserved the bump. Besides, the Pentagon is already silly with majors."

"Will I be working with you?"

"Probably. In some capacity. You'll have a week to relocate, and then you'll report back here. I don't know exactly what Bloomfield has planned for you, but I do know you'll be working with the Joint Chiefs. And that's part of the reason I wanted you to come to this party tonight."

In the excitement about her impending promotion and the news she wasn't getting booted, Zoey had almost forgotten they were headed to a function. "Where exactly are we going?"

"Julia Scott is throwing a birthday party for her girlfriend." They were stopped at a light and he glanced at her with an expectant expression. She rolled the name around in her head, but she couldn't quite place it without more context.

"I give up." The minute the words were out of her mouth, she wanted to reel them back in. "Wait a minute. Julia Scott, President Garrett's chief of staff? And her girlfriend…Addison Riley? Chief justice of the Supreme Court?"

"Those are the ones." He looked out the window and she was grateful he couldn't see her mouth was hanging open. "We're almost there, so if you have questions, ask them now."

"I guess the most obvious one is how did you score this invitation? I figure you've met Julia Scott at the White House, but defense briefings are a little different than social invitations."

"If you want to get ahead here, you have to learn to schmooze a little. You'll have plenty of opportunities to socialize, mark my words. But I got an invite because I'm an old family friend. I served with Addison Riley's father, and Margaret and I are godparents to her and her brother Jack."

"That makes you DC royalty, doesn't it?"

"Hardly," he said with a grunt of disdain. "But I know how to make nice when I need to. This party will be loaded with VIPs. It's the perfect opportunity for you to get to know some of them and make a good impression. I'll introduce you around, but have a little fun. After this week, you deserve it."

"Thanks. Speaking of Margaret, how are she and the kids? I'd love to see them. George and Luke have to be almost out of college by now, right?"

He drummed his hand on the armrest and craned his neck as Carl braked to avoid a car that turned late into the intersection in front of them. When they finally pulled forward, he replied to her question. "Marge is good. George has a year to go, but I'm not sure he knows what he wants to do with his life. Luke's at Annapolis, so he doesn't really have a choice."

Zoey nodded at the rundown but made a mental note that he didn't sound as enthusiastic as usual when talking about his family. George's lack of direction had to be a disappointment. She could relate, but for completely opposite reasons. Her family had been plenty disappointed when she'd announced she was joining the service. They'd acted like she was throwing her life away, but if she'd returned to their tiny Texas town after a full ride at Texas A&M, that would have been the true waste. At first she'd missed the easy comfort of small town life, but she'd quickly adjusted to the routine of military life and the built-in camaraderie. David and his wife had been particularly welcoming, and she'd come to think of them as her second family, but the one that came first when she needed the kind of comforts a family was supposed to provide.

A few minutes later, they pulled up to a large Tudor style house in what Sharp told her was Georgetown. Every window was lit and the massive sycamore trees were sprinkled with lights. They waited in a line of cars inching toward the valet stand. The team of valets worked quickly, and it wasn't long before a young man in a navy suit jacket opened her door and reached out a hand as she climbed out of the car. While she waited for Sharp, she took a moment to drink in the atmosphere, grateful for her uniform since, based on the attire of the other guests, she wasn't sure she owned any clothes dressy enough for this occasion. When they reached the door, a man in a butler uniform ushered them in and pointed out the way to the bar and buffet.

The house was exactly the kind of significant, but not ostentatious dwelling Zoey would expect for a high profile power couple. Chief Justice Addison Riley had been on the bench for a year and had already distinguished herself as a no-nonsense jurist, and Julia Scott, President Garrett's former campaign manager, had taken over the job as his chief of staff soon after he started his second term. When Addison and Julia started dating, gossip columnists across the nation made it the meat of their news reports for months.

"General Sharp, thank you for coming."

A striking red-haired woman headed their way, and Zoey pegged her as Julia Scott. Zoey didn't spend a lot of time following DC politics, but she didn't know any lesbian alive who hadn't soaked up the news about Julia and Addison's relationship with fervent interest. She could hardly believe she was actually here in their home.

David handled the introductions. "Julia Scott, meet Major Zoey Granger. The major is an old friend and she's in town—"

"For the hearings, I know," Julia said with a smile as she clasped Zoey's hand. "Major, it's nice to meet you in person. C-SPAN's cameras don't do you justice. You handled yourself like a champ last week. Thank you for your service."

Zoey returned the smile, hoping to hide the fact she was a bit disconcerted to know the president's right hand had paid attention to her testimony before the Senate. But it made sense Julia would have been briefed by someone from the Joint Chief's office. "Thank you, ma'am. It's easy when you have the truth on your side."

Julia winked at Sharp. "This is a good one. I hope you plan on keeping her around."

"Trust me, we want her working on our team," Sharp said.

"Well, don't let me hold you up. There are a lot of people to see and Addison is out on the back deck, but you should make your way to the buffet. I hear the tiny prime rib sandwiches are going fast. Feel free to use your uniforms to cut in front of everyone. I'm pretty sure Jack is over there now employing that strategy with great success." Julia waved as she wandered off into the crowd greeting other guests.

"She seems very nice," Zoey said.

"Until you piss her off and then she's a hellcat."

"I guess that makes for a perfect quality in a chief of staff."

"All a matter of perspective I guess." He gestured toward the bar. "Drink?"

"I thought you'd never ask." Zoey followed him as he cut through the clusters of people. She spotted several familiar faces, some from cable news and others she'd seen the past week at the Capitol. One of the latter grabbed her arm as she walked by.

"Major Granger, what a nice surprise to see you here," Senator Connie Armstrong said.

Zoey cracked a half smile, uncertain of the protocol. "Nice to see you too, Senator." She looked at Sharp who'd turned back. The senator tracked her gaze and waved the general off. "General, if you're headed to the bar, I could use a bourbon and whatever my friend here is having."

Sharp raised his eyebrows. "Major?"

Zoey turned to Armstrong. "Actually, I was—" She stopped talking when Sharp shot her a pointed look, hoping she was reading the signals correctly. "Red wine. Thanks." Sharp nodded and plunged back into the crowd, leaving her alone with the senator.

"Are you relieved the hearings are over, Major?"

"Honestly, I'm happy to be getting back to real work."

"And you don't consider keeping the legislature informed part of your real work?"

Zoey fumbled for a recovery, but apparently she'd used up all her diplomacy during the grueling sessions over the past week. She was saved from answering by a voice from behind her.

"Connie, leave the major alone. This is a party, not an inquisition."

She knew that voice. A second later, Rook Daniels appeared next to her, confirming her suspicion. Was everyone in DC at this event?

"You look surprised to see me," Rook said, her voice smooth and a hint of a grin playing at the corner of her lips.

"I am, but I guess I shouldn't be. Famous DC fixer. Of course you'd be where all the big names are."

"I'm not quite sure how to take that. I assure you I came by my invitation honestly. I'm not on the job tonight." Rook let loose with the grin. "That is, unless a beautiful woman needs to make a quick escape."

Connie waved a hand between them. "You two know each other?"

"Barely," Zoey said.

"Intimately," Rook said at the exact same moment.

Armstrong shook her head. "I learned long ago not to believe anything Rook Daniels said unless I hired her to say it myself."

Rook placed a hand over her heart. "Connie, you wound me."

"Save it for the camera, Daniels. Ah, here are our drinks."

Zoey tore her gaze away from Rook, and Sharp was standing next to them holding three glasses. She reached for hers, happy for the distraction. Rook was distracting enough, dressed in a sleek charcoal gray silk suit and oozing charm. As Sharp handed over her drink, Zoey couldn't help but notice a slight frown on his face, and she wondered at the cause. She didn't have a chance to ask before the senator whisked him away, leaving her alone with Rook.

"How honestly?" Zoey asked.

"Pardon?"

"You said you came by the invitation honestly."

"Yes, well, Julia is an old law school buddy of mine."

"You're a lawyer?" Zoey replayed the question back in her head and wished she hadn't injected so much surprise into it.

"Top of my class at Yale."

"But you don't practice law."

"You say that like it's a bad thing."

"I'm sorry. I didn't mean anything by it. I suppose I just wondered why anyone would go to all the trouble to become a lawyer, but not go into the profession."

Rook smiled, but Zoey read a note of frustration behind the expression. "Oh, I did. And I do. My practice isn't...traditional." She narrowed her eyes. "I wasn't aware you knew anything about me other than my skill at getting through airports undetected."

"And you are very skilled at that. If you learned that in law school, I'm quite impressed."

"I was very involved in extracurricular activities."

"I'm trying not to read too much into that."

"Then I must be failing at my job." Rook looked at a spot over Zoey's shoulder. "Have you met the guest of honor yet?"

Zoey followed her gaze and saw Addison Riley entering through two French doors that appeared to lead to a back deck. "No, but that's okay. I don't want to bother her. I'm sure there are a ton of people here who want to pay their respects."

"You say that like it's a funeral." Rook crooked her arm. "Come on, I'll introduce you. We can save her from the politicos posing as guests so they can try and backdoor all their issues."

Zoey stared at the crooked arm and shot a glance over at Sharp who was still getting an earful from Connie Armstrong. Something told her following Rook would be dangerous, but their interaction was nothing more than harmless flirting. Surely she could handle that on her own. She ignored the arm, but nodded. "Lead the way."

Rook shouldered her way through the crowd, acutely conscious of Zoey right behind her. Two times in as many weeks, she'd swooned over this woman in uniform. Something about Zoey intrigued her, and she was going to find out what it was if she had to spend the rest of the night at her side.

They were a couple of feet from the chief justice, but the group around Addison was like a wall with the outer edges ebbing and flowing, but never giving way. Rook reached back and grabbed Zoey's hand and raised her other one as she waved to Addison. Addison waved back and murmured excuses to the throng surrounding her as she edged toward Rook and Zoey.

"I need a stiff drink and a quiet place. Get me there, and I'll owe you for life," Addison whispered once she was standing next to them.

"I'd be stupid to refuse that deal." Rook noted Addison's questioning look in Zoey's direction, but she didn't pause to make introductions. "Point the way to the quiet place, and I'll get drinks."

"Up those stairs." Addison pointed toward the sweeping balcony, and the three of them climbed away from the growing crowd. Zoey reached for the banister and Rook instantly missed the warmth of her touch. She followed Addison's directions, down the hall, around the corner to a large wooden door that led to a beautiful library. The walls were lined with shelves, floor to ceiling, and filled with books and art objects. Rook was impressed, but Zoey appeared to be captivated. She walked over to one of the shelves and traced the spine of a volume of Emily Dickinson's poetry that Rook bet was a collector's edition.

"I'm amazed every time I walk in here," Addison said. "Feel free to look around."

Zoey jerked her hand back and came to attention. "My apologies, ma'am. I have a small book collection, but this..."

Addison wagged a finger at Rook. "Look at you bringing a woman with great taste to my party. And a soldier no less. I knew you had it in you."

Rook shot a look at Zoey to gauge her reaction to Addison's mistaken assumption and caught her shaking her head. "Madam Chief Justice, I'd like you to meet Major Zoey Granger, soon to be Lieutenant Colonel if the rumors are true. As much as I'd be flattered to claim her as my date, she is here as General Sharp's guest."

Addison reached out a hand. "Nice to meet you, Major soon to be Lieutenant Colonel."

"The pleasure is all mine," Zoey said. "And I'm afraid it would be a bit premature to believe any such rumors."

"Well, any friend of David Sharp's is a friend of mine."

Rook watched the exchange. Connie Armstrong had filled her in on the promotion request that had been filed by Sharp. She had no doubt it was true, but now she wondered if Zoey had known about it. She didn't look surprised at the pronouncement, but she did look slightly embarrassed. *Stop overanalyzing and enjoy the evening.* "Well, premature or not, I say we celebrate. Shall I go get us some fresh drinks?"

"Or we could just find the bottle of ancient Scotch Julia keeps hidden up here," Addison said, opening a cabinet door and pushing her way through the contents. "Somebody get the door before we get caught pilfering through her stash."

"I can do you one better," Rook said, spying the bottle with the red bow she'd handed to Julia at the door. She picked it up and handed it to Addison. "Happy birthday."

"Hey, sis, are you bailing on your own party already?"

A tall, handsome man who bore an unmistakable resemblance to the chief justice stood in the doorway. "You must be Jack Riley," Rook said, noticing Zoey perk up at the mention of his name.

"That's me." He walked in the room, his hand outstretched. Rook returned the firm handshake with one of her own. "Rook Daniels, nice to meet you." She pointed at Zoey. "And this is Major Zoey Granger, a fellow soldier. Any chance you two know each other?"

"I don't believe we've met," Jack said.

"We haven't," Zoey said. "But we have a friend in common. General David Sharp?"

"Ah, yes. Uncle David. Well, he's not really our uncle, but we've known him since we were kids. He served with our dad," Jack said, waving to include Addison in his remarks.

"He's been a mentor to me throughout my career."

"You couldn't find a better man for the job. Where are you stationed, Major?"

Zoey cleared her throat before speaking. It was a little thing and easily written off to allergies or the hours she'd spent talking while on the hot seat in the Senate, but Rook had noticed her doing it before and recognized it as a tell. Whatever Zoey was about to say wasn't entirely true. "Most recently Fort Hood after I detailed back from Bagram, but I won't get my new orders until next week. You?"

Jack nodded knowingly. "I've been detailed with JSOC, but I'm at the Pentagon for a while riding a desk." He pulled out a card.

"If they drag you back here, look me up and I'll show you my small part of the Puzzle Palace."

Zoey studied the card and placed it in her pocket. Rook watched the entire exchange with a small measure of envy. The tight-knit military club never failed to amaze her. These two had never met before, but suddenly they were fast friends.

"So here's where you're all hanging out." Julia stood in the doorway, shaking her head. "I've got a crowd of people screaming for cake and the guest of honor is nowhere in sight."

Addison raised her glass. "Sorry. All my fault. I corrupted this entire group, but I promise we'll be downstairs in five minutes. But first, a toast." She motioned for everyone to fill their glass. "To good friends and family. May we cherish what we have while we have it."

The group called out hear, hears and everyone drank to the toast. As they made their way back downstairs to the party, Rook sidled up to Zoey. "Having fun?"

"More than I expected." Zoey covered her mouth. "Sorry, that sounded rude."

Rook laughed. "Not at all. I spend a lot of time at parties, but they aren't my favorite things."

"Oh, really. You seem like a natural."

"Professional partygoer. It's on my résumé."

"What are your favorite things?"

"Pardon?"

"What kind of things do you like to do?"

Rook pondered the question. It wasn't hard, but she had a difficult time coming up with anything, probably because she hadn't done anything just for fun in a very long time. "To be perfectly honest, I spend most of my time working."

"Too bad. Your driver, George, recommended a nighttime tour of the monuments as one of the best ways to see DC and I planned to go tomorrow. Any chance you want to join me? I know it's probably cheesy to you, but it would be a small thing I could do to pay you back for saving me in the airport."

Rook started to decline. It was cheesy and she kind of hated to admit she'd never done any of the usual touristy things in DC. Not on purpose anyway. She didn't really see the point. She'd seen parts of the White House and Capitol most tourists never got to see—anything else seemed like a waste of time. Besides, she had absolutely no interest in developing a relationship with someone in the military. But then again, Zoey was only here temporarily—it wasn't like they were going to get involved for anything beyond the short-term. *It's not like you're going to war.*

"I'd love to join you."

❖

"I'm sorry I bailed on you back there. You'll learn soon enough no party in DC is purely about pleasure," Sharp said as they drove away from the party.

"Didn't take me long to figure that out." Zoey leaned back against the seat, reflecting on the evening. Her response wasn't entirely accurate since except for her initial encounter with Senator Armstrong, she'd spent most of the night in the company of Rook and Addison's brother Jack who'd regaled them with stories about his sister as a child. Zoey had felt like one of the cool kids for the first time since she'd blown the lid off the Nine Tech scandal.

Earlier in the day, she would've sworn it wasn't important to fit in, but that's what everyone who fit in said. For a fleeting moment she wondered what her family would think if she told them she'd spent the better part of the evening in the company of the chief justice of the Supreme Court and the president's chief of staff. But she knew she'd never tell since their response would evoke a tirade about liberal judges and a president who'd rather help people in foreign countries than his own citizens. Never mind they were always the first ones in line when there was a handout to be had, especially her able-bodied brother with his lazy wife who pretended to homeschool the kids to avoid getting a real job. Both of them would rather tear down the establishment they didn't really understand than do anything to fix it.

"She's respected in certain circles, but you'd probably do well to steer clear, especially until you have a bit more experience with DC politics."

Zoey looked at the general, hoping he didn't have a clue she'd zoned out for the last few minutes. She cycled through the faces of the people she'd hung out with at the party, wondering exactly who he was talking about. "Senator Armstrong?"

He laughed. "That one's almost impossible to avoid. She's got her nose in everything. Mark my words, you'll see Armstrong for President commercials popping up next year. She won't rest until she's at the top of the heap. No, I was talking about Rook Daniels."

With a guilty thought about the date she'd scheduled with Rook the next day, Zoey casually asked, "So I take it you know her pretty well."

"I know of her and that's enough. Not many people know her well. She's a chameleon. Worse than a lawyer. Her allegiance goes to the highest bidder."

Zoey laughed. "Sounds exactly like a lawyer to me."

"Except lawyers take an oath and have some accountability to the court. Public relations experts, which is what she calls herself, act with impunity to make their clients look good, right or wrong be damned."

Zoey resisted pointing out Rook was a lawyer since she sensed this conversation wasn't about facts, but impressions. Clearly, David Sharp was not impressed with Rook Daniels, which left her feeling a bit torn since she'd had exactly the opposite reaction.

but to Rook it was a necessity that allowed her to stay at the office whenever the team was in crisis mode. Her office featured a sleek leather sofa that folded out into a Tempur-Pedic bed on nights when she couldn't make it home, and the bathroom was another extension of the home away from home.

She brushed her teeth and finger-combed her short curls with a drop of product, wishing not for the first time they would obey her commands. The eyes looking back at her in the mirror were puffy and tired, and she dug through the drawers and found a bottle of eye drops. Other than the eyes, she supposed she looked okay. People told her she was handsome, which she took to mean not quite girly enough, but still good-looking. Her features were chiseled, which gave her a hard edge, and she'd spent many hours practicing an engaging smile so her audiences would warm to her for her clients' sake. She laid one on now and was surprised it came naturally. Whatever mixed feelings she might have about the circumstance, she was actually excited about seeing Zoey again. After a few moments of messing around with her wayward hair, Rook changed into a maroon cashmere sweater and light gray pants, and sprayed a light mist of cologne to finish out her transformation.

George was waiting at the curb, but she waved him back into the car before he had time to make it to her door. She sank into the cushy seat in the rear of the town car. "Did you manage to get everything?"

"Full picnic basket right up here. Wynn didn't have the wine you wanted, but she said this bottle is even better. Difference is on her."

"Thanks, George. You mind if I catch a few winks while you drive?"

"You must be tired. No documents to review or phone calls to make?"

"I think I might have reached my max for the day." Rook caught his look of surprise in the rearview mirror, but rather than explain, she took advantage of the time alone and closed her eyes, letting thoughts of Zoey fill her dreams.

❖

Zoey waited in the hotel lobby since Rook's text had said she'd be there at six and would come inside to get her. Zoey had offered to meet her at Union Station where the trolleys picked up their passengers for the tour, but Rook had insisted on this courtesy, and Zoey was glad not to have to navigate her way around, although she'd soon have to learn her new city.

Sharp's bombshell about the job at the Pentagon had left her with a boatload of logistics to consider. She'd been deployed for the last ten months, but many of her belongings were still at her base housing in Texas. She'd have the week to travel, pack, return, and find a new place to live. She'd spent the better part of the day online researching housing in DC. Thank God she was being promoted. She was going to need every dollar of her pay increase and step up in housing allowance to afford a place to live. If Sharp hadn't cautioned her to keep the transfer under wraps until it was official, she would ask Rook for advice about options.

Of course, she was ignoring Sharp's other advice about steering clear of Rook in the first place. She'd spent some time after he dropped her off at the hotel last night considering whether she should cancel her outing with Rook in light of the caution, but ultimately decided against it. It was a casual outing, not a date. There was zero chance Sharp would be on a tour bus in the town he'd called home for years, and if they did run into him, she didn't mind explaining she'd already made plans with Rook before his warning. Besides, she was perfectly capable of taking care of herself. A civilian like Rook Daniels was no threat to her.

She'd barely completed her thought when Rook strode through the double glass doors of the hotel lobby. She looked dashing in light gray wool slacks and a burgundy V-neck sweater that hugged her trim upper body. Zoey wrote off the accelerated beating of her heart to excitement about the tour, but she knew deep down she was fooling herself. *Not a date. Not a date.* She repeated the silent mantra in time with Rook's steps until they were standing face-to-face.

"You look amazing," Rook said, her eyes sweeping Zoey's frame.

Zoey shrugged off the compliment. For the first time since they'd met, she was dressed in civilian clothes, dark blue jeans and a heather green sweater. "I didn't pack much in the way of casual clothes. Of course, I assumed the tour would be casual, but you look anything but." She stopped talking, conscious of the fact she was rambling.

Rook looked down at her outfit. "This is pretty casual for me." She held out her arm. "Come on, I have a surprise for you."

Zoey's ears perked up at the word surprise—not her favorite word—but she took Rook's arm and followed her to the town car she recognized from the airport. Rook opened the door and Zoey slid inside, spotting George behind the wheel. "Hi, George. Remember me?"

"Not likely to forget, Major Granger. I see you took my advice about the best way to see the city."

"Indeed. I hear the weather is supposed to be perfect tonight. No clouds or rain."

"Perfect night for a picnic, indeed."

Picnic? Zoey looked over at Rook who had just slid into the seat beside her. "I just booked the basic tour, nothing fancy. I hope you don't mind."

"Well, that's the surprise. Now, I hope *you* don't mind, because George here has obtained the tour route and you'll get the same exact features, but without a busload of tourists. And," Rook reached around to the front seat and lifted a basket, "I have food and wine. I figured we'd take a little break between stops." She paused for a second. "I guess I should've run this by you first. I'll reimburse you for the tickets you bought."

Zoey stared at the picnic basket and then back at Rook, astounded by the thoughtfulness, even if it was a bit presumptuous. Presumptuous, hell. Rook had planned the perfect evening. Who was she to throw a wrench into it? "It's perfect. Really. And don't be silly about the tickets. This will be so much better."

"You say that now, but I'm afraid I only have a passing knowledge of most of these places." Rook pulled a book from between the seats. "I, or rather George, got us a copy of the *DC Lonely Planet Guide*, and I'll be happy to look up any questions you have."

Zoey had a ton of questions, but none of them about monuments or anything tourist related. Was Rook always this thoughtful? How had she managed to live in a city and know virtually nothing about its most famous venues? One question topped the list. If this wasn't a date, what was it?

❖

Rook watched Zoey run her hand along the granite wall, tracing the words. *The moral arch of humanity is large, but it always bends toward justice.* The Martin Luther King Jr. memorial was their third stop on the tour. They'd noshed a little in the car, but Zoey had insisted she'd rather see a few of the monuments before their picnic. Rook was pleasantly surprised to find she was enjoying herself and she'd actually learned a few things along the way.

"The book says those cherry trees over there were positioned to bloom in a particular spot so it looks like MLK is gazing at them," Rook said, pointing at the trees.

"I hear the cherry blossoms are a beautiful sight."

Rook nodded. "We locals moan about all the tourists who crowd the city to see them, but you can hardly blame them. Too bad you won't be around to see them."

"When do they usually bloom?"

"A few weeks from now, toward the end of March, beginning of April."

"Mmm," Zoey said. "What's next on the tour?"

Rook started to call her out on the quick change of subject, certain it was a cover for something but wasn't sure what. Could Zoey already be missing their connection? Silly really, since they'd barely met, but Rook had to admit the idea of Zoey jetting back to wherever she was assigned left her feeling unsettled. Was it possible

Zoey was feeling the same? "I'm a little hungry. Ready for a short break?"

"Sure."

They returned to the car and Rook told George they were ready for the next stop. When they pulled into the parking lot for Meridian Hill Park, it was deserted. Zoey looked around, the expression on her face making it clear she thought the destination was a no-go. Rook suppressed a grin and pulled out her phone. When the call connected, she said, "Hey, Nancy, we're here…Okay…See you in a minute."

She slipped the phone into her pocket and reached for the picnic basket. "Ready?"

Zoey's eyes narrowed, but she nodded and followed Rook out of the car. Rook told George she'd text when they were ready to leave and led Zoey to the gate at the edge of the property and waited.

"I hate to burst your bubble," Zoey said, pointing to a sign, "but I think they might be closed for the day."

"Oh, they're definitely closed. To the general public that is."

"And we're not the general public."

"Not tonight."

"Okay."

Rook didn't bother hiding her grin now, but before she had a chance to explain, Park Ranger Nancy Evers appeared at the gate.

"Hey, Rook, how're you doing?"

"Great, Nance. I'd like you to meet Major Zoey Granger. She's in town for a few days and is trying to see as much of our fair city as she can." She hefted the basket. "Beautiful night for a picnic, don't you think?"

"Perfect and you picked the best place in town for it." Nancy held the gate open and ushered them through. "Text me when you're done and I'll come back down and let you out."

"Will do." Rook waited until Nancy disappeared back into the park and took Zoey's hand. "Shall I give you a little history of the park while we find the perfect place to have dinner?"

"If you're trying to impress me, you can consider this mission accomplished. What is this place?"

"It's Meridian Hill Park. In 1819, John Porter erected a mansion here on Meridian Hill so called because it was on the exact longitude of the original District of Columbia milestone marker, set down on April 15, 1791. In 1829, the mansion became departing President John Quincy Adams's home. After its conversion to a public park, Union troops encamped on the grounds during the Civil War." She paused to catch her breath, but before she could go on, Zoey held up a hand.

"Got it. So, this is either your favorite place in the world or you memorized that out of a brochure or…"

"What's the last 'or'?"

"Or you bring all the girls here to impress them."

Rook laughed as she spread out a blanket and began to unpack the picnic basket. "Fair question, but I've never brought a girl here or anyone else for that matter. It's one of my favorite places, but it's always been just my place." Rook let the words trail off as the significance of her remark hung in the air between them. Zoey stared into her eyes, and Rook could swear Zoey was trying to read her mind. Good luck with that, she thought. She didn't know why she'd told Zoey about her affection for the park. When she played the words back in her head, they sounded private and intimate, like something lovers shared. Time to move this conversation in a different direction, preferably with the focus on Zoey.

"I guess you've traveled all over the world." Rook didn't wait for Zoey's response before pressing on. "What's your favorite place?"

Zoey broke their stare and looked off in the distance. "Hard to say. I was stationed in Okinawa, Japan, for a while. For a farm girl from Texas, it was quite a shock. Instead of acres of land with just a few people, there were people and buildings packed into every corner of that island. At first it felt suffocating, but then…" She stopped as if considering the right description. "Then it was comforting. Like when you wrap a scared dog in a blanket and pull it tight to soothe him. It was so easy to lose myself in the large crowds. No one cared that I didn't speak the language or understand the culture. I was just swept up in it all and eventually found my way." She focused back on Rook. "Does that sound stupid?"

Rook smiled. "No. I totally get it. There's freedom in anonymity. It can give you the space to be who you want to be." She reached for the bottle of wine. "I guess you don't have that anymore."

Zoey's laugh was hard and humorless. "You think? I noticed it even when I was playing tourist yesterday. People would stare. Most of them didn't have a clue who I was, but they knew they'd seen me somewhere. I even caught a few taking pictures, no doubt in case I turned out to be someone famous. Boy, will they be disappointed."

Rook popped the cork on the sparkling rosé and poured them each a glass. "Maybe. Or maybe they'll have a new hero."

Zoey made a face. "That sounds a little sappy, don't you think?"

"A little, but hey, a lot of people think you are a hero. I bet your parents are proud." No sooner had the last few words left her lips than Rook noticed Zoey's expression darken. "Sorry, that was insensitive. No parents?"

"Let's just say I don't think anyone's sitting at home in Imperial, Texas, watching C-SPAN so they could cheer me on because A, they wouldn't know where to find C-SPAN on the dial, and B, approving of me and my choices isn't in their playbook."

"Well, that sucks."

"It's my reality, but I try not to think about it too much." Zoey took a drink from her wineglass. "What about you? Family in the area? Do you come from a long line of fixers?"

"Fixer," Rook repeated. She hated the moniker since it made her sound like someone who built houses or worked on cars. "I prefer public relations specialist. My specialty is helping people and/or organizations who've found themselves in difficult situations navigate their way through the nightmare that public relations has become in this era of hundred-and-forty-character take downs."

"Nightmare is a good word for it." Zoey appreciated the frank assessment. She'd avoided Twitter and Facebook since she'd blown the whistle on Nine Tech, but she needn't have bothered. Every time she flipped on the news, social media feeds were the secondary source of the day.

"And I'm the first in my family to take on this particular business."

Zoey studied the hard lines of Rook's expression. "Let me guess. Your family doesn't approve of your occupation either?"

"They can't really deny my success, but they pretend they don't understand what I do. I get a lot of 'why did you bother to go to law school?' at family gatherings."

Zoey nodded, but she couldn't help but wonder what Rook's response to her family's question was. She'd gone to school on an ROTC scholarship, and without it she would've been stuck at community college. Graduate school had been out of the question, but thankfully, she'd had the Army to supply her with options for her career. No one else in her family had attended college, let alone law school.

As if she could hear Zoey's thoughts, Rook added, "My family has a history of producing fat cat lawyers who work at large firms, billing big bucks to keep their clients out of trouble. No matter how hard I try to explain the similarities, my particular niche is lost on them."

Zoey sensed there was a deeper story about Rook's motivation to avoid the family business, but she simply said, "That must be hard."

"It was, but I solved the problem by being as successful as I could and not caring what they think. Needless to say, we don't spend a lot of time together." Rook reached into the picnic basket. "Now, enough depressing, dysfunctional family talk. I'm starving."

On cue, Zoey's stomach growled and they both laughed. With the change in tone, Zoey decided to abandon drilling deeper into what made Rook tick. Rook pulled out a selection of cheeses, crackers, charcuterie, and olives, and they dug into the food. Zoey couldn't help but wonder if both of them were avoiding conversation until they could steer it to something innocuous, but for her part, she wasn't sure where to begin. She liked Rook's sense of humor and her easy manner. If they were different people in different roles, she might even consider seeing her again despite the vast disparity in the way they approached the world. Rook had grown up with every opportunity but wasted her talents helping famous people cover up their problems. Zoey had grown up with nothing and had dedicated her life to service so the world could be a better place. Okay, perhaps that wasn't a fair comparison, but she'd seen real problems that created real news, not the gossip column problems of the rich and famous that Rook was hired to spin. Boiling it down that way made it hard to deny the striking difference. She decided to enjoy the moment and put aside deeper thoughts. "This cheese is amazing. What is it?"

"It's a Manchego with truffles," Rook said. "One of my guilty pleasures." She sliced another piece and placed it on a cracker. "Try it on this. I plan on having this at my last meal."

Rook reached toward Zoey's mouth with the cheese-laden cracker. Zoey held a hand out to take the food, but before she could, Rook's fingers grazed her lips and her traitorous mouth opened on cue and her tongue touched Rook's skin sending currents of pleasure throughout her body. If this hadn't been a date before, it sure felt like one now.

A loud buzzing interrupted her thoughts, and Rook reached into her pocket with a sheepish look on her face. "Sorry," Rook said as she answered her phone. "Daniels here."

Rook's expression hardened as she listened to the voice on the other end of the conversation. Zoey sipped her wine and tried not to eavesdrop, but the urgent tone and clipped phrases pulled her in.

"You're kidding…How long?…And they don't know?…Be right there." Rook slipped the phone back in her pocket. "I'm sorry, but I have to go."

"Is something wrong?" Zoey asked, hoping Rook's worried frown wasn't a harbinger of some dire personal emergency. "Is there anything I can do?"

"No, it's work. I'd send someone else, but this particular client demands my personal touch." Rook packed up the picnic basket as she spoke. "I'm so sorry to cut our d—outing short." She stood and held out a hand. "Rain check for next time you're back in DC?"

Zoey took Rook's hand and climbed to her feet. They were standing only inches apart, and the heat she'd felt earlier flared up again. Rook had been about to call this a date and, in every way except this abrupt parting, it was one. But it was the last one. She would've understood if Rook had raced off to care for an ailing relative or to help someone in need, but a 911 for PR trouble on a Sunday night? Nope, Rook's priorities were all wrong, and even if neither one of them was willing to call this night what it was, there would be no repeat performance.

Chapter Six

A week later, Zoey stood outside the Shake Shack at Pentagon City, the shopping mall situated one Metro stop from the government building it was named for. Building was really a misnomer for the Pentagon considering it was the size of a small city that housed about fifty times more people than the West Texas town where she'd grown up.

Zoey had two more days of freedom before she started her new assignment, and while she was both excited and nervous at the prospect, she had more pressing issues to face. First up was defying all odds to find a place to live before she reported to her new assignment on Monday morning, and she'd enlisted the perfect person to help her.

Margaret Sharp showed up on time, exactly what Zoey would expect from a career officer's wife. She'd first met Margaret when she was still very green after David had taken her under his wing. She'd spent many Sunday afternoons eating way too much pot roast and then playing pickup games of touch football with the entire Sharp family at her first base assignment, Fort Bragg. Margaret had regaled her with stories about all the exotic overseas assignments David's career had taken them on, and later took credit for Zoey's wanderlust, but at the time Zoey was just happy to have pseudo family to call her own. The ease with which she'd fit in amongst them almost made the pain of her own family's indifference bearable. Almost.

"I love this place," Margaret said. "But every time I think of it, there's always a huge line. This worked out perfectly. I figure we can eat now before the crowds and then spend the rest of the day narrowing down the search for your new home."

Home. The word sounded so permanent, so real. Zoey hesitated to entertain the idea this assignment might result in her staying in one place for any length of time long enough to consider it home, but the prospect was inviting. She'd spent her career moving from base to base and taking every deployment opportunity she could get. Roots were for people with spouses and kids. The only long-term relationship she'd ever been interested in cultivating was with the service, and a week ago she'd thought her affair with the Army might be coming to an end. Now that she was assured a more permanent assignment, the idea of setting down roots was actually appealing.

"I don't need much," she said. "A simple apartment, maybe with an extra bedroom for a study."

"How about a townhouse? Colonel Peters is transferring to Fort Benning, and his place is up for sale. You'd have some of the benefits of living in an apartment—no yard work, neighbors close by, but you wouldn't be tossing your money away on rent and you'd be building some equity. We've been out there a couple of times and it's a really nice place. It would be perfect for you."

Zoey fixated on "neighbors close by" and started to rethink the whole apartment idea. She'd lived her life in the close confines of the various bases she was assigned to, and until this moment, she assumed that was all she'd ever wanted, but that was before she'd turned on her peers and become a pariah on base. Even after she'd transferred stateside from Bagram, she'd noticed the whispers and side-eye glances from fellow soldiers at Fort Hood. Close quarters meant closer to rejection, and she could do without the reminder she was alone in a crowd.

"You know, I think I might like to look at something different. An actual house with a yard. I realize real estate can be a little off the rails here, but I have quite a bit in savings. I'm open to renting for now just to have a place to live, and then taking some time to find something more permanent if things work out for me to stick around."

"House it is," Margaret said. "We should be able to make this work." She drummed the table with her fingers as she worked through the change in plans. "I'm thinking Fairfax or Vienna would be good places to start." She reached a hand across the table. "And I have a feeling things are going to work out for you to stick around for a long time. David is so very happy to have you close by. He couldn't stop talking about you after he got back from the party Saturday night. I swear he couldn't be more proud of you if you were his flesh and blood." The buzzer signaling their food was ready lit up and skittered across the table. "If you'll pick up our burgers, I'll run a few quick searches at MilitaryByOwner."

Zoey complied, happy to leave the details to Margaret. She had no idea where Fairfax and Vienna were or what MilitaryByOwner was, but she was confident Margaret would make sure she found the amenities she wanted in close proximity to her new office. The only surprising thing about their conversation had been Margaret's revelations about her husband. Zoey hadn't been certain how to read Sharp's reactions since she'd been called on the carpet two weeks ago, and she'd suspected her promotion was more for show than because anyone in Army command thought she deserved a reward. To hear he was proud of her, even if she didn't hear the words directly from him was a welcome accolade, and she tucked the warm fuzzy away in case she needed a reminder at some point she wasn't alone.

Zoey stood behind a crowd all waiting to pick up their food, and her eyes were drawn to a copy of the *Washington Post* on the abandoned table next to her. The headline blared *REPUBLICANS CALL FOR SENATOR NEWMAN TO RESIGN.* She didn't spend a lot of time dwelling on politics, but like everyone else in the country, she'd heard the name and couldn't resist skimming the story while she waited.

Youthful and dashing, Steve Newman was a big deal in DC. Having soared to a governor's seat in Ohio at the young age of thirty-three, he'd foregone a third term to take his father's Senate seat when the elder Newman met an untimely death at the hands of a shooter at a mall in Columbus. The younger Newman had been pegged as a Bill Clinton type, and as early as a month ago, his name had been floated as a potential standard bearer for the Democratic Party when President Garrett was forced to retire in two years. His path to success was one of the most watched spectacles in the country. And so was his demise.

Last week, a woman came forward, not to make a sexual assault or affair allegation as was often the case for a popular politician, but to say she'd been a passenger in a car that had plowed into a young woman one snowy night last year in downtown Columbus. This witness told the press the driver of the vehicle had been none other than Senator Newman, and he'd driven from the scene without even checking to see if the girl was okay. She died before help arrived.

Zoey shook her head. The woman might have lived if he'd stopped to call an ambulance. What had been so worth hiding that he'd chosen to flee the scene rather than face the consequences of his actions? He'd probably been drinking, she surmised, and like an echo of her thoughts, her eyes caught the next few lines of text in the article. Senator Newman strongly denied that alcohol played a factor in the incident.

"Senator Newman doesn't drink, but that's not the point. He was not responsible for this tragic death, and there is no credible evidence to support the allegation that he was," said Rook Daniels, spokesperson for the senator.

Zoey dropped the paper back onto the table. She'd thought about Rook several times since their aborted date, wondering what might have happened if she hadn't been summoned away, but she'd filed the missed opportunity under things best left undone. The sight of Rook's name scattered her neatly tucked feelings in several different directions—curiosity, longing, regret—but something about the news story nagged at the back of her mind. She picked up the paper again and skimmed the rest of the article as well as the sidebar, and when she had devoured every word, she was certain the call Rook had taken the night they were at Meridian Park had been about this case.

"Is everything okay?"

Zoey looked up at the sound of Margaret's voice and then over at the counter where a tray of food sat waiting. She had no idea how long she'd been standing here, reading the article, letting their food grow cold in the window. "Sorry, I started reading this article and got completely distracted."

Margaret glanced at the paper. "It's a sad story for everyone involved. That poor girl and now Senator Newman's career is ruined over a snap decision made in the heat of the moment. I guess you never know when your entire world will spin out of control."

Zoey nodded as she grabbed the tray of food. Apparently, Rook Daniels lived her life in the eye of the storm, and Zoey was grateful she hadn't allowed herself to be swept away.

Rook tipped the coffee mug to her lips, but only a trickle of the caffeinated magic met her lips. She had no recollection of drinking the entire cup, but she was going to need a lot more if she was going to make it through the day. She swung her legs off her desk and trudged, zombie-like, toward the office kitchen, colliding with Lacy as soon as she reached the entrance.

"Lacy, you scared the hell out of me. What are you doing here?"

"I could say the same to you. Last I checked you own a pretty nice townhouse, but I doubt you've seen it in a week. You look like hell, Rook."

"Thanks for the pep talk, but seriously, it's Sunday. Don't you have family stuff?"

"I made pancakes and bacon for the kids and now Ron's responsible for entertaining them the rest of the day. Blake's already here. I called Harry and Eric and they're on their way. You have a team for a reason. Let us help you."

Rook weighed her options. Normally, she'd have no qualms about calling in the whole team to work on a weekend, especially when it was a big case with a high-profile client, but she'd chosen to pull the overtime on this one by herself for a very good reason. "You know I'm working on the Newman case, right?"

Lacy rolled her eyes. "Yes, Rook, I read the papers, just like everyone else. It's a case, just like any other. What do you always say? Personal is our business. Now we get to test that, so let's get to work."

She crossed her arms and her expression dared Rook to challenge her. The truth was, Rook did need her. The press requests alone for information about Newman's situation had her buried, and Lacy was much better suited to sorting through and prioritizing who she should talk to and when. Every major network wanted to book the Newmans for their Monday morning shows, and she needed to make some decisions fast.

But she hadn't wanted to involve Lacy. Holly, Lacy's daughter from her first marriage, had been run down in the street and left for dead as she walked back to her dorm after a particularly raucous fraternity party. Lacy had to fight the police to find the perpetrator when all they wanted to do was blame her daughter, claiming her blood alcohol content was the reason she was in harm's way. Her marriage had been ripped apart by the loss of their only child.

Lacy had come a long way since then. She'd remarried, had twins, and embraced a new life, but Rook knew her past grief always simmered just below the surface. Lacy had told her more than once that she viewed the work they did as a means of revenge—when they represented the good guys. But this wasn't one of those times. Newman might have been a good guy in the public eye before—a champion of the disenfranchised, the poor, a change-maker—but his favorables had plummeted since this story broke, and Rook wasn't sure she could save him no matter what she did. But she'd taken the case, so she had to try, and if trying was painful for the people she cared about, she'd shield them as best she could.

"Okay, to be honest, I could use the help." Rook handed over a stack of notes she'd scribbled on various bits of paper. "Interview prep. If you could type that up and make it look like a semi-intelligent outline, I'll be forever in your debt. The Newmans will be here at five, so I need it before then."

"Are you doing the full rounds in the morning or are you putting all your eggs in one basket?"

"Jury's still out on that, but I'm leaning toward the one basket approach. The Newman kids are home from spring break, and if I can get the whole family to go on camera with a female anchor, I think we'll get the best spin." She ran a hand through her hair. "If it isn't too late."

"I have to say, I was heartbroken when the story broke. He's been quite a force in the Senate."

"Tell me about it. Never would've seen this coming."

"I'll have this back to you in less than an hour." Lacy paused in the doorway. "I'll order up some food. Why don't you grab a shower or a nap or both? You probably have another thirty minutes before everyone gets here."

Rook shook her head, secretly happy for Lacy's intervention. Her desk was covered with projects, and every single one was critical. She was a complete hard-ass when it came to evaluating which cases she would take on, but lately it seemed every single one was impossible to turn down. From old friends calling in favors to the rare instance, like this one, where her ideology demanded she give her client the benefit of the doubt. Her appearance at Addison Riley's birthday party seemed to have rousted a few new clients despite the fact she'd spent most of the party flirting with Major Granger instead of networking.

She wondered what Zoey was up to. She'd sent her a text to apologize the day after their aborted date and she'd sent flowers to the hotel, but the florist had informed her Zoey had checked out, probably headed back to her base and whatever normalcy she could find after her week taking center stage on C-SPAN. Rook didn't envy her the transition, but she did wish she'd had the full evening to spend with her. Rook had been drawn to Zoey despite her allegiance to the military, but considering how her work schedule had heated up over the past week, it was probably best Zoey was no longer in town to distract her.

Her phone buzzed and she glanced at the screen, smiling when she saw it was Julia. "Hey you," Rook said. "Let me guess. Your party went so well, you're planning another one."

"You're hilarious, although I did make a splash in *Reliable Source* and not on my boss's behalf for once. Helena Andrews said

Addison's party was the 'it' place to be last weekend, which means I have a backup plan if my current career doesn't work out."

"I hate to be the one to break this to you, but the clock is ticking on your present position. You might want to go ahead and start marketing your event planning business to get a jumpstart."

"Some days that actually sounds like a perfect plan. What are you doing right now?"

Rook's ears perked at the abrupt change of subject and she answered cautiously. "The usual. Helping the oppressed."

Julia's voice dropped to a whisper. "I need to see you."

"Sounds ominous."

"Today."

Rook looked at her antique Rolex. "I have a meeting at five, but you're welcome to stop by if you can get here before then."

"Yeah, it's not a drop by and see you kind of thing. I'm sending a car for you. I'll have you back in plenty of time for your meeting."

Rook wasn't in the mood for cloak-and-dagger even when she wasn't exhausted, but she resisted the urge to tell Julia no, partly because she was curious and partly because she didn't have the energy to argue. Julia wasn't known for taking no for an answer which was precisely why she made a perfect chief of staff. "Fine, but I'm warning you, I'm tired and grumpy, so be prepared to make this worth my time."

"If you can be ready in fifteen minutes, I'll even guarantee you a sandwich. The car will be waiting downstairs."

Julia clicked off the line before Rook could respond. She was still holding the phone when Lacy poked her head in the door. "We're ordering Thai. You want me to get you something?"

Struck by the coincidence, Rook shook her head. "Actually, I have to run out for a little bit." She hesitated, pondering whether she should mention where she was going before she recalled she didn't know. Rather than share the vague details she did know, she glossed over the particulars. "Quick errand and I won't be long. I'll grab something while I'm out." She pulled her jacket off the back of her chair and strode to the door, ignoring Lacy's curious stare. "See you in a bit."

The big black SUV waiting at the curb with the motor running told her what she needed to know. Whatever Julia wanted to see her about was official business. Julia wouldn't have sent feds to get her if she'd been asking for a personal favor. While Rook was glad her friend didn't need her services to get out of a personal jam, she braced for the blowback when she turned down the request for help. President Garrett seemed like a nice guy, but the White House was a behemoth, and no way was she going to get caught up in a bureaucratic maze.

She had a twenty-minute ride to practice saying no. She spent part of that time marking the route, and it didn't take her long to realize the driver, a man of few words whose expression she couldn't make out because he wore dark aviators, was purposely driving in circles. Whatever Julia wanted, she didn't want anyone to know she'd summoned Rook on official business, which suited her just fine. If word got out she was working for the White House, chances were good a lot of potential clients would seek help elsewhere figuring she'd be too consumed with a bigger case. Sure, there might be a long run benefit, but she wasn't interested in taking the chance.

They were near Dupont Circle when the SUV pulled to the curb. "This is your stop," Mr. Not-Talk-Much said as he reached back and handed her a folded piece of paper. Rook grasped the note and pushed her door open, waiting until she was on the sidewalk before reading the contents.

Bookstore. By the travel guides.

She crammed the note in her pocket and glanced around at the buildings until she spotted the bookstore, silently vowing to end this treasure hunt if Julia wasn't waiting inside. She nodded to the cashier by the door and wandered through the shelves as if she were a curious customer. She heard Julia before she saw her.

"Rook Daniels! Oh my God, it's good to see you. What have you been up to?"

Rook resisted looking around to see if they had an audience because it was pretty clear Julia was playing to one. She decided it wouldn't hurt to play along, a bit. "Nothing special. How about you? Oh wait, I forgot, you're running the world. Guess they gave that most likely to rule the world award to the wrong person in our law school class."

Julia playfully slapped her arm and then slipped her hand through it. "I'm sorry I didn't get a chance to talk to you at Addison's party. Do you have time for coffee? I'd love to catch up."

Rook recognized the play-acting for a cover and looked at her watch even though she knew it was a rhetorical question. "Sure."

"Great. They have a place here." Julia didn't wait for a response, instead leading Rook by the arm to the back of the store where a few scattered tables and an espresso machine constituted the cafe portion of the establishment. On a normal day, Rook would have suggested they bag this place and partake at one of the better known coffee shops this area boasted, but the faster she could hear what Julia wanted, the faster she could turn her down and get back to her real client.

They ordered at the counter and took the table closest to the back of the store. Rook caught sight of a tall guy in a navy suit, standing a few feet away and she jerked her chin in his direction. "Do they go everywhere with you?"

"No, thank God. I'd go insane. Or quit. Probably quit."

"So are they here because I'm a badass?"

"You're not as badass as you would like people to believe. They're here because what I want to talk to you about is very sensitive and they can give me a heads up if they think someone might be listening in."

Rook couldn't help it. All the clandestine activity had her mildly curious, but she feigned nonchalance. "Gotcha. So, what's up?"

"What I'm about to tell you is top secret. Not classified top secret, but between you and me top secret. Even if you turn me down flat, which you won't, I need your word that whatever I say won't go any further than this table."

Rook raised her right hand. "I solemnly swear not to divulge your secrets." At the sour look on Julia's face, a sense of dread flashed through her and she leaned forward and whispered, "This isn't about Addison, is it?"

"No. God no," Julia hissed. "Throw some salt over your shoulder or whatever. I can't believe you even said that."

Thankful her gut feeling had been wrong, Rook pressed on. "Then what is it?"

"A group of students at McNair got caught with some high dollar escorts at one of their parties."

Rook scanned her memory. McNair National Defense University was located on the army base with the same name at the confluence of the Potomac River and the Anacostia River. "Isn't that a grad school? Higher level training for warmongers and the like?"

Julia stuck out her tongue. "Don't be an ass. It's a highly regarded master's program for 'joint professional military education.'"

Rook put up her hands in surrender. "Fine. But I don't get why a bunch of quote unquote professionals hiring escorts should be on your radar. Unless…Wait, is one of them related to the president?"

"No. That I could handle. I mean, it's not like he's ever going to run for anything again. One of them is General Bloomfield's youngest son."

Rook took a minute to process the detail. She generally prided herself on staying up-to-date on all the scuttlebutt in the Beltway, but it was simply impossible to keep up with everything and she had a tendency to focus on the things that naturally captured her interest. The military wasn't one of them. Still, the name Bloomfield sounded vaguely familiar. "Bloomfield. That's one of the guys Garrett is considering to replace Daniger, right? Head of the Joint Chiefs?"

"That's right."

"How have I not heard about this development?"

"I'm thinking that up to now the press has been distracted by the Nine Tech hearings."

"'Up to now'?"

"Yes. Arnie Wilkins from the *Post* has started digging around, but we've managed to hold him off. We've back-burnered the Joint Chiefs' announcement, but Daniger's ready to move on and we can't leave the position vacant. Not with everything going on in Syria right now. Once we announce his replacement, everyone's going to start digging."

"And Bloomfield's one of the guys in the running?"

"He's not one of the guys, he's *the* guy. Garrett has already settled on him."

"Well, that's easy. Get him to unsettle and go with your second choice."

"Not happening. Garrett has known him forever. He promised Bloomfield the position and thinks going back on his word because of his son's indiscretion is a show of weakness. By all accounts Bloomfield himself is as clean as they come."

Rook sipped her coffee, her brain churning. Julia hadn't brought her here, under Secret Service protection, to tell her all of this was a foregone conclusion. There was more; there had to be more. The key was whether she wanted to ask and potentially dig into a situation she had no interest in pursuing. She tapped her fingers against her leg while the silent standoff between them played out.

Julia broke first. "Aren't you going to ask what I want?"

"If I ask, it implies I have some interest in getting involved. Which I don't. I have plenty of work, and it sounds like you have this little matter under control."

Julia glanced around and then hunched closer. "You'd be wrong."

Rook had known Julia a long time. A veteran campaigner and a fearless political advocate, Julia didn't scare easy, but Rook spotted a trace a fear in her eyes. The question was, could she resist knowing what had put it there?

CHAPTER SEVEN

Zoey pushed through the turnstile and followed the uniforms up the steps at the Pentagon Metro stop, thankful for the anonymity the crowd granted her. Unlike the last few times she'd been here, she was no longer a visitor, but an employee, stationed to this base of sorts for an indefinite assignment.

It would take some getting used to. She'd lived off base a couple of times during her career, but it wasn't her preference. The commute back and forth was a waste of valuable time. Time she could be working, serving. Time she didn't have to wonder what to do with herself. But living on base wasn't an option here, and with Margaret Sharp's help, she'd been lucky enough to find a rental in Vienna, a simple Metro ride away. She'd fallen in love with the house at first sight, thankful for the large fenced yard, situated well apart from the other houses on the street, unlike the apartments she'd occupied in the past where her nosy neighbors took advantage of every opportunity to observe her comings and goings. The new house was the nicest place she'd ever lived, and she could hardly believe it was hers for as long as she was stationed here.

She walked through the Pentagon entrance and looked around, trying to decipher which of the many lines she belonged in. Whenever she'd been here in the past few weeks, Sharp had had a sergeant greet her with a badge, but she wasn't a guest any longer. Her orders said for her to check in at security, but the windows at the front of the line all looked the same. She turned back and forth, looking for a friendly face to whom she could direct a question and found herself face-to-face with Jack Riley.

"Major Granger, nice to see you again."

"Nice to see you too, Major," she said, breathing a sigh of relief. "When you said you worked here, I didn't imagine there was any way I'd wind up running into you on my first day."

He tilted his head. "You're working here too? I thought you were headed back to Fort Hood."

She felt a twinge of guilt at not sharing her new assignment with a fellow soldier, but then she remembered she'd been following Sharp's orders. "Last-minute change of plans. Guess they decided I'd stay out of trouble if they kept me close, although I don't know where I'm going, so they may have been wrong about that."

"I'll help you out. Do you know which office you're assigned to?"

"Joint Chiefs, reporting to General Sharp."

"You're in luck because I'm headed in that direction and I know exactly where Sharp's office is."

She remembered Sharp telling her he was Jack and Addison's godfather. She held up a hand. "I got a little ahead of myself. I need to check in with security and personnel first. I don't want to keep you. If you'll just point me in the right direction."

"Nonsense. I'm early for a meeting, so I'll get you where you need to go. Come on."

She followed Jack to a window around the corner and waited as he explained the situation to the officer checking IDs. The entire lobby was teeming with people, from a crowd of what were obviously tourists to a group of men and women wearing the uniform of the Brazilian Air Force that she assumed were here to tour the building as well. She provided her credentials to the man at the window and nodded as he explained where she should report next to get her badge, relying on Jack to know the specifics. He motioned for her to follow, and they walked through the checkpoint metal detectors and up the escalator to the main level.

"Any of this look familiar yet?"

"Vaguely, although I have to confess, I feel like someone blindfolded me and turned me around in circles since the last time I was here." She looked over to her right at the candy shop. "Now that I remember. Is that chocolate in the window as good as it looks?"

"Better. They call this whole row Make Up Alley. Flowers, candy, cards—everything you need to apologize for any transgression. If you're lucky enough to have someone to go home to, that is."

"I take it you're not married?"

"Not even close," Jack replied. "I haven't exactly lived the kind of life conducive to relationships. You?"

"Married to the Army. She understands me." Zoey shook her head. "At least until lately."

"I imagine things got a little rough for you after you came forward about Nine Tech."

"Nothing I couldn't handle." The moment the words were out, she regretted her clipped tone.

He held up his hands. "Oh, I have no doubt, but it couldn't have been easy. I've been around long enough to know soldiers turn on one of their own if they think they're in danger of getting caught. For the record, I fully support your decision to come forward. Sharp must too if he brought you in."

She thought it likely Sharp's decision was more complicated than a mere evaluation of her performance, but she didn't feel like making excuses. "There's a better than even chance I'm here because no one else will have me."

"Their loss." He stopped in front of a door. "Here's your stop."

"You're not coming in?"

"I've got a meeting down the hall. I'm sure I'll run into you again soon. You still have my card?" At her nod, he added, "This place can be a little crazy to get used to when you've been out in the world. Call me if you need anything. Any friend of Addison's is a friend of mine."

He was gone before she could point out that she barely knew his famous sister. She shook her head and walked into Sharp's office suite. She fully expected to meet with one of his aides to get more information about her exact assignment, but the lieutenant at the desk just outside his door motioned for her to go into his office.

"Have a seat, Major," Sharp said, barely looking up from his computer. "Although I won't be calling you that for long." He slid his keyboard aside and picked up a folder. "Here's the paperwork for your promotion. Shouldn't be long now."

"Thank you, sir." She took the folder from his outstretched hand and glanced inside at the official documents. It wasn't a done deal yet, but as with every promotion before, she experienced a surge of who should I call, who can I tell, but the musings vanished as quickly as they came. Getting the commission had to be good enough on its own.

"Ready for your next assignment?"

"As long as it doesn't involve sitting across from the Senate Armed Services Committee for a grilling, I'm all yours." She grinned as she delivered the words, but she couldn't have been more serious. She was ready to be tucked away in some corner of the Pentagon, content to be a cog in the massive military machine.

Sharp chuckled. "I think we can manage a small break from the rabid senators, but I'm afraid there might be some grilling." He reached for another file on his desk and pushed it toward her. "We have a small situation that some folks across the lake think might blow up into something bigger. General Bloomfield was impressed with the way you handled yourself up on the hill and has directed me to assign you to Public Affairs for the Joint Staff." He waved his hand. "Sounds worse than it is. You'll head our internal investigation and act as a liaison with the White House to keep them informed. Take an hour to review the file. Major Dixon will accompany you to briefings at first, mostly to help you find your way around and assist you with anything you need, but you're his senior and this is your show."

Zoey ran her fingers along the file folder in her hands, itching to get a look inside as she slowly digested the specifics of her new assignment. White House. Briefings. Public relations. Apparently, there would be no hiding out in her new position. Not for a while anyway. "Are you sure I'm the right person for this? I'm a bit of a lightning rod after the Nine Tech mess. And I kind of expected to stay in logistics."

"Not my call, but I can't disagree with Bloomfield's judgment. Folks on the Hill loved you. You were the very model of the perfect soldier in their eyes. I expect the White House will love you too."

Zoey focused on what she didn't hear, which was whether he actually agreed with Bloomfield's decision. Agreement was decidedly different from not being able to disagree. She wasn't sure why she cared either way. Aside from a deployment to some base where no one knew her or had access to C-SPAN, being tucked away here was probably her best chance at putting Nine Tech behind her. But Public Affairs sounded suspiciously like the kind of work Rook did, and the prospect caused her gut to churn. Was she going to be expected to find the best spin for news involving the military? She knew some news stories needed to be massaged to make them more palatable for the general public, but she was known for being a straight shooter not a smooth talker. *Maybe that's why they picked you.* She took a deep breath and decided to go with that. "Thank you, sir. I'll do my best."

"I have no doubt." He stood to signal the meeting was over, and she scrambled to her feet. "Margaret said you found a place."

Damn. She'd almost forgotten she was supposed to meet the landlord around noon today. She started to mention that to Sharp, but decided she'd just have to figure out a way to work it in. "Yes, sir."

"You've never lived off base, have you?"

"No, sir."

"I think it might be good for a change. Allow you to stay out of the fray."

"Yes, sir." She resisted the urge to ask exactly what he meant by fray.

"Lieutenant Louden, out front can show you to your office, and Major Dixon will be by to collect you." He paused after the words of dismissal and his stare was penetrating. "I'm counting on you, Major. Don't let me down."

She nodded and turned to leave, uncertain where she was going or what was behind the cryptic message. Chances were good she was trying too hard to decipher a hidden meaning to his pointed words. General Bloomfield might have picked her for this job, but Sharp had probably made the recommendation based on the years he'd known her. Letting him down wasn't an option.

Louden was on the phone, so she lingered just far enough away from his desk to let him know she was waiting but not be obtrusive. When he finished the call, he grinned her way. "Ready to see your new digs?"

The friendly demeanor was a blessing. "Absolutely." She held up a file. "I'm already on a deadline."

"Right this way."

She followed him down the hall, through a twisting corridor. She tried to memorize every picture and display along the way like they were breadcrumbs that would lead her back to Sharp's office, but eventually she gave up. Maybe having to ask her way around would help her develop some relationships since it was clear she was going to need assistance getting used to the differences between this place and the life on base she'd grown accustomed to.

"Here you go." Louden held open a door, and Zoey took in her new office. It was plain, but spacious. Desk, bookshelves, computer. "Your phone is working and IT has already hooked you up for access to the system, but you'll need to contact them to set up your passwords. There are basic supplies in the desk, but if you need anything else, just fill out one of the forms I left. You'll get things a lot quicker than you're used to on base."

"Good to know. I'm supposed to have an appointment with Major Dixon in an hour. Will he know where to find me?"

"I'll make sure of it. I highlighted my extension in case you need anything to get settled. I assume you have your personal effects being sent over?"

"A few things. I've been pretty mobile over the years and kept a pretty bare-bones office when I had one."

"Well, now that you're settling down, you'll probably start collecting stuff. That is if you plan on sticking around."

She smiled by way of answer since she didn't know her plans and hadn't allowed herself to think past this moment, this day. "Thanks for your help, Lieutenant. I'll call if I need anything."

When he was gone, she shut the door and took a moment to drink in the new space, wanting to embrace the permanence, but careful not to let it sway her too much. This was just an assignment, like any other. At any moment, she could be called up and sent anywhere in the world. All her life, that possibility had been intoxicating, but right now, in this moment, she wanted to stay here and see what she could make of this world.

❖

"I don't know why Ms. Elias is saying those things, but I was not the driver of the car that hit that woman."

"But you know Candace Elias?" Robin Roberts's voice was even, but her expression was braced as if to show she wasn't afraid to ask the tough questions.

"Yes, I do," Newman said, his eyes trained on the screen in front of him showing Robin sitting in the New York studio. "She worked on my campaign for governor, and although I haven't seen her in years, I always considered her a trusted colleague and friend."

"Are you friends now?"

To his credit, Newman didn't flinch. "Well, Robin, that's a bit of a loaded question. I don't know the motivation behind all of this which makes it difficult to attribute any malice to her actions." He stopped and turned to face the camera, his face fixed in a grim but pleading expression and his hand firmly gripping that of his Jackie-like wife who sat close beside him. "Candace, you and I both know I was not involved in the tragic accident that killed Sheila Edgar. I sincerely hope you will recant your allegations and, if you do have information that could assist the police in finding the person or persons responsible, you will come forward now so this young woman's family can finally find peace."

Several yards away, Rook turned to Harry. "I would have preferred we do this in studio with Robin, but I think it went pretty well. What do you think?"

"He's smooth."

"Blake polygraphed him. Spent an entire day, but he didn't break during the interview. The test results were inconclusive."

Harry let loose a low whistle. "So he's either telling the truth or he's a stone cold psychopath."

"Or the truth is somewhere in between. Maybe he wasn't driving the car." Rook pointed to the screen where Robin was playing footage of an earlier interview with Candace. "Maybe she was, and he's protecting her."

"Well, if he is, his gallantry is a bit misplaced considering she's throwing him under the bus. Hard."

Rook appraised her associate. Harry was the newest member of their team. She'd always had one other lawyer on staff, but her last law partner had left last year citing the need to find a calmer, less crisis-driven occupation. Luke Gidry was now handling estate matters for the rich and famous and couldn't be happier. The idea of wading through the administration of an estate, no matter how lucrative, made Rook yawn. His response was to tell her how happy he was to leave his office at six o'clock, go home to his wife and kids, and never worry about a late night call asking him to make magic out of a mess. She'd picked a younger lawyer when she hired Harry, and discrimination laws be damned, she had Blake run a thorough background check to make sure he was single, had no kids, and was fit enough to work as rigorous a schedule as she did. He'd measured up in every category, but she hadn't tested him full tilt yet to see if his stamina matched his brains. Newman would be his first test.

"They're wrapping up," Rook said. "I'm going to need you to debrief with Newman. He'll be insecure. Hold his hand and tell him he did great. Make sure he knows no more interviews, no social media. I want radio silence from the entire family, kids included. If you have to stay at his house and guard their phones and computers, do it."

He nodded, but she could read the trace of panic in his eyes. "I have an appointment across town and I'm running late already. Call me if you need anything, but, Harry?"

"Yes?"

"You got this." She clapped him on the shoulder and took off, anxious to get away before the Newman family descended. Harry would do fine. Or he wouldn't, in which case, she'd have to work some magic to fix whatever he broke, but since that was her specialty, she wasn't worried.

George was waiting at the curb. She waved him off as he started to get out of the car and let herself into the backseat. He looked at her in the rearview mirror. "White House?"

"Yes. We should be on the list at the gate."

Rook took the time in the car to reflect on everything Julia had told her yesterday. What had initially started as a routine investigation of student misconduct at Fort McNair had begun to snowball. The exclusive escort service General Bloomfield's son and his pals had used to "alleviate stress" was normally very discreet, but because of the vetting Bloomfield was getting, someone, probably NSA, had gained access to their records and found their client list included more than a few flag officers who worked at the Pentagon. If made public, the list could prove embarrassing to the brass as well as the current administration, an unwelcome distraction on the heels of the Nine Tech mess, and especially untimely since the president was negotiating with Congress for funds to mount an offensive in Syria. All of this, on top of the upcoming confirmation hearings for Bloomfield, created a perfect storm, and Julia had tugged hard at the strings of their friendship to get Rook on board to help put the right spin on the investigation.

"You know I'm not a fan of the military, and what you've told me isn't doing anything to change that. The military bureaucracy is a big ole boys club, playing with people's lives." Rook said. *"Why not let them implode?"*

"Just pretend for a minute it's not about them," Julia said. *"It's about a president that even you respect, trying to get something accomplished to quell the very serious turbulence in the Middle East with a military establishment that makes everything we do like wading through quicksand. The Pentagon has already started their own internal investigation, but you and I both know that'll go a big*

fat nowhere, and when word gets out, Congress is going to yank funding from every project we have in the pipeline."

"So what exactly do you want me to do?"

"Oversee the investigation for us. Just work with whoever they assign and make sure they don't do anything super stupid that makes us all look bad."

"Julia, really. I do crisis management, not babysitting. If you want to call when this goes tits up, I'll consider helping, but right now it sounds like a bureaucratic snooze-fest."

"Grow up, Rook. Real people do boring stuff sometimes, because a bunch of boring links make a pretty strong chain. It's called being an adult. Adults make things, they don't just fix them."

Rook had walked away from the meeting telling Julia she'd think about it. As the hours wore on during her meeting with the Newman family, Julia's words had stung, partly because they echoed the disapproval of her father who'd never understood how she could throw away her law degree to, as he put it, tilt swords with the likes of the *National Enquirer*. She liked to think she'd long since stopped caring what Richard Daniels expected of her, but old insecurities died hard.

Ultimately, her decision to work with the White House wasn't about her father's expectations. She'd been intrigued by what Julia had told her and she'd been even more intrigued by what she hadn't said. There was more to this story and she intended to peel back the layers until she found out what was really going on.

Thinking of layers brought Major Zoey Granger to mind. Julia had mentioned several times how the Nine Tech scandal was the primary reason this story was likely to garner more attention than it would in a regular news cycle. Zoey had done a great job pacifying the Senate Armed Services Committee with how she'd reported the fraud immediately upon discovery. She presented well, her testimony was articulate and forthright, and she'd risked her career to expose the crime. But the hooker scandal had no central hero, only a cast of dumbasses who put their libidos and egos ahead of duty. If Julia wanted Rook to spin shit into valor, it wasn't going to be easy.

The guard at the White House security gate checked their names off his list and directed George to a parking space, but Rook suggested he take off.

"I'll wait."

"I don't know how long I'll be."

"It's okay." He pulled into the spot and cut the engine, closing the discussion. "I'll be here when you come out."

Rook shook her head and climbed out of the car, stopping by George's window before she walked to the portico. "Thanks."

He nodded and pulled a copy of the latest Harlan Coben novel out of the console. "I'm pretty anxious to find out what happens, so you're really doing me a favor."

Rook laughed. A few minutes later, she showed her ID again to the Marine officers manning the entrance. She was issued a visitor's badge and provided an escort in the form of a young male intern who could only be described as super pretty. As he walked her through the halls, he asked if she'd been in the building before.

"A few times, but mostly in the East Wing for social functions." She could tell he wanted to ask for details since West Wing interns probably didn't attend a lot of White House galas, but instead he gave her a rambling narrative of the various rooms they passed.

He was on his third spiel, "And this is the Roosevelt Room. Most people don't know it's named for both Franklin and Theodore Roosevelt," when Julia appeared in the hall about ten feet in front of them.

"There you are. The gate said you'd checked in, but I was beginning to think you'd snuck off to the bowling lanes."

"Actually, that sounds like a great alternative." Rook placed a hand on the intern's shoulder. "Clancy here was giving me the full tour." She could feel his tension and wanted to keep him out of trouble. "The guy really knows his stuff."

"Better him than me. I can recite the Constitution and have the entire Congressional delegation memorized, but I can't for the life of me tell you which Roosevelt that damn room is named for. Clancy, thanks for your help, I've got it from here."

Rook watched her guide amble off and wondered if she'd be better off joining him, but she dutifully followed Julia to her office.

"Saw your guy on *Good Morning America*," Julia said.

"He's not my guy."

"He is now. You own the entire family and the drama that comes with them until someone fesses up to killing that girl."

"Any theories?"

"Don't try to drag me into your drama. Not unless you want to give me a cut of what I'm sure is the very exorbitant fee you're collecting from the congressman."

"I'd bring you on as a consultant, but you look like you might be a bit busy." Rook walked into Julia's office. "Wow, this is huge."

"Biggest office in the building. Don't worry, there's no coup. The big guy still runs the place from his tiny little oval command center."

Rook sank into one of the cushioned chairs across from Julia's desk. "Okay, so I'm here. Tell me exactly what you want me to do."

"So, you're in?"

"I'm here, aren't I?"

"I'm still processing that after you shut me down yesterday. Rook, if you take this on, you have to stay with it until it's done. No matter what bright, shiny new client comes your way."

"I get it. I haven't talked to my team yet, but I'm sure they can pick up any extra slack. I'm not sure this is going to be as complex as you think, but I'm in it for whatever you need. Now, let's get started."

Julia tilted her head, and Rook sat still during the examination. Finally, Julia smiled and said, "Welcome aboard. The first order of business is to introduce you to the liaison from the Joint Staff."

Rook followed Julia to a conference room down the hall. When they reached the door, she hung back and let Julia enter first, giving the poor schmuck inside time to get used to the idea he was going to have a handler for the duration of his inquiry. When Julia waved her forward, she stepped into the room and her gaze swept over the personnel sitting at the table. Two people, both uniformed, but one made her stop in her tracks. "Major?" she said, unable to form any other words.

Both Zoey and the man beside her looked up and they each said, "Yes?"

At the exact same moment, Rook had a feeling she was in over her head.

Chapter Eight

What was *she* doing here? Zoey offered a polite smile, but her gut was churning at the sight of Rook standing in front of her looking like she owned the place. She didn't have time to process her feelings before Major Dixon spoke up.

"I'm Major Dixon," he said with his hand stuck out in greeting. "And this is Major Granger."

Rook shook his hand, but her eyes were on Zoey the entire time. "Major Granger," she said, her voice rising in question. "Nice to see you."

Zoey nodded, acutely conscious of Dixon's eyes on both of them, and she wished the floor would rise up and swallow him whole. He'd been annoying since the moment they met, feeling the constant need to explain the inner workings of the Pentagon in a way that was designed to make him look superior. Even Sharp, who'd accompanied them to make introductions, seemed to find his salacious manner a distraction. Zoey had already made a mental note to figure out a way to shake him.

They'd arrived a half hour earlier, and Zoey had concentrated on acting like it was no big deal to file in past the Marine guard and be escorted into the inner echelons of the West Wing. Funny, a couple of weeks ago, she'd checked into the possibility of a White House tour only to be told she would have to go through a member of Congress which could take several weeks to get approved, and the "tour" was only a self-guided walk-through of the East Wing.

Deciding she'd probably seen more on TV than she'd see on the pseudo-tour, she'd abandoned the idea only to wind up here just a few yards from the Oval Office for an initial meeting with the president's chief of staff, Julia Scott.

Julia had acknowledged her with a simple "nice to see you again," and left them alone to go get "someone who would be assisting with the investigation." Zoey had wanted to use the time to grill Sharp about why he'd assigned her to this job, but Dixon's constant presence robbed her of the opportunity, and ultimately Sharp had left them to handle the rest of the meeting on their own. Now Julia was back with Rook in tow and Zoey had way more questions than answers.

"So, here's how this will work," Julia said, settling in at the head of the table. "I know you've been instructed to conduct a full investigation, but it's imperative that we be kept in the loop, especially considering the link to General Bloomfield's son. Ms. Daniels and her team will need complete access to conduct interviews, review documents, whatever she deems necessary. You will consider her an arm of the White House for this internal investigation. Understood?"

"Yes," Zoey answered before Dixon could jump in. "Our orders are unequivocal. We're to cooperate with whoever the president designates."

Rook smiled. "Well, that would be me." Her expression turned serious. "The first thing I want to do is interview everyone in uniform that has any connection to…" She glanced through the folder in front of her. "Lorraine Darcy Inc." She looked over at Julia. "Who uses their own name to run an escort service?"

Julia shrugged. "Who knows? Someone who's really proud of her work, maybe?"

Zoey watched as they shared a laugh. The joke was funny, but she didn't dare join in lest she send the wrong message to Dixon. There was plenty of misogyny to go around already.

"What's the process here?" Rook asked, her gaze trained on Zoey. "I mean, do your guys all lawyer up or are we free to question them without counsel?"

Dixon started to answer, but Zoey cut him off. "Everyone under our command will cooperate with you. We'll want to be present, of course, and anyone you interview will have the right to have a JAG officer present as well." After Nine Tech, the procedures were etched in her mind.

"Fair enough. I have a few things to take care of, but I can be at your office this afternoon to get started."

Zoey felt Dixon twitch beside her. She didn't want Rook to show up so quickly either, but she wasn't about to tell her no after they'd just promised her complete access. "Perfect. We'll have interviews lined up. Is there anything else we can do for you?"

Rook raised her eyebrows slightly, and Zoey braced for a personal remark, but all Rook said was, "Not at the moment, but I reserve the right to let you know if something else comes up."

Rook's comment was easily interpreted as professional, but Zoey knew it was more complicated than that. "Would you like to discuss anything further right now?"

Rook looked at Julia before turning back to her. "Actually, no. I'd like to go into the interviews without a lot of preconceptions about what they're going to say."

"Then I suppose we're done here," Zoey said, grasping for some control. She stood and Dixon stood alongside her. "We'll make the arrangements and have an escort meet you at the main entrance at fourteen hundred." Remembering not everyone spoke military time, she added, "That's two o'clock in civilian terms."

Rook grinned. "Got it. I look forward to seeing you, Major Granger." She paused for a few beats. "And you too, Major Dixon."

Zoey walked to the door feigning confidence she didn't feel. Nothing about the meeting had given her any sense of control. For a second, she wanted to bolt from her newfound responsibilities, but she dug deep for fortitude and injected a confident and commanding tone into her voice as they followed an intern down one of the long and confusing corridors back to the entrance. "Make sure Ms. Daniels and her team are cleared to enter the building when they arrive this afternoon. Have at least two of the students from McNair ready to be interviewed today, and we'll get to the others in the next few days. If they've been assigned JAG counsel, get them here too because I don't want to have to toss these interviews because we didn't follow regs. We'll need a conference room. See if Lieutenant Louden can arrange something."

Dixon's head bobbed, but Zoey read conflict in his eyes. She got it. They might be the same rank, but she had seniority and Sharp had made it clear she was in charge. Was he jealous of her command and access or was this his usual demeanor? She didn't have the time or energy to figure it out and she wasn't sure she cared either way. If she cared more about making friends than doing her duty, she never would have come forward about Nine Tech. Determined to focus on the task ahead instead of worrying about whether she was liked, she picked up her pace, but the sound of a voice calling her name thwarted her plan for a quick getaway.

❖

Rook was beginning to wonder if power walking was a requirement for everyone in uniform, but she finally caught up to Zoey and her surly fellow officer. "Major Granger, could I speak to you for a moment?"

"Of course." Zoey's clipped voice conveyed the exact opposite.

Rook took a breath and shot a look at Dixon who was looking between them with way too much curiosity. "If you could come with me, please. Major Dixon, we'll only be a moment." She spun around without waiting for a response and walked back to Julia's office.

As they crossed the threshold, Zoey asked, "Did Ms. Scott need to see me about something else?"

"Julia's in the Oval. I'm the one who wanted to see you about something else."

"What can I do for you?"

Rook studied Zoey's stoic expression and wondered if it was a natural extension of her personality or the result of years of training. Either way, she desperately wanted to pry beneath the stone and find the soft side she'd witnessed at Meridian Park. "We'll be working together for the foreseeable future, do you really plan to act like you don't know me the entire time?"

Zoey's breath hitched slightly, a tiny fissure, so small it might have gone unnoticed, but Rook caught it before Zoey replied "But I don't know you. Not really."

"Would you like to?"

"What I like or don't like doesn't matter. As you said, we'll be working together. Key word working."

"I'm going to pretend you'd like to know me if you were allowed to."

Zoey frowned, and Rook wondered if she'd bristled at the "allowed to." Why was she so focused on getting a rise out of Zoey? Was she having a childish reaction to Zoey practically ignoring they'd been on a date? *A date you abandoned.* No wonder Zoey was pissed. A woman like her probably never got stood up."I'm sorry about our aborted picnic."

Zoey smiled, but the expression didn't reach her eyes. "You had to work."

"I did."

"And work comes first."

The characterization stung, but Rook couldn't deny it was true. "I suppose it's a hazard of owning my own business."

"We all make choices we can live with. And I'm sure you understand how my first allegiance is defined by duty and whatever orders I receive."

The message was clear, but Rook stubbornly wanted to hear Zoey say the words. "So, this attraction between us just disappears because the Army put you on this case?"

"Something like that."

"I don't believe you." Rook hadn't pulled Zoey aside for this. All she'd planned to do was apologize in person and clear the air between them, but now that Zoey was singularly focused on ignoring they had ever shared a connection, she was suddenly hell-bent on making her acknowledge its existence.

"I suppose I'll have to live with your disbelief." Zoey looked at the door. "Did you need something else from me?"

She should make something up. Something provocative to tease back the Zoey she'd met at the airport, at Addison's party. She hadn't imagined their connection, but apparently she had no power to reignite it. She'd find another way to burn off the heat that consumed her when Zoey walked into the room. There was no shortage of women in the city who'd gladly fill the role. Ignoring the voice inside that whispered Zoey was different and other women weren't going to cut it, Rook responded in the only way she could and keep her dignity. "No, Major. I think we're done."

Zoey nodded and walked out of the room past Julia who entered with a curious expression. Julia shut the door behind her. "What is it about women in uniform?"

"Excuse me?"

Julia waved a hand in front of her eyes. "Earth to Rook. Uniform equals hot. I might be in a relationship, but I'm not dead. Don't tell me you didn't notice."

Oh, I noticed, Rook thought. Zoey Granger had her attention, but she wasn't going to cede all the power that easily. She feigned nonchalance, but she was going to have to work hard to keep her libido in check during the course of this investigation or risk losing her heart and her reputation.

Chapter Nine

Rook returned to the car and contemplated her schedule while George navigated back through the guard gate. In order to make the appointment at the Pentagon, her afternoon was going to undergo some serious shuffling. She should never have allowed Julia to goad her into taking this case, but now that she had she was determined to wrap it up in short order. A few interviews today, a few over the next week, and then a report detailing their findings which she imagined to be something like, military men chose to use dicks instead of brains when exercising judgment. No new story there—the list of sex scandals in the military was longer than she had time to recall.

She wasn't judging. If she were forced to live a life so confined by rules and authority, she imagined she'd eventually succumb to making decisions based on pure pleasure as well. The students at McNair might be professional soldiers like Julia said, but they were probably still much like any other college students—academically smart, but stupid when it came to thinking about how one dumb decision at a party might pop up during a job interview years down the road and derail their whole career. Today's soldiers had likely been lulled into a false sense of well-being with troops pulling out of Iraq and both houses of Congress insisting they didn't want to get involved in Syria. The students likely viewed their time at McNair as a boondoggle complete with drinking games and expensive hookers. She, however, didn't have that luxury, and picked up the phone to check in with the office.

"Rook, where have you been? Eric's been looking everywhere. He's got some news about Diamond Credit."

"Put him through." Rook listened carefully, stopping Eric's report only to interject a few pointed questions. When he finished, she gave him instructions and then directed George to drive her to Diamond Credit's headquarters. "This won't take too long," she told him when he pulled up to the building. "Grab us some lunch, and I'll text you when I'm done."

Rook punched the button for the twentieth floor of the sleek steel and glass building where Melissa Mendoza, the CEO of Diamond Credit, and all the other C-Suite Diamond execs had their offices. The receptionist didn't recognize her, but when Mendoza's assistant came out to the plush, top floor lobby to see who was trying to get in to see her boss without an appointment, Rook was ushered directly back to Mendoza's office.

Melissa looked up from her desk as Rook strode into her office and called out, "Tell me you're here because you have some good news."

Melissa was a crisp, no-nonsense woman, which was exactly why Rook had taken her company on as a client. She didn't waste a lot of her time, she gave Rook a wide berth to do her job, and she paid well. Rook liked her and wished she was here to give Melissa what she wanted. "I have news. Let's leave it at that for now. How fast can you get your CIO and CFO in here?" Melissa answered by pressing a button on her phone and instructing her assistant to interrupt whatever the two other execs were doing and get them to her office, pronto. She leaned back in her chair. "Any chance I get a preview of what you're about to say?"

Rook shook her head, instead fishing out her phone and initiating a FaceTime call with Eric. When his face appeared on her phone, she showed it to Melissa. "This is my chief information officer, Eric Pryor. He's been working to try and discover the source of the hacking."

"I trust our IT department has been helpful," Melissa said.

"In a manner of speaking," Eric said. "I haven't actually talked to any of them."

Melissa shot Rook a what the hell look, and she held up a hand. "I asked Eric to employ some special methods." They both looked up at the sound of a knock on the door. "Let's wait to let him describe it once we have the others in the room," Rook said.

Two men strode in and Melissa introduced Mike Anders, chief financial officer for Diamond, and Harvey Linus, the chief information officer. After a few minutes of small talk, Rook turned the show back over to Eric. "Tell the group what I asked you to do and what you found."

"You asked me to check for any backdoors to the system." Eric took a moment to explain a backdoor, using the kind of layman terms that Rook preferred and then described how he'd conducted his search. "I found two methods a hacker could use to get into the area of the servers that house your customers' sensitive information. One appeared to have been written into the system on purpose to allow for data retrieval in the event of an accidental system lockout."

"And the other?" Rook prompted him.

"The other was a breach. The information that was released last week came from the breach."

Melissa leaned across her desk. "Linus, did you know about either of these?"

The CIO shifted in his seat. "I knew about the built-in backdoor. The other access point is news to me."

"Well, that's just great," Melissa sighed. "Why didn't the hacker just go in the backdoor that was already set up? Seems like it would be easier to take the path of least resistance."

"Good point," Rook said. "Eric, any theories?"

"Actually, yes. One reason might have been to avoid leaving tracks."

"I don't understand. If they are accessing through a path that already exists, how would they leave tracks?"

"I guess the best comparison I can think of is those TV crime shows where the person who lives in the house jimmies the window from the inside, forgetting that the burglar would have jimmied it from the outside. If there was a burglar, that is."

"You're saying this was an inside job?"

"I'm saying that even though there are two access points to reach the data, I believe that data was only transferred via the breach, but that's not enough information, on its own, for me to conclude whether the breach came from someone inside the firm or an outside hacker."

Rook heard the clues loud and clear, but she waited for Melissa to home in on exactly what Eric was implying. It didn't take long. "But you have reached a conclusion, haven't you?" Melissa asked. "You have other information, right?"

They all stared at the screen on Rook's phone and Eric stared back, seemingly unfazed by the information he was about to impart. Even Rook, who already had a heads up about what he would say, was on pins and needles waiting for Eric's conclusion. Finally, he cleared his throat and started talking.

"Your system is vulnerable to outside hacking and there are a number of safeguards you can make that I'd be happy to share with you. But in this particular instance, I believe this was an inside job."

Linus slammed a hand on the arm of his chair. "Dammit, Melissa. I would've appreciated the opportunity to be part of this investigation. If we need to, we'll polygraph the entire department, but next time I demand to be involved from the outset."

Before Melissa could respond, Rook broke in. "Hang on a minute. I don't think Eric was finished. Eric, you want to tell them how you arrived at your conclusion?"

"Sure, Rook. It was pretty simple, really. Once I established that someone was trying to throw me off their tail, I figured I would look at who had the most to gain from the data breach."

"You mean someone from my department sold the information?" Linus asked.

"Actually, no. I was looking at bigger picture transactions."

"He's talking about short sales," Rook said. "While Diamond's stock was in free fall last week, an upstart hedge fund was making a killing short-selling your stock. Do any of you happen to be familiar with the name SA Investments?" She looked at each of them. Melissa's and Linus's expressions registered genuine ignorance, but the other guy started to shift in his seat. "Eric pulled their SEC records and found that the manager's name is Samuel Anders."

"That's your son," Melissa exclaimed, staring at the CFO.

"I don't know anything about this," Anders said, raising his hands in protest. "Besides, are you really going to believe some hacker who's probably sitting in a basement somewhere, violating a dozen federal laws?"

Rook held back a laugh and injected a fierce tone into her voice. "Back down. Eric Pryor is sitting in my offices right now and he's the best computer specialist you'll ever meet. Of course, I don't think you're ever going to meet him or anyone like him where you're going." She turned back to Melissa. "You need to get your in-house counsel in here right away and lock down Anders's office. But call the SEC first, so you can be first in the door."

Rook gave them a few more instructions, including not talking to anyone in the media until she had time to craft a statement for the press, and then she left. George showed up within minutes of her call and handed her a sandwich as she settled into the car.

"You have about an hour and a half until your meeting at the Pentagon," he said. "You want to go back to the office?"

If she went back to the office, it would be easier to make calls and get a press release ready to go, but she'd likely get wrapped up in a ton of other cases vying for her attention. What she really wanted to do was have a little time alone to shift gears before she saw Zoey again and before she had to become immersed in the bureaucracy of the Pentagon. Once again, she pondered why she'd agreed to take this case. Would she have agreed if she'd known Zoey was going to be involved? Didn't matter now since she'd already committed, but she was more committed than ever to making sure she finished the work quickly so she could extricate herself from the morass of military bureaucracy. She shivered at the idea she would have to spend any time at the Pentagon and decided she needed to steel herself for the afternoon ahead.

Rook made a snap decision. "George, let's head to Arlington. I'll text Lacy and let her know the change in plans."

The trip from Diamond Credit's offices across the river only took about thirty minutes, during which Rook called the office and dictated a draft of a press release about how Diamond's CEO's diligent efforts had uncovered the source of the data breach and she was working with the appropriate government agencies to ensure their obligations were met. She also called an old pal with the SEC and gave her the heads up that Diamond's CFO was the target of their internal investigation. She typed a few emails on her phone and then leaned back in her seat to relax before they reached their destination.

Without being told, George pulled into the parking lot of Twin Towers Florist and kept the car idling while she wandered around inside and selected a bouquet of fresh flowers. She returned to the car, and within five minutes, they pulled into the parking lot at Arlington National Cemetery. George showed their permit at the guard gate and drove directly to the spot they'd stopped at many times.

"I'll be back in a few minutes," Rook said.

"Stay as long as you like."

Rook didn't bother answering. There was no "like" to these trips although she made them often. Every single time was a horrific reminder that her brother Rory was gone and he would never be back. She pulled a plastic cone for the flowers from the receptacle near the roadway that ran through the massive cemetery and trudged toward his headstone.

When she reached her destination, she knelt in the grass and let her gaze sweep the property. The long, white rows of sameness always struck her with their stark reminders of the cost of war, and her stomach roiled as she relived her own loss. Struggling to focus on something besides her grief, she forced her vision back to her brother's headstone and murmured the words she'd memorized years ago. Rory had died on the battlefield, and even though his death hadn't come at the hands of the enemy, the basic details— name, rank, branch of service, date of birth, and date of death—were followed with chiseled proof of his heroism, Purple Heart and Silver Star. She traced the words with her finger, truth and lies, blending together to tell a story that had ended too soon.

The rest of the ritual was easier now that she was grounded. She told him about her meeting at the White House, the stupidity of the soldiers at McNair, and she even mentioned Zoey. He would have teased her unmercifully about being attracted to a soldier. When she was done talking, she nestled the plastic cone in the grass and inserted the flowers one at a time, taking care to arrange them in a beautiful display that Rory would have scoffed at. Today's flowers were lilies. The florist had been stuffed with them, no doubt because of the impending Easter season. As ubiquitous as they were, Rook found comfort in their beauty, their soft, white purity.

Her thoughts were shattered by the sharp crack of gunfire. She shook and braced for the rounds to follow—seven guns, three volleys in a row, twenty-one rounds to commemorate a death. She remembered thinking, during Rory's funeral, how off balance it seemed that gunfire was used to honor him when gunfire was the reason his body was waiting to be buried. More irony—Rory was the only one in her family who would enjoy the joke.

She finished arranging the flowers and stood, smoothing her rumpled clothes. Maybe someday she would find answers to the questions she had about his death, but in the meantime, she would visit and pay tribute to a life she believed had been given in vain.

❖

Zoey took the keys from the landlord and only half listened as he rattled off all the things he thought she needed to know about the house. When he finally left, she took a few minutes to wander through the empty rooms. Somehow it looked smaller without all the furniture that had been here when she'd seen it the first time, but the thought of purchasing furnishings felt daunting. The movers would arrive later in the evening with the few boxes of books, clothes, and other personal effects she hadn't been able to fit in her 370Z coupe, her one luxury. Their small load would barely fill a couple of closets in this house. Had she made a huge mistake not renting a cozy little apartment?

Too late now. She'd signed the lease and this place was hers for the next year unless she wound up being shipped out. She checked the time, pleased to see that the entire process of this commitment had only taken fifteen minutes. If she drove back to the Pentagon, she could even stop and grab some lunch along the way. She locked the front door, climbed into her car, and drove off, scouring the side streets along the way for something quick that wasn't fast food. She'd driven a few miles without finding any options when she spotted a sign for Arlington Cemetery, the one big item on her list of DC landmarks she hadn't made it to yet. The cemetery was only a few miles away. If she skipped lunch, she could go by, pay her respects to fallen friends, and make it back to the office in plenty of time to prepare for the first round of interviews. A small nagging voice told her she was avoiding her new responsibilities, but she ignored it and took the next turn.

After she parked, she walked around until she found the visitor center where a Marine corpsman showed her how to locate a particular grave using the app on her phone. She spent a few minutes looking up names and located one of the men she'd served with in Afghanistan. She'd lost others, but they must have been buried elsewhere. Unfortunately, after the bodies were returned home, she'd lost track of what happened, having returned her attention to the work at hand. She'd always intended to go visit the families of her fallen comrades when she returned to the States, but now that she was back, it felt awkward to show up at a stranger's door, stirring up memories that were, to her mind, best left buried. She'd pay her respects now and not make similar promises in the future.

Zoey hailed a shuttle and gave the location to the driver. After a few more people boarded, he took off through the grounds, stopping to let passengers off and on as they drove past the perfect rows of white headstones, lined up by the thousands. She'd read in the visitor's center that approximately thirty funerals were held here each day, and while she knew many of the dead were aging veterans, she couldn't help but be overwhelmed by the marble markers of loss surrounding her.

She found Lieutenant Kyle Peavy's headstone fairly quickly after the shuttle driver stopped to let her out. Unlike the other markers she saw that contained endearments like "loving father" or "dutiful son," Kyle's headstone matter-of-factly listed his name, rank, date of birth, date of death, and nothing else. She'd known him as well as she'd known most of the people she served with, but she was embarrassed to admit she didn't know if he had a family. What she knew could be summarized by her observation that Kyle had been a hardworking officer, dedicated to his work, but always finding time to have fun. She fished back through her memory and settled on a memory of Kyle pulling a prank on one of their fellow officers the day before a suicide bomber exploded on the sports field where Kyle and a few others were playing a pickup game of soccer.

She kneeled in front of the white marble, wishing she'd thought to bring flowers, a flag, some tribute to a life that had been cut short. A life too quickly forgotten. "Dedicated soldier. Liked by all." She whispered the words that should have been on this headstone, words she wished she'd said to him and vowed she wouldn't forget again.

A different shuttle picked her up for the ride back to the main gate, and it took a winding path through the cemetery, stopping to drop off and pick up other visitors along the way. Zoey stared out the window lost in memory and sadness. How could anyone work here each day amid the constant reminders of death and sacrifice? Suddenly, she spotted a familiar figure sitting in front of a headstone. No, it couldn't be…could it? She squinted against the sunlight, certain her eyes were tricking her, but as they drove closer, she spotted the familiar sedan she'd ridden in the day she arrived in DC. Rook was hunched over a grave, her face drawn and her shoulders quaking.

The shuttle stopped to let someone out, and Zoey kept her eyes trained on Rook who was fully focused on the headstone in front of her. In the distance, the crack of rifle shots pierced the weight of silence. She flinched at the unexpected sound, and Rook did too. In that moment, Zoey felt the kinship of loss and filed the image of Rook, standing next to a grave, looking lost and alone, under things they had in common. The realization was strangely comforting.

Chapter Ten

Zoey pushed through the door of her office, acutely conscious of Dixon on her heels.

"We need to figure out a way to keep Bloomfield's son out of this," he said, his voice a grating burr.

She ignored him and sat down behind her desk, the universal position of power. When they'd left the White House that morning he'd been itching to talk about their approach, but didn't dare for fear their fellow passengers on the Metro would listen in. Now, it was like he'd been lying in wait for her to get back to the office so he could share his ideas about how the investigation should go.

"We're not figuring anything out. We're going to make sure Roo—Ms. Daniels and her team have whatever information they need to conclude their investigation so General Bloomfield can put this behind him as quickly as possible."

Dixon studied her hard for a moment, but she didn't flinch, hoping he couldn't read any of the raw emotion she still felt after seeing Rook at Arlington less than an hour ago. He nodded slowly as a smile crept across his face. "I get it. You're right. The quicker we get them out of here, the better." He looked at his watch. "I'm going to grab some chow. You want to come with?"

"No," she answered quickly, relieved he had misinterpreted her response. She softened her tone. "I'm good. I'll meet you back here at two." She was starving, but she'd rather go hungry than forego the opportunity for a break from Dixon's chattering.

She sent a quick email to Lieutenant Louden, to confirm he'd have a conference room ready later that afternoon. An hour wasn't nearly long enough, but it would have to do. What she needed was a time warp to take her back to before she'd met Rook, before she'd become attracted to her, because that was the only way she was going to be able to focus on the task at hand.

How had her worlds collided? She'd honestly thought that night at the park was the last time she'd see Rook again. The idea hadn't been unreasonable—DC was a big city and they didn't run in the same circles. Hell, she didn't have any circles. Truth was she'd experienced a moment of relief when she'd spotted not one, but two familiar faces at the White House, but Julia and Rook were not her friends, no matter how friendly they might seem. Something was off about this whole thing, and Zoey was convinced Rook's involvement meant there was more to the whole McNair scandal than she'd been told.

She reached into her desk and pulled out the notes she'd made while reviewing the file. Lieutenant Donald "Donny" Bloomfield and three of his fellow officers had been suspended from the graduate program and brought up on conduct charges at McNair after a bust at a venerable luxury hotel in Maryland. Hotel security, responding to complaints from other patrons, had kicked Donny, his pals, and the girls out without contacting the police. But the room had been registered in Donny's name, and it was probably just a matter of time before the press figured out Donny Bloomfield was none other than the well-known general's youngest son. While the simple fact the general's progeny had been tossed from a fancy hotel would be embarrassing, it wasn't a career-killer for anyone involved. But when reporters started asking questions and found out high paid escorts were at the party, things would get sticky.

Zoey flipped through the pages but didn't find much else. In her view, the White House's decision to hire Rook was overkill. You don't flash a lot of cash if you're trying to act poor, and you don't hire the biggest gun in spin if you don't have anything to hide. She might not possess the same skill set as Rook, but she knew how to conduct an investigation and she knew how to keep a secret, despite what many of her peers might believe. She supposed Rook might be helpful if they wound up having to navigate DC politics, but this entire case was nothing more than an embarrassing incident that should be handled internally.

Even as complicated as things could get, Zoey had to admit she was looking forward to seeing Rook again. Spotting Rook at the cemetery had spurred her curiosity and given her a glimpse of Rook's vulnerability—a far cry from the commanding presence Rook displayed in public. If she had a chance, Zoey was going to try to peel back some of the layers behind the very public persona of the charming Rook Daniels, but for now she needed to focus.

Zoey finished looking through the file and then pushed it aside and rummaged in her bag for one of the PowerBars she usually kept on hand. Banana. Not her favorite flavor, but she'd been down to the last ones in the box and she'd jammed this one in her purse as she rushed out of the house this morning. Her alternative was to wander the halls looking for food, but she didn't want to get lost with only an hour until her meeting with Rook, and Dixon would be back before that. She tore open the wrapper and bit off a hunk of the protein-filled wonder. She was still chewing when the knock sounded on her door.

"Come in." Annoyed that Dixon hadn't waited the full hour, she didn't try to hide the exasperation from her voice.

Lieutenant Louden poked his head in. "Sorry to bother you, Major, but Rook Daniels is here for your meeting."

Zoey looked at the clock on her computer and back at Louden. Rook was an hour early. She was all about the motto that early was the new on time, but this was crazy. Suddenly, she wished Dixon were around to act as a buffer because she had no desire to wind up alone in a room with Rook. Or did she? "Thanks, Lieutenant, tell her I'll be there in a few minutes."

Louden cleared his throat and pushed the door open a bit farther. "Sorry, Major, I guess I wasn't entirely clear. She's here, as in right here."

Zoey looked past his shoulder at Rook's face and barely resisted the urge to tell him he should've led with that information.

Damn. "Come in, Ms. Daniels." She started to dismiss Louden but mentally calculated how long she'd have to deal with Rook on her own and had an idea. "Lieutenant, where's the closest place to get a sandwich?"

"Food court." He used hand gestures to give her directions. "If you get lost, just ask someone along the way."

She had no intention of asking anyone in front of Rook, so she hoped his instructions were as easy as he said. After she dismissed him, she stood up. "I'm starving. Come with me to get something to eat." She didn't wait for Rook to respond and instead took off walking down the hall. This was the perfect opportunity to set some boundaries and assert her authority, and as long as she didn't get lost, it might work.

The choices in the food court were all waist-thickening nightmares of the fast food industry. Making a mental note that she needed to start bringing her own lunch, she scanned the menus for the least stroke-inducing item and finally settled on a salad with grilled chicken and vinaigrette dressing.

"Is that all you're having?" Rook asked after Zoey placed her order.

"Yes. Are you eating?"

"I'm…No, thanks."

Zoey took the paper cup the clerk offered and started to turn toward the soda fountain, but instead she focused on Rook's face. No familiar grin or knowing looks. Rook seemed tired, subdued and Zoey imagined what she'd witnessed at the cemetery had something to do with her current state. She started to ask, but decided the one question would lead to many. She settled on a simple, "Are you okay?"

"What?" Rook asked before shaking her head. "I'm fine. Let's just say this isn't my favorite building in the city."

Zoey stared a little harder, convinced there was more to it but didn't want to push. Her mission didn't involve learning more about Rook's feelings and it certainly didn't involve soothing them. The personal peeling of layers would have to wait until a more opportune time. Still, she felt a little rude for eating in front of Rook. "I guess

I should have asked you before we headed down here, but if I don't eat, I can't be responsible for my actions."

"I hear you." Rook flashed a hint of a grin. "One of my associates is the same way. I keep her desk stocked with candy bars for that very reason."

Zoey picked up her tray of food and led the way to an empty table. "How many associates do you have and why aren't any of them here with you?"

"Five, including George." Rook fiddled with a napkin, rolling it between her thumb and forefinger. "They're all working on various projects, and I haven't had time to fill them in on this one yet. Besides, I figured I could handle the first round of interviews on my own."

Zoey looked around. She didn't need a security breach on her first day, but she didn't see anyone seated close enough to overhear their conversation. "You think we'll need to interview them more than once? I was under the impression they'd already been interviewed extensively by the MPs who investigated the initial complaint."

Rook's brow furrowed. "The MPs only interviewed the students from McNair, not anyone else."

Now it was Zoey's turn to be confused. "Who else would they interview?" She shook her head. "Never mind. Dumb question. You mean the escorts, right?"

Rook's puzzled expression remained. "I don't think they're going to let you parade a bunch of call girls in here. I mean the other officers who've been visiting Svetlana and her pals."

Zoey's head swam and she desperately wished she was better at hiding her surprise. Rook wasn't making fun. A girl named Svetlana was mentioned in the report she'd reviewed—probably not her real name—but she didn't have a clue what Rook meant by "other officers."

"You're looking at me like you don't know what I'm talking about."

Zoey took a bite of salad that tasted closer to cardboard than the real thing. She stubbornly chewed to the end, preparing to square off. "Maybe you should take me at face value. What officers are you talking about?"

Now it was Rook's turn to look surprised. "They sent you to the White House without being fully briefed?"

That wasn't the point, and Zoey was annoyed that Rook was trying to push the issue. "Will you just tell me and spare the lecture?" She instantly regretted the outburst, but not more than she wanted answers.

"Someone prowled around in the," Rook glanced around to see if anyone was listening, "*working* women's records and found they have other uniformed customers who aren't students, and a good many of them work right here in this building. After we talk to your graduate students, we need to start interviewing the higher-ups to see how far this goes."

Zoey sensed a storm brewing. She'd rather be on the hot seat in front of the full Senate talking about Nine Tech and whistle-blowing on her pals than dealing with a sex scandal that might cost a four-star general a White House post.

"You had no idea?"

Rook's voice was gentle, caring, but Zoey couldn't help thinking it strange a civilian knew more about a scandal that was supposed to be dealt with internally than one of the military officers assigned to it, and the idea made her angry. She was being irrational, because it wasn't Rook's fault, but she didn't even try to rein in her anger. "No, I didn't. Unlike you, I don't spin things for a living, so if you get information from me, it's going to be the truth and nothing but. Understood?"

Rook held up both hands, palm side out. "Hey, don't shoot the messenger. I promise not to be the one who shuts you out of the loop. Okay?"

Zoey spent a moment rolling Rook's promise over in her head, but the syntax left her wondering if someone was indeed trying to shut her out of the loop and why.

❖

Rook looked at her watch. She'd only been at the Pentagon for two hours and it already felt like twelve. The three officers they'd interviewed so far had ostensibly acted like they were happy to cooperate, but they all said the same thing. They didn't know anything about anyone else who'd used the services of Lorraine Darcy Inc. To a man, none of them had a specific recollection of how they'd found the name of the agency, but they were pretty sure they remembered seeing an ad online.

Of the men who'd been at the party, the only one they hadn't talked to yet was General Bloomfield's son, Donny. She was saving him for last on purpose.

"Any more questions, Ms. Daniels?"

She looked up at Zoey and saw only cold indifference reflected back. The lieutenant in the hot seat right now looked like he was about to piss his pants, and Rook doubted he actually had any new information to offer. Maybe when he left the room, she could get Zoey to tell her why she was giving her the cold shoulder. Yes, Rook had abandoned their one and only date, but she'd had an excellent reason. Besides, Zoey didn't seem like the type to harbor a grudge. Maybe she was still mad about being left out of the loop regarding the depth of the investigation, but Rook didn't get why she was the one bearing the brunt of her anger.

Whatever it was, she'd have to wait until Dixon left to get to the bottom of it. He'd been hovering all afternoon. He was trying to read her notes right now, and she hoped he got an eyeful from the doodles she'd sketched of a naked woman lounging by the beach—something she wished she were doing. Her reliable memory meant she didn't need to take notes, but she always pretended to since it gave interviewees the impression she'd never forget what she'd been told.

"No, Major," Rook said. "I don't have any more questions." She waited to see what Zoey would do after she'd dismissed the soldier. Now that they'd finished with the students, it was time to start down the list of higher-ranking officers Rook had given her, a much stickier subject, especially since Zoey hadn't been fully briefed.

"Major Dixon, please go check with Lieutenant Louden about the records I requested and see if Colonel Mitchell is available now for his interview." Dixon responded to Zoey by pointing to the phone on the conference table. "The operator can connect you," he said, his tone barely hiding derision at her authority. Zoey didn't even look at the phone. "I'd rather you ask him in person," she said, waving a hand toward the door. "Thanks."

Dixon stood in place for a moment, clearly taken aback by the dismissal, but well-trained enough not to disobey a direct order from a more senior officer. "I'll be right back," he muttered as he left the conference room.

"That guy hates that you have seniority."

"I guess that's it. Maybe he just doesn't like me."

"As if. How long have you been stuck with him?" Rook asked.

"The entire time I've been here, but it feels like forever."

Rook contemplated the vague response and pressed for more. "How long have you been here, exactly?"

"I started this morning."

"Kind of a lot for a first day. Sudden reassignment?"

"Excuse me?"

"Nothing." Rook tapped her fingers on the table. It wasn't nothing. Had Zoey known she was going to be transferred to the Pentagon a couple of weeks ago, and if so, why hadn't she mentioned it?

Zoey read her mind. "I didn't tell you because I was asked not to mention it at the time."

"Orders?"

"A good soldier always obeys them," Zoey said, a smile playing over her lips.

"And you're a good soldier?"

"So I'm told. Now, do you have anything else you want to ask me before Dixon gets back?"

Rook was torn between formulating a strategy for interviewing the officers that had been mentioned in the Darcy Agency's files and taking the opportunity to confront Zoey about the shift in her mood.

She settled on a compromise. "I suggest we take up the rest of the interviews tomorrow, but you have dinner with me tonight so we can formulate a plan."

"I don't think that's a good idea."

Zoey was probably right, but Rook couldn't resist the urge to spend some time alone with her. "You're just not thinking it through. This place is all about sucking up. What better way to show you're willing to go above and beyond than to work overtime with the woman hired by the White House to make the military's problems go away?" She watched Zoey's face for a reaction, but she couldn't get a good read and wondered if they taught stoicism in boot camp or was it advanced officer training? She resisted asking. Barely.

"I don't think it's a good idea for us to talk about any of this at some restaurant."

Rook started to protest but quickly changed tactics. "Agreed. We'll have dinner at my place." She held up a hand. "Before you say no, you should be aware that my speed dial is set for all the best DC restaurants."

"Not much of a cook?"

"Let's just say I'd like you to live to work another day."

"Low bar. I might have conditions."

"Name them." Rook was prepared to agree to pretty much anything, in part to get out of this building and away from Dixon's watchful gaze. Zoey started to answer, but Dixon chose that moment to walk back in, his hulking frame casting a shadow over their conversation.

"He didn't have the records, and Colonel Mitchell isn't available. He said he'd speak to you on his own terms," Dixon bellowed. "Told you we should have called before I traipsed all the way over there." He stood between them, staring daggers at Zoey.

Behind his back, Rook rolled her eyes and watched Zoey struggle to suppress a grin. "I need to get back to my office anyway," Rook said, stuffing her notepad into her briefcase. "Let's start up again tomorrow. Major Granger, why don't you let me know when and where?"

She didn't wait for an answer before she started for the door. She'd hoped Zoey had been about to take her up on her offer, but there was no way they could make plans with Dixon in the room. It was probably best this way since she had a ton of work to do. Senator Newman had probably blown up her phone with messages. Powerful people weren't used to her going off grid, and they paid dearly for the privilege of being able to reach her no matter what. She'd agreed not to use her phone during the meetings today, but she wouldn't agree to it in the future. If the military had a problem with it, they'd have to talk to the White House.

She was two steps out the door when she felt a grip on her arm. She turned around and came face-to-face with Zoey. "What are you doing?"

"I think the more appropriate question is what are *you* doing?"

Rook jerked her chin toward the corridor. "Heading out. Did you have a change of heart?"

"About?"

Zoey's expression was genuinely curious, and Rook started to think she was losing her game. "Dinner? My place?"

"I came to escort you out of the building. Rules."

Zoey's determined expression made Rook feel feisty. "It's your first day. Do you even know the way out?"

"I'm finding my way around. Are you scared I'll get you lost?"

"Maybe I'm scared you'll get us both lost." Rook felt like they were talking about something other than navigating their way through the halls of the Pentagon.

"Only one way to find out." Zoey didn't wait for an answer. She took off down the hall, and Rook followed. When they reached security, Rook hung back for a moment, unsure whether she should try to resume their earlier conversation. Zoey saved her the trouble.

"I only have two conditions," she said.

"Let's hear them," Rook said, bracing for some huge caveat.

"I pay for my own dinner and it can't be tonight."

"Another date?" Rook asked before holding up her palm. "Wait, no, don't answer that. So, tomorrow then."

"Yes, but I'm serious about going dutch."

"Really?"

"It's business. I can tell you're used to a certain level of...Let's just say fancy meals, expensive drinks, and cars idling curbside to take you anywhere you want to go. Anyway, that's not me. I'm pretty basic, and if we're going to hang out, you'll have to get used to that."

"So, we're going to hang out?" Rook smiled and then spoke quickly for fear Zoey would change her mind. "Okay, burgers and beer it is. We'll settle on the details tomorrow." She didn't wait for an answer before walking away. Zoey might think of herself as simple and basic, but Rook sensed there was a lot more to the major than allegiance to country. Tomorrow night she'd find out what made Zoey Granger tick.

❖

Zoey looked up to see David Sharp standing in the doorframe of her office.

"Everything going well?" he asked.

Well wasn't exactly how she'd define her first day. More like a scorching introduction to military politics. The trip to the White House, being saddled with Dixon, and learning key facts of the investigation from a civilian had Zoey feeling she might be in over her head. Not to mention Colonel Mitchell blowing off their appointment and refusing to return her phone calls. But Sharp wouldn't want to hear any of that, and she wasn't about to ask him to bail her out. "Yes," she answered simply.

"You don't sound very convincing." He strode in and sank into the chair across from her desk.

Zoey considered her next words carefully. "I appreciate this opportunity. I really do, but I suppose I am curious about why you chose me."

"You want the truth or the sugarcoated answer?"

"Truth, sir."

He ticked off the reasons on his fingers. "One, you needed to be off base for a while because the people you work with are pissed off at you. Two, you might not have official experience, but you did solid work on Nine Tech, which brings me to reason three. The suits on Armed Forces like you, so I figured the White House would too. And finally, I trust you to look out for the best interests of your fellow soldiers. Is that enough?"

She resisted pointing out that her fellow soldiers probably thought investigating them was antithetical to looking out for their interests. "Yes, that's enough." She blurted out the next question without deference. "Is there a reason you didn't tell me this case doesn't just involve students at McNair, but also some flag officers stationed here at the Pentagon?"

His look of surprise appeared genuine. "I thought that was in your briefing materials. Are you sure it wasn't?"

She'd only had an hour with the packet before Dixon had shown up to escort her to the White House, but she'd reviewed everything again after Rook left for the day and she'd seen no mention of anyone other than the students at McNair. The omission was probably an oversight, to be expected in this giant bureaucracy. "I'll check again. We'll resume interviews in the morning."

His nod was the only additional acknowledgment of her concern. "So, how's it going? Anything interesting come to light?"

She paused for a second before answering, naturally hesitant to disclose anything while the investigation was ongoing, but quickly shook away the thought. He'd assigned her to the case and was her direct command. Of course he had a right to know how things were progressing. "Nothing so far. Looks like a bunch of guys with poor judgment, but that's it. Of course we've only interviewed the officers who were enrolled at McNair and we haven't talked to Donny Bloomfield yet. Some of the other officers seem a little reluctant to talk to us."

"That's to be expected. I'm sure you'll figure it out." He stood and started toward the door, waving her back to her seat when she started to stand as well. "Don't work too late. Nobody expects you to solve the world's problems on your first day." He paused with his hand on the door. "And don't let Rook Daniels bully you. This is our investigation and she's here as a courtesy to the president."

As the door shut behind him, Zoey processed his words, focused more on what he didn't say. He hadn't told her to back off, but he hadn't encouraged her either. Neutrality was to be expected and she tried not to read anything into it, but he was in a precarious position, since his promotion was tied to his boss's future. General Bloomfield was definitely the one with the most to lose if this scandal escalated, but she couldn't fault him with any interference since he'd given her this job and not reached out since.

Sharp's reference to Rook was mystifying, but it wasn't the first time she'd gotten mixed messages from a commanding officer. When your only directive seemed to be "do no harm" it wasn't easy to navigate the politics, especially since she didn't know much about the internal issues between the Pentagon and this administration. Word was President Garrett was supportive of the military, but no one could blame him for being wary about any hint of scandal.

Another knock on the door interrupted her musings, but this time the person knocking didn't wait for an invitation before barging in.

"Are you Granger?"

She quickly assessed the silver eagle on the uniform of the shorter than average man in front of her. "Colonel Mitchell?"

"Damn right. Where do you get off trying to drag me into your little game? Tell your pal Dixon to quit calling my office and take me off your list. I didn't have anything to do with those women and I've got nothing to say to you or your little lackey about it. Understood?"

She nodded, not because she understood, but because she figured any other reaction would send him running. "I think we got off on the wrong foot. I'm just following orders, talking to everyone whose name came up in the records of the Lorraine Darcy Agency." She could sense he was about to erupt again and held up a hand, careful to keep her voice low-pitched and calm. "It's very likely your name was in their records by mistake, but I have to talk to you to get that sorted out. Are you sure you can't find time to meet with us before I finalize the report?"

His shoulders relaxed slightly, but his face remained curled into a scowl. "It's a big mistake. Likely one of those damn kids who got into McNair because of their name not their potential is trying to drag me down. I'm a hard grader, but I'm not about to advance piss-poor soldiers just because of some supposed birthright. I have a family, for God's sake. There's no way I'd do the things they wanted me to do."

Zoey struggled to keep up, but Mitchell was speaking in riddles. "I'm sure no one expects you to do anything that isn't right. I'm only interested in pursuing the facts, but to do so you have to be willing to talk to me so I can sort out fact from fiction." She paused to think through her strategy. Protocol demanded she not interview anyone on the list without someone else present to witness what was said. Dixon was long gone, and she had no idea where Rook was or even if she could make it back to the building quickly. Maybe she could get some preliminary information and schedule a full interview for the next day. "Why don't you give me a rough idea of what's going on, and we can talk more about it tomorrow? If you don't want to include Dixon, I'll have someone else on hand who might be more responsive to your concerns."

He backed toward the door, his body shaking, and spat out his final words. "Leave. Me. Alone." The slamming door shook the frame and Zoey stared after him, completely mystified by his strange appearance and exit. On impulse, she picked up the phone and pressed the button that would connect her to Lieutenant Louden. When he picked up the line, she didn't waste any time.

"It's Major Granger. Can you tell me if I have access to a personnel file for Colonel Mitchell?"

"Hmm, let me check." She heard the sound of tapping on a keyboard in the background. "He's on your list of interviewees, right?"

"Right." Zoey resisted the urge to gossip about the strange visit from Mitchell. More tapping. "The system says his file is restricted," Louden said. "Must be a mistake in the system. I can check into it and get back to you tomorrow if that works."

"Thanks. Probably overkill on my part, but it doesn't hurt to be prepared."

"I'll email you when it's ready. Anything else?"

"No, thanks. Have a great evening." Zoey hung up and surveyed the files on her desk. She was at a stopping point and needed to leave now if she was going to be on time to meet the movers. What she would rather be doing was meeting Rook for dinner. If the movers were quick, maybe she could make that happen. She pulled out her phone, but before she could type a text, years of discipline took hold. She'd meet the movers and then prepare for Donny Bloomfield's interview. Resigned to her boring but industrious evening, Zoey packed up her desk and headed for the parking lot, unable to deny the growing excitement about the prospect of seeing Rook again very soon.

Chapter Eleven

Rook's phone started ringing at six a.m. She was on her way to the treadmill, located on the top floor of her townhouse, and for a second, considered ignoring it until she got in her exercise for the day. But the second passed and she checked the screen and took the call. "Good morning, Senator Newman."

"Do you have any updates for me?"

Fine. She didn't want to waste time on niceties either. "Matter of fact, I do. I spent last night reviewing the tapes of the morning shows and my team performed an analysis of the resulting press coverage. Your favorables are up five percent since the story broke. If we keep—"

"Five percent?" His voice rose. "I get a five percent bump when I kiss babies on the campaign trail. You can't seriously think that's progress."

Rook rubbed her pounding forehead. "Senator, this isn't a campaign for votes. It's a campaign for your future and maybe even your liberty if the DA decides to open a criminal investigation. Every tenth of a percentage point we can elevate your image is a potential juror deciding you're too nice, too sincere to convict on a manslaughter charge. Trust me when I say that we are making progress."

"I'm sorry," he said, sounding more resigned than apologetic. "Jeanine is not happy about all this attention. The press is following

CARSEN TAITE

us everywhere and they're scaring the kids. I can't get to my office without a Capitol Police escort."

Rook searched for a solution, and something she'd seen on one of the news segments last night came to mind. "Didn't Jeanine graduate from Columbia?"

"Yes. She grew up in Manhattan. Her parents still live there. But I don't understand what that has to do with—"

"Bear with me a second." Rook put the senator on hold and dialed Lacy on another line. "Lace, I know it's early, but there's some kind of women's conference going on at Columbia this weekend. Farah Hamil is one of the organizers. I need you to contact Farah and get her to invite Jeanine Newman to attend. Small speaking role, not one where she'll be subject to questions, just something to give her and the kids an excuse to be away from DC for a while. Get Harry to start working on her speech. Something along the lines of you can be a strong, modern woman and still stand by your man. I want to see copy by noon."

"Got it. I have until noon to roll back decades of feminism."

"Very funny." Rook knew Lacy was kidding. Mostly. "If Farah balks, have her call me."

"Will do. What time will you be in?"

"Not sure. This new case is going to have me running around for a few days."

"The one from Julia?"

Rook appreciated Lacy's discretion. "That's the one. I'm not sure I need to involve the rest of the team right now, but I'll keep you posted." After Lacy hung up, Rook switched back to Senator Newman. "Your wife is about to be invited to speak at a women's conference at Columbia. She'll go and take the kids for a visit with their grandparents. In the meantime, you'll go back to Ohio and schedule meetings with as many of your constituents as possible. You'll do town halls and pancake breakfasts as if you're running for office. You'll answer every question that comes your way until the press is tired of talking about it or until some other story splashes across the headlines."

"But I thought you didn't want me talking to the press anymore?"

"I changed my mind. We're going to divide and conquer. You two will represent like the power couple you are, and since you'll be in two different places, the press will be spread thin. Every time you get a question about the case, you'll give your stock answer and pivot to a pressing issue, like healthcare or the economy. Harry will work with you on exactly what you can and cannot say about the pending case. You'll be so visible, the press will get sick of you. There's nothing they like more than a slammed door because it means there's something to dig for. You and Jeanine are going to show them everything and nothing all at once."

"Are you going to be in Ohio with me or New York with her?"

Rook held back an audible sigh. "Neither. You don't need a big gun if you don't have to guard against big damage. Having me visible is a liability. Harry will be dedicated to whatever you need. Trust me, it won't be long before the press is sick of you."

Rook added a few more encouraging words to their pep talk and clicked off the line. A few miles at a fast clip on the treadmill provided a welcome release, and by seven thirty, she'd showered and settled in to eat breakfast and watch the morning news. She'd taken her first bite of grapefruit when her phone buzzed with a text.

Morning. Hope it's not too early to text.

She smiled at Zoey's message with its spelled out words and punctuation, and typed her reply. *I've been up for hours. You?*

Always. Hard habit to break. A few beats passed and then Zoey wrote: *I was hoping to do that other interview offsite. What's your schedule?*

Available anytime after noon. Rook hesitated before hitting send, pondering whether she should include anyone else from her team in the interview of Donny Bloomfield. She reasoned with fewer people involved he'd be more likely to open up, but a small part of her nagged that she just didn't want to share her time with Zoey. This case didn't appear to be a big one, but the fact that it came from the White House elevated its importance, and normally she would have held a team meeting to discuss it before she'd ever met with

Zoey. But she hadn't and she didn't want to now. Rationalizing that her team had a lot of other stuff going on right now and she wasn't merely trying to spend time alone with Zoey, she sent the message and impatiently waited for Zoey's reply. She didn't have to wait long.

Perfect. Meet me at McNair at one.

❖

Zoey sat on the hard plastic seat on the Metro train, focusing her energy on ignoring Dixon's grating voice. He'd been talking for the last fifteen minutes about how he'd wanted to be deployed, but someone stateside was always in need of his skills, so he'd had to serve his country here at home. He seemed to be working very hard to keep his tone from being defensive, but it was pretty clear he was comparing his own experience against hers—overseas, in combat zones—and failing to measure up. After the first few minutes, Zoey had started concocting fantasies, the most appealing of which involved her pushing him through the doors at the next stop and waving gleefully as the train pulled away. Pipe dream.

Next her thoughts roamed to Rook and their dinner plans. She'd spent the morning wavering about her yes to dinner, and she'd come close to texting Rook to say she'd changed her mind. If she had she wouldn't have to spend the entire day in eager anticipation. How was she supposed to concentrate on interviewing Donny Bloomfield when all she could think about was hanging out at Rook's place pretending to be entirely focused on their work when she was incredibly distracted by the mystery of Rook's public and personal personas?

The train lurched to a stop at Waterfront Station, and she stood too quickly, almost falling into Dixon.

He grabbed her shoulder and steadied her with a grin. "You'll get used to it." She grimaced a smile of thanks and walked briskly from the train, leaving him to follow or not. She could get used to a lot of things, but she was certain he wasn't one of them.

They walked a few short blocks to McNair where the sergeant at the gate checked their IDs and waved them through. A few minutes later, they were escorted into a classroom where Rook stood to greet them. Like every other time Zoey had seen her, Rook was dressed like she'd walked off the pages of a fashion magazine. Today she wore a slim, tailored black suit with a crisp pale yellow shirt, open at the collar. She looked dashing and confident, and Zoey was certain if good looks were a gateway to success, Rook's clients got their money's worth. She opened her mouth to say so before she remembered Dixon's presence and bit her tongue. "You're early," she said instead.

"So are you. I just happen to be earlier."

Rook barely gave Dixon a glance, for which Zoey gave a silent cheer. "Is Lieutenant Bloomfield on his way?"

Rook sat back down and shrugged. "So they say, but I don't have your kind of pull around here. Maybe you should check with whoever's in charge and see if they'll give you more than a 'wait here, ma'am.' I don't think I've been ma'amed so much in my entire life."

"Welcome to my world." Zoey paused, unsure what to do next. She'd spoken to the provost to arrange the interview with Bloomfield, but she didn't know where his office was or even what he looked like. She started to pull out her phone to call him when Lieutenant Bloomfield came through the door.

Donny approached Dixon first and offered a salute. He had to know that she was the one who'd arranged the interview, but he deferred to the only male in the room, immediately losing points in Zoey's estimation. When he finally turned and saluted her, he wore a cocky, fraternity boy grin and she braced for a confrontation. "Let's get started, Lieutenant."

"Sure," he said. "The sooner you can clear all this up, the better off we'll all be, right, Major?"

She ignored the implication that they were merely going through the paces to give his father a break and introduced Rook. "Ms. Daniels is here at the request of the White House. Anything you can say to us, you can say to her. Understood?" She watched him give Rook a once-over, his gaze lingering longer than she liked. She couldn't tell if he found her attractive—he'd have to be dead not to—or if he was sizing up a challenge. Either way, she wanted to move this along.

"Tell us about the night at the Ivy Hotel. Was that the first time you used the services of the Lorraine Darcy Agency?"

"Wow, you really cut to the chase, don't you?"

"I have a job to do." Zoey didn't bother to hide the growl in her voice, although she was walking a fine line considering this kid, arrogant as he was, was also the son of a four-star general who was about to become one of the most powerful people at the Pentagon. But she wasn't used to subordinates being so informal and it was disconcerting. Nothing she'd witnessed from General Bloomfield would have led her to believe his son would lack discipline, but maybe being the youngest child in a military family was kind of like being a preacher's kid. She decided to take a different tack, relaxing her posture and leaning in like they were old friends. "Look, I get it." She waved her arm. "Being you can't be easy. You have a lot to live up to, and I'm guessing there's always someone riding you about fulfilling your legacy. Your dad's a tough guy, and with the Senate hearings on his confirmation coming up, I bet there's even more pressure than usual. Am I right?"

Donny shifted in his chair and looked around the room, everywhere but at her. She'd struck a nerve, but didn't want to press too hard for fear the pain would send him running rather than get him to open up. Besides, there was no telling how Dixon might spin what she'd said when they got back to the office, and she didn't need Bloomfield thinking she was running him down to his own son.

Spin. The word had become part of her lexicon since she'd met Rook. She'd hated it before, having considered it useful for nothing but covering up a lie or making something unpleasant sound exactly the opposite. But now she found she was developing spin of her own, already thinking about the way she would describe this interview to her superiors. She shot a look at Rook who nodded encouragement. "Lieutenant?" she said.

"It wasn't a big deal."

"Sure it wasn't," Dixon broke in. "You were just having fun."

Zoey gave him a murderous look and then caught Rook smiling at her, seeming to enjoy her discomfort. Ignoring them both, she pressed on. "Just tell me where you got the contact for the agency, if you or any of the others contacted them before, and what was your arrangement with them?"

He grinned. "If that's all you want to know, that's easy. One of the guys, I don't remember which one, saw an ad online, you know, on one of those lonely heart, matchmaking sites. Pretty sure it was his first time and I'd never heard of them before. As for the arrangement, it wasn't anything special. We invited some women to a party and they came. They drank and hung out with us. Some asshole thought we were having too much fun and called the cops. End of story."

It was far from the end. Zoey opened her file and pulled out photos of the hotel room the manager had taken after the police were called. She wondered if the reporter from the *Post* already had copies of these and why he hadn't run them yet. Probably waiting to see if he could get evidence about more senior officers partaking of all that the Darcy Agency had to offer and saving it for publication until after the president made his nomination of Bloomfield official. She spread the photos out on the table and pressed her finger on one depicting nearly a dozen liquor bottles in a pile by the side of the bed. "Is that part of what you mean by too much fun?"

"So now we're in trouble for drinking?"

She ignored him and jabbed a finger at another picture of a lacy thong hanging from the lamp by the side of the bed. "You pay extra for the decor?"

"Guys having fun on a Friday night. Surely even you cut loose from time to time."

"Absolutely. I make a point of it every time I return from a battle zone," she said, a raw enjoyment at the blow she struck with the dig. The most combat he'd ever seen was probably in that hotel room. She let a few beats pass. "But I never have to pay for it."

"Lucky you," he said, his voice dripping with sarcasm.

She waited, thinking he would say more, but he clammed up. She had more questions to ask, but he probably wasn't going to respond truthfully, so she chose the most important one, the one she'd been dreading. "Has your father ever used the services of the Darcy Agency?"

She heard Dixon stifle a gasp, but Rook's face, to her credit, didn't change from her neutral, I'm just soaking all this in, expression. Bloomfield, on the other hand, stood so fast, he sent his chair crashing to the ground.

"I hope you enjoyed this little outing, Major, because it's going to be your last," he said.

"Maybe so, but at least I'll have done my duty."

Donny shook his head, made a show of saluting Dixon, and marched out of the room. Zoey looked down at the table. Her knuckles were white from gripping the side, and she took a few long, slow breaths to calm down. Her role as a ball-buster was a complete facade, and once General Bloomfield heard from his son, she was probably going to be reassigned to a post in the middle of nowhere for the rest of her career, assuming she still had one.

"Well, that went well," Rook said, breaking the silence.

"I should go talk to him," Dixon said, staring longingly at the door.

Zoey snapped to attention. "You'll do no such thing." She could tell Dixon was practically foaming at the mouth to corner Donny and commiserate about her tactics in a ploy to find a way to suck up to Bloomfield Senior and undermine her command. "We'll talk to him again, but not today. He's a hothead and needs to calm down before we get any decent information out of him."

"I agree," Rook said. "Besides, there are other ways to get the information we need." Before Zoey could press her on the point, she changed the subject. "Anyone else here we need to talk to?"

Dixon shuffled through his file. "Colonel Mitchell is on the list. He wasn't there that night, but his name was on the list of possible 'clients.' He's a professor in the, get this, Information and Cyberspace department. We asked him to come by yesterday, but he wasn't available. Maybe he's on campus today."

Zoey picked up her phone and dialed the provost to ask if Mitchell was available. She probably should've mentioned he'd come by her office yesterday and chewed her out, but she'd written it off to posturing on his part and forgotten about it until now. She'd wanted to wait until Louden got back with her about Mitchell's file before pursuing an interview with him again, but Dixon was right, they may as well see if he was around while they were here.

The provost was in meetings off campus for the rest of the afternoon, but his secretary said she would take a message and have him call her tomorrow. Deciding they could wait one more day before poking the beast, Zoey told her that would be fine. "Mitchell's going to have to wait until tomorrow. I guess it's time to start working through the rest of the names on the list. Shall we head back to the office?"

"Actually," Rook said, "I'm supposed to meet with Ms. Scott to update her about our progress and I'm sure she'll want to hear from you directly. Perhaps Major Dixon could pull the files we need, and we could start in on the rest of the list tomorrow?"

Zoey looked at Dixon who was shaking his head no, which only made her want to do the opposite. Telling herself she was only agreeing to Rook's plan to irritate Dixon, she said, "That sounds like a great plan. Major, we'll see you tomorrow." Without waiting for a response, she followed Rook from the room, full of renewed energy at the prospect of spending the rest of the day with her.

Rook held the door to the car open and waved Zoey in, happy she'd managed to wrangle her away from the annoying presence of Major Douchebag. Clearly, Zoey found Dixon as annoying as she did, and she'd admired the way Zoey had put him in his place. While Zoey might feel it was her duty to put up with another afternoon being in a room with Dixon, Rook had no such allegiance and no one could pay her enough to suffer his presence any longer today. As she settled into the car, George asked where they were headed next. Shooting a look of contrition at Zoey, she gave him an address in Maryland.

"We're not meeting Ms. Scott at the White House?" Zoey asked.

"Please don't call her Ms. Scott. She'll get a big head. And actually, we're not meeting Julia at all. Not today, anyway."

Zoey's brow furrowed. "Any chance you want to tell me where we're going?"

"We're taking a field trip to the offices of the Lorraine Darcy Agency. I thought it might be fun to drop in and see what kind of women make otherwise upstanding officers act like fools." She paused and stared at Zoey's expression. "You look mad. Are you mad?"

"Mad is not the word. I guess I'm not sure why you felt compelled to lie."

"It wasn't a lie so much as a cover, a way to get you away from Major Marshall Dixon, who I'm hoping you find as annoying as I do."

"Trust me, he's not my favorite person by any means, but what if he asks me later about the meeting at the White House in front of General Sharp or Bloomfield?"

"He won't. Guys like him—all that promise and nothing to show for it—don't like feeling inferior and there's no way he'll draw attention to the fact you were called to the White House and he was left behind."

"How do you know so much about him?"

Rook spent a moment considering how much to share. She'd had Eric dig into Dixon's background for no other reason than she wanted to know more about the people she was working with, but Zoey was likely to take offense at the intrusion. What she'd found hadn't been all that interesting. Dixon had graduated from West Point and served his required five years of active duty at Fort Irvine and Fort Polk, respectively. A West Point graduate relegated to two of the most despised posts in the service likely meant he'd always been as much of a douche as he was now. He'd started working at the Pentagon a year ago, and Eric hadn't been able to find anything about why or how he'd gotten the reassignment. "Remember what I said about other ways to get information? Well, I did a little research. I like to know who I'm working with."

"And what about me? Did you do a little research about me too?"

Rook swore she detected a hint of flirtation in Zoey's voice, but she wasn't sure she could trust her reactions where Zoey was concerned. She tested the waters with some mild flirtation of her own. "Maybe," she said with a grin. "Is there something special you'd like me to know?"

"Where is this place we're going?"

With the question, Zoey edged slightly away, subtle enough to deny, but Rook noticed it just the same. Okay, so they were back to business. She was going to get whiplash from the back and forth, but two could play this cat-and-mouse game. "Interestingly enough, the agency has an actual office in the business district." She pointed out the window, recognizing the building from the pictures Eric had emailed to her. "It's in that building over there." She told George to park on the street in front, and when the car stopped, she turned to Zoey. "You ready?"

"I'm not sure this is a good idea. What if we go in there and rattle the cage and one of them talks to the press? Wasn't the whole point of this investigation to control the flow of information? Once we start asking questions of a bunch of civilians, there's no putting that back in the bottle."

"Trust me. I have a plan." Rook climbed out of the car and held out a hand. Zoey hesitated at first but then grabbed on and followed her. The building was older than she'd expected, architecture from the early seventies with nicks and blemishes in the facade that spoke of being left behind for newer, fresher office space. Somehow Rook had thought the high dollar escort service would be in one of the fancier, trendier buildings that had popped up over the last year, but maybe high dollar was a relative term. As they walked through the doors, Rook said, "Let me do the talking. Just stand there and look gorgeous."

Zoey bristled at the remark, and Rook felt like a heel, wondering how often people assumed Zoey's good looks outweighed her sharp intellect. "Sorry, that was rude. I'm just trying to keep you out of trouble. If anyone asks if you were here, you can deny you said anything to anyone, and say it was all me. Fair enough?"

"Let's do this thing before I change my mind." Zoey took off without waiting for a response.

The registry in the lobby listed the Lorraine Darcy Agency offices on the tenth floor. They were the only two people on the elevator on the way up, but they rode in silence. Rook felt like every time she opened her mouth, she risked pushing Zoey further away, which was probably for the best, but the quiet between them was noisy with unanswered questions. Thanks to Eric's skills, she knew all about Zoey's lifetime of service, but she knew little about her life outside the Army. What kind of things did she like to do? What were her favorite foods? What kind of women did she like to date and why wasn't she with someone now?

That last one was high on the list, but she supposed she could guess the answer. Zoey probably liked women who were as committed to duty as she was and she wasn't dating one of these women because she had impossible standards. Rook realized she had no real basis for the supposition, but she'd bet the entire big ass retainer she'd made from Senator Newman that she was right.

The elevator stopped and Rook stepped out, leading the way. Contrary to what she'd told Zoey, she didn't have a plan in mind, but experience told her there was no substitute for a surprise visit. They walked down the well-worn carpeted hall to Darcy's suite, and Rook noted several vacant offices along the way.

"I guess I never imagined prostitutes having office space," Zoey said. "I mean what could they possibly use it for? Interviewing applicants? Training?"

Rook placed a finger over her lips and whispered, "You're hilarious. Don't you dare make me laugh before I go in."

"Before you go in? Don't you mean 'we'?"

"Sure, but remember the rule."

"Right, no talking without your permission." Zoey rolled her eyes and pointed at the door. "Are we going in or not?"

Rook pushed through the door and quickly realized they wouldn't be talking to anyone at the Lorraine Darcy Agency today. The large open area was littered with haphazardly placed furniture and desk phones. File cabinet drawers stood open, their emptiness apparent from yards away. Rook spun in place, looking for something, anything to give her a clue that this space had been the headquarters for a group of escorts, but all she saw was the same kind of detritus that could have been left when a CPA or some other equally boring business moved out.

Zoey knelt and picked up an envelope off the floor. She read it and then handed it over. "You think this means anything?"

Rook took it from her, letting her fingers linger on Zoey's for a few seconds longer than necessary before she reluctantly pulled away. The envelope had been slit open cleanly and the contents slid out easily. Rook skimmed the page twice before handing it to Zoey.

Zoey thumped the paper with her finger. "This is an eviction letter."

"Yes," Rook answered simply, her brain churning. "Look at when it's dated."

Zoey traced the typewritten words. "That's the day after the incident at the Ivy."

"Exactly."

"What do you think it means?"

"I don't know," Rook answered. She didn't know, but she had some ideas. "Maybe someone reported their little run-in at the Ivy to the building management."

"But that's not what you really think, is it?"

Rook shook her head, surprised Zoey was able to read her so well. "It's logical, for sure, but I kind of doubt the management of this particular building cares who does what as long as they have the opportunity to rent out the space."

"Good point."

Rook grinned. "That might be the nicest thing you've said to me all day."

"You don't strike me as the kind of person who needs people to say nice things to fuel your ego."

"My ego's fine, thank you very much, but it's always nice to get compliments from smart, accomplished women."

"Are you always this smooth?" Zoey asked with a skeptical tone.

"Hardly ever, but don't tell anyone because I have a reputation to uphold." She reached for the envelope to turn the conversation back to business. "Don't go all rules and regulations on me, because I'm taking this with me. It feels like a clue." As her hand touched Zoey's again, she let it linger this time. The letter might feel like a lead in their investigation, but the charge she felt whenever Zoey was near was a signal of something else entirely. Something she wanted very much to explore.

Chapter Twelve

Later that evening, Rook checked the fridge for the third time, but the beer she'd stowed hadn't moved. Beer had been her first choice because of how she'd sold the evening as a casual work meeting, but maybe Zoey would prefer something different like a nice Malbec, a Champagne, or whiskey. She picked up the phone to call in a liquor order, but then set it back down again. She had wine and hard liquor on hand, and Zoey sure didn't seem like the Champagne with burgers type. What she needed to do was figure out why she was so damn jumpy about having Zoey over in the first place. Her mind wandered back over every moment they'd shared earlier in the day, reliving the spark she'd felt at every glance and touch and she had her answer.

Her phone rang and she grabbed it off the counter, hoping it wasn't Zoey, calling to cancel. Eric's number showed up on the display. She answered on the second ring. "Tell me you have some intel."

"I'm emailing you a file with all the information I've gathered so far, but it isn't much. I couldn't find a copy of a lease for Lorraine Darcy Inc. for any space in that building. Doesn't mean it doesn't exist. It just wasn't in the files where I expected to find it."

"I hear you." Rook was used to listening to the undercurrent of Eric's reports. He'd likely hacked into the leasing company's files and seen where they kept their leases, but didn't find one for Darcy Inc. "Maybe it's under another name?"

"Nothing matches that suite number. If the office is rented out, it's not in the books. Not the official ones anyway. What I sent you is all the information I could find about the leasing agency, the building's other tenants, and a copy of the building management's letterhead."

"Go ahead and spoil it for me. Is the eviction letter legit?"

"You have some reason to think it isn't?"

She didn't have a reason, not a good one anyway, but her gut told her something was off. The doorbell rang. "I have to go. Keep digging, and I'll talk to you later." She disconnected the call and looked at the clock on the wall, noting Zoey was exactly on time—precisely what she'd expected. Happy she didn't have to spend any longer contemplating her inadequate hospitality, Rook glanced around the room one last time to make sure she didn't have any client files lying around.

She didn't spend a lot of time in her townhouse, which was a shame because it was actually pretty dreamy. Open and airy with lots of sunlight, it was the perfect place to enjoy a Sunday morning brunch or tea on the terrace. Rook didn't indulge in either of those things, but she liked knowing she could if she wanted. This place had turned into a stopover between her office and those of her clients, a place to house her clothes and the trappings of wealth she'd accumulated over the years. Her dates were spent at luxurious DC restaurants and overnights were for hotels or her companions' homes where she could make a quick getaway when the inevitable text, email, or phone call came, summoning her back to her first love, the business she'd created.

She pulled the door open at the first knock and lost her composure for a moment at the sight of Zoey, framed in the doorway. Like the night they'd gone to Meridian, Zoey was out of uniform, but this time she was dressed a little more formally, in slim black slacks, loafers, and a crisp, cornflower blue shirt, rather than the casual picnic wear she'd had on for the tour of the monuments.

"You said tonight, right?"

Zoey's smile was captivating, and Rook couldn't help but return it. "Yes." She swung the door open wider. "Come in."

Zoey walked in and her eyes swept the interior. She sucked in a breath, and Rook felt compelled to say, "I know, it's a little on the big side."

"You could say that. I'm terrified to know how much something like this would cost." Zoey instantly put her hand on her mouth. "Sorry, that was rude. It's just that I've been looking at real estate and this part of town was on my don't even look at it list."

"No worries. I bought it quite a while back so I got a steal." Rook allowed herself the small lie. Even though she had purchased during a down market, the price had still been exorbitant. Time to change the subject. "So you're looking to buy?"

"Leasing for now, but maybe someday."

Rook motioned for Zoey to follow her to the kitchen. "If you'd like some tips, I know the entire area pretty well."

"I appreciate the offer, but General Sharp's wife has been an invaluable resource. I found a place in Vienna. I'm still in boxes, but it's home." Zoey waved an arm. "Besides…"

Her voice trailed off, but Rook got the point. "You're thinking we don't have the same taste."

"Don't get me wrong. It's clear you have impeccable taste, just different."

"What can I say? I like nice things." Rook cringed as the defensive tone crept into her voice. She did like nice things, even if she worked so hard she rarely had an opportunity to enjoy them. Her father had sworn she'd never make anything of her choices in life, but her six-bedroom townhouse in Dupont Circle rivaled the Manhattan apartment where she'd grown up.

Zoey was looking at her, a questioning expression on her face, but when she mentally replayed the story of her rivalry with her father, it didn't bear telling. She rushed to change the subject. "Speaking of nice things. I promised you burgers and beer. Does that still sound good?"

"Sure, I'll take a beer."

Rook reached into the fridge and grabbed the growler George had picked up from the new local microbrewery everyone was raving about. She started to tell Zoey about the place and how hard it was to get the stuff before it ran out on any given day, but she had a feeling Zoey would file such a story in the category of things that impressed most people, but didn't impress her at all. Rook had planned on ordering burgers from another hot, new place in town, but as she poured them each some of the creamy stout, she made a last-minute change of plans. She handed Zoey a glass. "Let me know if this is okay."

She watched as Zoey tipped the glass to her lips. She took a small sip at first and her eyes fluttered. A soft moan escaped and she pulled a deeper draught, sighing after she swallowed. "That's delicious. Best brew I've ever had."

Rook tore her gaze away from the sensual tableau of Zoey's desire. "Trust me to order dinner?"

"Absolutely."

Rook pulled up her favorite food delivery app and placed an order, and then invited Zoey to join her in the living room. Zoey glanced between the couch and the two club chairs opposite and chose one of the chairs. Okay, Rook thought, she's here for business. That's exactly what she should be here for. All for the best. Rook settled onto the couch and fished for light, pre-dinner conversation. "So, when did you find out you were being reassigned to the Pentagon?"

"The night of Addison Riley's birthday party. General Sharp asked me not to say anything until it was official."

"Speaking of official, I hear congratulations are in order on your upcoming promotion." Rook watched Zoey's eyebrows rise and added, "Senator Armstrong told me the request is sailing through."

"She seems like the kind of person that knows a little bit about everything that's going on in this city."

"More than a little bit and more than just this city. Connie Armstrong is a bulldog. Nothing gets past her. She's a good person, though, and if she's on your side, there's no stronger ally."

"Good to know." Zoey swallowed a taste of the beer. "This is really good. I have high expectations now about your choice in burgers."

A knock on the door cut off Rook's reply. She tipped the delivery guy and walked back in holding two bags. "Shakeburgers and fries from Shake Shack. Simple, but tasty."

"Winning endorsement." Zoey grinned and set her beer down. "Tell me where the plates are, and I'll get us set up." She pointed. "Kitchen table okay?"

"Perfect." Rook set the bags on the counter and started pulling out the burgers and fries. "The city's full of well-known burger joints, but I'm a big fan of this one."

"Me too."

"Oh, you've been there before?" Rook supposed it was silly to think she was introducing Zoey to something new. "I was hoping I would be your first introduction to the Shack."

"You're a really close second. Margaret Sharp took me to the one at Pentagon City when we were house hunting, and I've been jonesing for another burger ever since."

"Allow me to feed your addiction." Rook portioned out the food and helped Zoey carry the plates and their beer glasses to the table. For the next few minutes they dug into the food like hungry wolves, and Rook realized she hadn't eaten anything since a half a sandwich grabbed during a working lunch, hours ago. A third of the way through her burger, she felt fortified enough to ask Zoey if she was enjoying her food.

"It might even be better than the first time, which doesn't bode well for my waistline."

Rook let her gaze roam over Zoey's figure, taking special note of her trim hips and tapered waist. "I think you're a few hundred burgers shy of an intervention." She handed her the bag. "And you should eat more of these fries before I finish them off." Zoey reached into the bag and pulled several fries. Rook watched her sigh with pleasure as they crossed her lips. She needed to change the subject quickly or be in danger of trying to kiss those lips. "So, you've known General Sharp and his family for a long time?"

"Is that more gossip or do you already know the answer?"

"It's partly what I hear and partly what I've observed." Rook wasn't lying. She'd asked Eric to conduct a simple online search for information about Zoey, and Sharp had come up in her past on several occasions. It was clear he'd taken a personal interest in her career, which explained why he elected to reassign her to the Pentagon.

"He was my first CO—commanding officer."

"I know what CO means," Rook said, letting a slight chiding tone creep into her voice.

Zoey shrugged. "Some people don't, and I have a tendency to forget not everyone speaks Army. But I guess it was silly to assume you wouldn't know the lingo. I mean why else would the White House have hired you for this job if you weren't familiar with the military?"

"I think they probably hired me despite my familiarity with the military." Rook cocked her head. "I'm actually a little surprised Sharp didn't mention anything to you about my past encounters with the Pentagon." The look on Zoey's face told her maybe she should have kept her mouth shut.

"Encounters?"

"More like run-ins. The brass probably has more colorful words to characterize their interactions with me. Let's just say I don't have a lot of fans in your new workplace." The painful memory of the last time she'd had to interact with the folks at the Pentagon punched her in the gut, and she cast about for a way to keep her composure. She pointed at Zoey's plate. "Can I get that out of the way for you?" Zoey nodded, and she took both their plates and hurried back to the kitchen, anxious to put some distance between the painful subject and this opportunity to get to know Zoey better. She took her time, scraping the few remains from their dinner into the garbage, taking long, slow breaths to calm her anger and remind herself that Zoey might wear a uniform but that didn't make her an enemy.

"Are you okay?"

Rook dropped a plate in the sink, instantly feeling stupid for being startled at the sound of Zoey's voice. If anything, her tone was soothing, but Rook couldn't seem to keep her own from being clipped and stark. "I'm good."

"Right." Zoey brushed close and picked the plate up out of the sink. She didn't move away, instead she lifted the faucet handle, carefully rinsed the plate, and stacked it in the dishwasher. "You know, if we're going to work together, it might help for us to clear the air."

Zoey's tone was light, but Rook shied from the portent. If only clearing the air was as simple as she implied. "I think you know it's a little more complicated than that." She wagged a finger between them. "It's no secret I'm attracted to you, right?" Zoey nodded slowly. "I never would have acted on that if I'd known we were going to be working together and I should've never acted on it in the first place since I knew from the get-go you're so gung ho about your job."

"I get the working together part and I completely agree, but I don't get what you have against the Army."

"Army, Navy, Marines—you're all the same. Closing ranks to protect your own. Don't mistake anything that your Pentagon buddies may have told you. They're cooperating now because the White House is watching, but if we look away for just a second, they'll be back to their old tricks." Rook delivered the proclamation with fire in her voice, and Zoey backed away from her like she was recoiling from a snake. For a second Rook wondered if she'd gone too far, but she couldn't help adding, "Why in the hell did I agree to take this case?"

"Maybe you shouldn't have," Zoey fired back. "Why don't you go back to your more important work and leave the men and women who risk their lives for you to their own devices?"

"Oh, plenty of you risk your lives, but the danger is closer than you think. You of all people should know you have to watch your back."

"Is that a threat?"

"I'm no threat to you, but your kind eat their own on a regular basis. You think your fellow soldiers have your back? You need to think again."

Rook felt her cheeks burning, and Zoey was looking at her like she'd lost her mind. This wasn't at all how she'd planned this evening to go. She'd overstepped, but she didn't care. In spite of all her combat experience, in the ways of politics, Zoey seemed naïve, and nothing but trouble could come from innocence. They stared at each other for what seemed like forever until Zoey broke the silence.

"I'm going to leave."

Rook looked at the door, just a few steps away. Was it this case or this woman that was causing her to lose her edge? She either needed to figure out what it was fast and solve it or tell Julia she was done. Bottom line, she wasn't going to figure anything out if Zoey walked out the door.

"Please don't go."

"I feel like you're playing tug-of-war with me. First I'm in, then I'm out." Zoey's eyes reflected hurt. "I don't know what's going on with you, but if I did something to piss you off, I'm sorry."

"It's not you. You're right. I never should've taken this case."

"Because of your deep-seated hatred of all things military?"

"Because they killed my brother."

❖

Zoey shot a look at the door. She needed to make a decision now and stick with it, but Rook's words were weighted with pain, and only a heartless bastard would walk out on her now. Acting purely on impulse, she grabbed Rook's hand and led her to the couch.

"Where's your liquor?"

"I need to stay focused."

"You need something to take the edge off."

Rook leaned back and listlessly pointed to a cabinet across the room. Zoey opened the doors and surveyed the contents. There wasn't a whiskey under twenty years old, so she poured a couple of glasses of booze she would've had to save for special occasions. She carried the heavy glass tumblers back to the sofa and sank down beside Rook. "Drink up and tell me what's going on." At the last minute, she bit back the words "that's an order," sensing the phrase might send Rook over the edge.

While Rook took a sip she did too, savoring the slow, smooth heat of the expensive alcohol and wondering what it was like to have a cabinet full of expensive liquor in an expensive townhouse in one of the most desirable neighborhoods in the capital. Apparently, none of these trappings were enough to mask any troubles one might have.

She waited as the minutes ticked by. Rook continued to sip slowly from her drink, but she didn't appear to be inclined to talk. Finally, Zoey took charge. "What was your brother's name?"

"Rory."

"Older or younger?"

"Older."

Zoey studied Rook's face, searching for clues. Her drawn features and the faraway look in Rook's eyes spoke of difficult memories, and Zoey wondered if digging deeper would only unearth more pain. Deciding it was better to get the poison out, she pressed on. "You were close?"

"The closest. He was my best friend. The first person I came out to and the only one in my family who didn't give me shit for not wanting to go into the family business."

Zoey remembered Rook's mention of her family full of lawyers during their picnic at Meridian Park. "So, I'm guessing he wasn't a lawyer."

"Oh, we're all lawyers. He was a third-year associate at Chamblee and Ives." Rook paused, apparently detecting the blank stare and then added, "It's a white shoe law firm in midtown Manhattan."

Zoey nodded even though she didn't have a clue what "white shoe law firm" meant.

"He'd been at work for several hours when the north tower was hit," Rook said. "By the time the second plane struck the south tower, he was organizing a group of associates from his firm to head downtown to do whatever they could to help out with the rescue effort. A year later, he quit the firm, and after ten weeks of Officer Candidate School at Quantico, he was shipped out to Afghanistan."

"Marines?"

"The few, the proud—that's the one. Rory fell for the whole line."

Zoey started to say maybe he really believed he was joining a worthy institution, but she was certain the observation would only upset Rook. "You want to tell me what happened or should I look it up?"

Rook grunted a mirthless laugh. "Good luck with that—looking it up. If you find anything in the official record, it won't be true."

Okay, now they were getting somewhere. Zoey still didn't have a clue what was going on, but now that she'd identified the source of Rook's anger, she was ready to press further. "Rory died in service and the information about the circumstances of his death has been sealed?"

"That's one way to spin it. But it would be more accurate to say Rory was killed *by* the service and the information about the circumstances of his death have been manipulated to protect the men who killed him."

Zoey schooled her features to keep from exhibiting the shock Rook's proclamation elicited. She took a deep drink from the whiskey and set the glass on the coffee table, settling on the kind of direct approach she believed Rook would employ with one of her clients. "Are we going to keep dancing around each other?"

She watched Rook shift in her chair and figured there was an equal chance she'd either fess up or completely shut down. The seconds ticked by and Zoey let the silence hang between them, certain if they didn't clear the air now they never would. Wasn't like she had anywhere else she needed to be. The only furniture in her new place consisted of piles of boxes, and if she was being honest, she didn't really want to be alone. Working with Rook, rocky as it may have been so far, made her feel a part of something, a feeling she hadn't experienced since she'd blown the lid on the Nine Tech scandal. Even before she'd come forward, she'd been feeling isolated in her command, having moved around so many times she no longer had a core group of friends or even acquaintances with whom she could socialize or commiserate. Watching Rook struggle with her demons, she wondered if Rook felt isolated too. She softened her tone. "Look, you don't have to talk to me, but—"

Rook's voice, low and deliberate, stopped her. "Rory's unit was attacked in an apparent ambush on a road outside of the Tani District of the Khost Province, near the Pakistan border. After valiant efforts to save the other soldiers in his unit, Rory succumbed to enemy fire."

"I'm so sorry." Zoey flinched inwardly at the empty phrase of sympathy and reached for Rook's hand. She squeezed, certain she'd heard only the scrubbed up version of events. "I assume there's more to it."

"You mean like how he received a posthumous elevation of rank and was awarded a Silver Star and a Purple Heart for his efforts? Oh, and let's not forget that I got a neatly folded flag."

Rook's voice dripped sarcasm and she punctuated her remarks by pointing across the room at the bookshelf where a triangular shadow box displayed a flag given to relatives at military burials.

Zoey was certain she'd only just started to peel back the layers and braced for more. "I'd like to say all the losses we suffered over there were for a good cause, but I get it's hard to see that considering how things are still so messed up."

Rook jerked to attention. "Is that your official version? Things are bad, losses are hard, sacrifice for the greater good?" She stood and started pacing. "I just want to make sure I'm clear on the official version, because it can change on a dime. A few weeks after Rory's funeral, some of his fellow soldiers were drunk and mouthing off in a bar about how his death was actually the result of friendly fire. Apparently, another squad patrolling in the region either didn't know or was too careless and wound up barraging Rory's unit with firepower under the mistaken impression they were all Taliban smugglers."

"Let me guess," Zoey said. "They weren't just mouthing off."

"Bingo, Major. They were telling the truth. Part of it anyway."

"So his death was the result of friendly fire?"

"Yes, but the mystery remains regarding which of his 'friends' fired on him and why it happened in the first place."

"You have some reason to doubt the revised story?"

"I have a bunch of reasons." Rook stopped pacing and counted out her points. "There have been dozens of friendly fire incidents during the war in Afghanistan, but this is the only one we know of where servicemen actively hid the facts. They burned Rory's body armor, his journals, and his command rushed to award him the Silver Star and Purple Heart which they have yet to revoke even though he didn't earn either." Her voice cracked. "We weren't informed Rory was shot by one of his own until two months after we buried him."

"What was the official line?"

"The usual. 'Evidence has come to light.' 'Further investigation revealed.' All the usual catchphrases authority uses to create spin."

Zoey bit her lip to keep from pointing out that spin was what allowed Rook to live in a house like the one they were sitting in now. "Did you ever find out what really happened?"

"No, but not for lack of trying. I've filed countless FOIA requests. Connie Armstrong personally requested the file, but what they gave her was so heavily redacted, it was like trying to get insight from a block of Swiss cheese. I've never been able to get a complete list of the soldiers who were in the unit that laid down the fire. I have a lot of clout in this town, but if a US senator can't get access, I don't have a chance."

"Have you thought of asking Julia?"

"It's one thing for the chair of the Armed Forces Committee to ask for information about a soldier's record, but for the White House to get involved?" Rook shook her head. "I'd tell any client of mine similarly situated to swing wide away from this one."

Zoey nodded like she got it, but she didn't. Julia Scott was arguably the most powerful person in the country aside from the president. Surely there was some way for her to get what Rook needed without causing a backlash, but it wasn't her place to argue the point. It was time to face where things stood between them. "I can't even imagine the pain you've suffered." She paused and then plunged into the hard part. "I'll concede you've got decent reasons to hate anyone in a uniform, but you accepted this job so I'm guessing you don't think we're completely irredeemable."

"No, not all of you," Rook said, shooting her a half smile.

Zoey met the smile with one of her own, feeling the air ease between them now that she understood Rook's reluctance to work with the military wasn't about her personally. "I can assure you I'm not interested in being part of a cover-up. Should we get to work?"

Rook stopped pacing and shot her a half smile. "You're good at that, you know?"

"Good at what?"

"Focus. I thought I was the master of drilling down, but you're better."

"Years of being whipped into shape will do that to you."

Zoey was instantly sorry for the flippant remark, but Rook greeted it with a smile so she supposed it was okay. Rook settled beside her on the couch. "Can you focus here or should we move into my study?" Rook asked, this time with a full, broad smile.

The voice in her head, the one that kept her life ordered and on track, said she should ease away and insist on structure, boundaries to guard against her growing feelings, but a much louder voice, one that usually gave in, yelled for her to stay here on the couch, by Rook's side. Zoey cast for the right words to state her honest feelings. "I have no idea if I can focus, but I want to be here. With you."

"Good," Rook murmured as she drew closer. She slipped her hand over Zoey's and gently extracted the heavy tumbler still full of whiskey. She set it on the coffee table with her other hand, never letting go of Zoey's. When she turned back to face her, her gaze was dreamy and she said, "There are times that focus is overrated."

The heat of attraction melded them closer. Zoey tugged at Rook's jacket and drew her in as the differences between them receded against the urgent need to touch her, to feel her lips pressed against hers. She was focused all right, like a laser tracking its target.

When their lips touched, Zoey groaned with pleasure, certain she'd never felt this good before and never would again. This moment, this mind-numbing pleasure, was the perfect erasure, removing the lines she'd been so careful not to cross. She dipped her tongue between Rook's lips, seeking, claiming, wishing for more, and Rook met her with forceful strokes, stoking their heat to new levels.

"You taste so good," Rook murmured, trailing kisses along her neck. "Best ever."

"You can say that again," Zoey said, sucking in a breath as Rook found the sensitive spot just below her ear.

"You're ticklish," Rook said with glee, diving back in to kiss the spot.

"Ticklish isn't the word I'd use for it."

Rook drew a long, slow circle around the area with her tongue. "What word would you use?"

"Imagine a line going directly from the spot you just discovered to…" She didn't get to finish the sentence before Rook was back at the spot. Zoey gripped her shoulders, certain if Rook kept it up much longer there would be no such thing as focus ever again.

A piercing ring filled the air, startling them both.

"Your phone," Zoey murmured, but Rook seemed determined not to stop.

"It can wait," Rook whispered, but her voice was already starting to resume its crisp professionalism.

Zoey gently eased back, out of Rook's grasp. "You should get it. Maybe there's been a development." She hesitated adding, "Or maybe someone else needs you."

Rook looked up into her eyes, and Zoey saw kindness and compassion mixed with raw desire. The blend was nice, new, and completely unfamiliar to her. She didn't want Rook to answer the phone, but she also didn't want to be the kind of person who stood in the way. She picked up Rook's phone, slid the answer button, and handed it over.

Chapter Thirteen

Rook tore her gaze away from Zoey and spoke into the phone, adopting a casual tone like doing so would keep her friend from knowing she'd just been lusting over her Pentagon liaison. "Hey, Julia, I was just sitting here with that liaison from the Pentagon, Major Granger. I'm happy to report, we seem to be working well together." She shot Zoey a smile, but it faded quickly at Julia's no-nonsense tone.

"Rook, I need you and your team to get to this address, right now." Julia's voice was thick with urgency. "One of the people on your list of interviewees is dead."

Rook listened as Julia filled her in and then reached for a piece of paper and scrawled the address. After she hung up, she sent a quick text to Blake, studiously ignoring Zoey's curious gaze. Once she'd sounded the alarms and notified George to pick her up downstairs, she slipped the phone into her pocket.

"What was that all about?" Zoey asked.

"I need to go." Rook leaned in and kissed her softly. "I'll call you later."

"Has there been some kind of development?"

Rook had made a split-second decision she was going to handle this on her own, but it wouldn't hurt to have a little more information first. "Did you or Dixon wind up talking to Colonel Mitchell this afternoon?"

"No," Zoey said emphatically. "I mean, he came by my office late yesterday and yelled at me for even trying to talk to him, but I don't think that counts."

"Yesterday? Why didn't you mention that when we discussed him this morning?" Rook shook her head, instantly zooming from zero to furious Zoey hadn't shared this detail with her. "Never mind. What exactly did he say to you?" Rook watched while Zoey cycled back through her memory and wasn't surprised when the slow burn of realization hit. "He told you something about the case, didn't he?"

"He said something about how he knew the students that were involved with the Lorraine Darcy Agency, but he didn't have anything to do with them. Blamed his name being in their files on the fact he is a hard grader and his students might want to get him in trouble. He sounded like he was posturing a little, trying to keep out of the fray. Why? What's going on?"

Rook shook her head, and Zoey pressed harder. "You can't keep me in the dark. This is my investigation too. One way or another I'm going to find out."

"You're right," Rook said, not disguising her annoyance. "We're supposed to be working together, which is why you should've told me he came by your office. I'll do you one better than you did me. Colonel Mitchell put a bullet through his head this evening, so whatever conversation you had with him was the last. I hope you're prepared to answer questions about exactly what you two discussed."

Rook was instantly sorry she'd delivered the harsh words when she saw Zoey's shocked expression. She sincerely doubted Zoey had anything to do with the colonel's death, but she had to be suspicious about everyone until they were eliminated, whether she'd kissed them or not.

She'd planned to head to Mitchell's house on her own, but with Zoey's revelation that she'd spoken with Mitchell the day before, she had second thoughts. Before she could change her mind, she said, "Come with me, but know this: I don't care about your rank. I'm in command on this particular operation. Get it?" She didn't wait for an answer before heading to the door, hoping she wouldn't regret any of her decisions this evening.

❖

Zoey sat in the back of the car with Rook, steaming. She needed to call Sharp, but she didn't dare make the call when Rook or George, for that matter, could overhear her every word. Damn Rook for trying to shut her out, especially after their kiss. She felt like a fool for letting her guard down.

Rook was on the phone the entire ride to Mitchell's residence, talking to everyone but her. From the sound of it, she was rounding up an enormous team to deal with any contingency. Zoey started to rethink her decision not to call Sharp, but before she could act on it, the car stopped and George announced they'd arrived at their destination.

Rook started to open her door, but she turned back to face Zoey. "Follow my lead and don't say anything to anyone without running it by me first. Understood?"

The harsh tone, the bossy words—everything about Rook's changed demeanor—put Zoey on the defensive, which was exactly the opposite of where she needed to be. She was here as an officer of the Army, a direct report to the Joint Chiefs, and she wasn't taking orders from a civilian, no matter who she thought she was. She assumed a sharp tone of her own. "No. I'm not here to follow your lead. I'm in charge of this investigation. My bosses might report to the White House, but none of us report to you. If Colonel Mitchell's death is related to this case, then we can talk about how we'll work together, but if it isn't, then the local police can investigate and we can move to the next name on our witness list. Understood?"

For a second, Rook looked surprised at her blowback, but then shook her head. "Okay, Major. Come on in. I think you're going to be in for a big surprise."

Zoey scrambled to follow Rook up the walk. The house was a modest two-story with a wraparound porch decorated for spring with newly planted flowers in bright ceramic pots. Zoey was indeed surprised not to see any signs of police activity on the street. Maybe they'd parked in back? The front door had a gatekeeper, a tall, thin man in a dark suit with an earpiece. His lips were moving, and Zoey wondered if he was telling someone they were coming in. Rook flashed her ID and leaned in close to whisper something, after which the man propped open the door and motioned for them to go inside.

The place was swarming with activity. A few men in suits were busy searching every nook and cranny while a huddled group consisting of a woman and two children that Zoey pegged as Mitchell's family stood in the corner. Rook walked over to one of the men. They spoke in low, whispered voices, and then Rook strode toward Mitchell's family and took the woman's hand. "Mrs. Mitchell, I'm so sorry for your loss. President Garrett asked me to give you his condolences. You can be assured your husband will receive a service befitting his command, but right now we need to deal with some housekeeping items. Do you have someone, a family member maybe, that you could stay with for a few days?" At Mrs. Mitchell's nod, Rook turned to one of the men in suits and signaled for him to come over. "This gentleman is going to take you and your children wherever you would like to go."

Zoey watched their frightened faces, clearly hesitant to follow the stranger from their house. Deciding it was time to contact Sharp and involve the Pentagon, she pulled out her phone and scrolled to find his number. Before she could connect the call, Rook grabbed the phone from her hand and pulled her into the hall.

Zoey struggled from her grasp. "We have protocols when an officer dies. I need to make some calls."

"Don't even think about it. No calls, no texts, no emails."

"Not your decision to make," Zoey said, reaching for her phone. "Either you give me back my phone or I'm out of here."

"What do you plan to do when you leave? This death didn't occur on a base and it's not your jurisdiction. It's being handled."

"By whom? I don't see any DC Police." Zoey pointed to one of the suited men searching the house. "I don't know who these people are."

"Trust me, you don't want to."

"What about the family? Should we have spoken to them about what happened?"

"They came home and found him already dead. Arrangements have been made for them to give full statements, but not here, not now." Rook pointed down the hall. "Come with me."

She took off, and Zoey watched her go, torn between protocol and practicality. Fact was she didn't know what to do in this situation. For all she knew someone well above her pay grade was already involved. Should she trust that they knew what they were doing, or was not calling Sharp a dereliction of her duty? Either way, it appeared that if she wanted to get to the bottom of why Mitchell was dead, her only hope was to go with Rook and find out what she could.

Rook, face grim, stopped her at the door and shoved a pair of paper booties at her. "Put these on and don't touch anything. Prepare yourself. It's not pretty."

Zoey leaned down to slip the booties over her shoes and nearly slipped. Rook grabbed her hand, gently this time. "Here," she said, motioning to her shoulder. "It's easier if you hold on."

"Thanks." Zoey held on tight to Rook's shoulder and managed to get both booties on her shoes. With no further reason to hold on, she let go and immediately felt a sense of loss at the broken connection from Rook's grounding force. Rook was so in control and in charge, like she visited scenes of violence every day. Zoey pointed into the room. "Is this where he…?"

"Yes. Step carefully and stay right next to me."

Zoey followed Rook into the room, sweeping her gaze slowly and carefully from side to side to take everything in. The space looked like a study with a large roll top desk against the far wall and bookcases lining the rest of the room. As she looked around, the sour, metallic smell of blood hit her nostrils, but it didn't entirely prepare her for the gruesome scene that served as the focal point.

The man on the floor lay on his side, a macabre sight. The profile of his face was recognizable as Colonel Mitchell, but the back of his head was a large, gaping mass. Gray matter and blood were splattered to the rear of the chair situated in the exact middle of the room. If she hadn't met him, she might be able to hold back a reaction, but this man had been in her office only yesterday, pleading with her not to involve him in her investigation. Guilt gripped her, but she'd had no reason to think his entreaty was a matter of life and death. "Did he leave a note?"

"We're not sure yet." Rook's dark eyes bored into her own. "We're not ruling anything out at this point. We don't have to stay in here, but I thought it might be helpful if you were present when we went through his desk, you know, in case we find something that you might have special knowledge about."

"You mean top secret military stuff?"

"Something like that."

Zoey nodded, but Rook's words about not ruling anything out played on a reel in her head. Was there some reason to think Mitchell's death wasn't a suicide? She wanted to ask, but the presence of the other people in the room gave her pause. "I can look, but I don't think I'd know if anything he has is important. Where should I start?"

Rook waved at a woman on the other side of the room. "Major Granger, this is Blake Wyatt. She'll stay with you and process anything you find that might be helpful."

Zoey assessed the stranger. Tall, blond, and model-thin, Blake wore a skin-hugging midnight blue dress that hit mid-thigh and she looked like she'd come straight from a party. General instinct told Zoey not to trust a civilian, but despite the way she was dressed, this woman's rigid posture and economical movements screamed some kind of law enforcement and maybe even a military bearing. With no specific reason not to trust her, Zoey decided to play along for now. "Show me what you've found."

Blake led her over to the desk. The roll top was pulled back, and Zoey asked if it had been like that when they arrived.

"Yes. Everything is exactly how we found it. The paperwork I'd like you to look at is there and there." She pointed at two desk drawers and then proceeded to tug them open with her gloved hands. "I'll hold the paper while you read. Okay?"

Zoey nodded and resisted the urge to hurry her along as Blake slowly opened the drawers and extracted an envelope from each drawer. She meticulously opened them and pulled out a few sheets from each. Zoey recognized the first one immediately as it bore the seal of the Department of Defense, denoting orders. She motioned for Blake to hold it closer and she skimmed the page and then read it again more carefully. Colonel Mitchell was being reassigned to the base in Kobani, Syria, effective the following day.

"What is it?"

Zoey looked back at Rook who was reading over her shoulder. "I'm not sure." She had a theory, but she didn't want to say it in front of the woman. Like a mind reader, Rook jerked her chin at the woman. "I'd trust her with my life. You can speak freely."

"Let me think about it." Zoey wasn't going to be pushed. "Let's just say this is important and it should be collected. Let me look at the other one, please."

The second piece of paper didn't bear an official seal, but was on Colonel Mitchell's official letterhead and it shocked her from the very first line. The rest of the words were a blurry mess, and she shook her head as if by doing so she could clear the words on the page like shaking a Magic 8 Ball. It didn't work.

❖

"It's okay." Rook focused on keeping her voice gentle and soothing, which was difficult considering what she'd managed to glean from a skim of the page. "You don't need to read it now. Blake, make sure you pack this one up with the other. I'll meet you at the office." She started to steer Zoey away, but she stayed firmly in place.

"No, I need to know what it says."

Rook caught sight of Blake shaking her head, but she knew a simple denial wasn't going to be enough for Zoey. "Let me have it," she told Blake who handed her a pair of latex gloves and waited for her to put them on before giving her the letter. Rook read the contents, taking her time to digest each word. Mitchell's message from beyond was a sucker punch of near revelations. When she finished reading, Rook moved the paper into Zoey's sightline. "I don't understand all of this, but maybe you will." Rook held the single sheet of paper steady, reading the words along with her.

Major Granger,

I don't know if you realize the Pandora's box you've opened, but now that it's done, you will have to face the consequences. There really isn't anything I can say to help except to warn you to trust no one. Anyone who professes to be on your side or offers to be of assistance to you is very possibly an enemy of the state and will likely view you as a threat once you begin to discover the truth.

I'm telling you all of this because despite your current position as inquisitor and the way I reacted in your office yesterday, I admired the fact you took a stand and chose to reveal the dishonesty going on in front of you. But know this: the fraud perpetrated behind the scenes is a thousand times worse than anything the public sees, and the consequences of standing up to the forces that drive it are dire. I did not have what it takes. Maybe you will, but no matter what, you will not escape unscathed.

Rangers lead the way,
Colonel Nicholas Mitchell

Rook watched Zoey's face for signs she'd finished reading, and when her eyes shuttered, Rook handed the paper to Blake and mouthed for her to keep searching. The agents were still conducting their search, and Rook guided Zoey past them until they were at the front door where Harry stood waiting, his eyebrows arched in question. Behind Zoey's back, Rook shook her head, willing him not to ask any questions. "Major, this is one of my associates, Harry Etheridge. Wait here with him. I'll be right back."

Rook strode back to Mitchell's study and pulled Blake aside. "I'm going to go. I need to get a statement prepared and figure out who's going to give it." She gestured at the desk. "You think there's anything else in there?"

"If there is, we'll find it."

"You have access to whatever resources you need. The suits are doing their thing and eventually they're going to want in here, but I don't want that letter to leave your sight. Understood?"

"Got it. Are they NSA?"

Rook flashed back to her conversation with Julia in the car. NSA had picked up chatter about the shooting when Mitchell's wife placed a call to 911, bawling that she'd come home to find her husband lying dead in his study. Because Mitchell's name was on the list of potential witnesses to be interviewed in the McNair case, whoever was monitoring the chatter ran the information up the line, all the way to Julia who'd sent in the troops, but instructed them Rook's team would have carte blanche at the scene. She had no idea how they'd circumvented the local cops and she wasn't sure she wanted to. "Yes, but it doesn't matter though. We're in charge. Consider yourself deputized by the president."

"Deputized is a strong word," Blake said. "It's a suicide, not a crime scene."

"Maybe not, but treat it like it is. Eric's on his way over to copy all the hard drives. Have him search for any reference to Zoey on any of the computers here at the residence."

"Zoey?"

Rook silently cursed the misstep. "Major Granger. She's a key to whatever's going on." She pressed on. "Bonus points if Eric can bust the Pentagon's firewall and connect to Mitchell's account there. If we assume no one there knows he's dead yet, we should have a little time to gather what we can."

"On it." She waved Rook toward the door. "Go on, we got this."

Rook walked back through the house toward the front door where Zoey was waiting. She had full confidence in her team, but under normal circumstances she would stay here with them, triaging information as it was gathered. But the circumstances weren't normal and one of the key pieces of information was Zoey Granger. Whether she knew it or not, Zoey held some piece to the puzzle and it was up to Rook to coax it forward.

Zoey was standing straight and tall, but her hooded eyelids and mussed hair gave away her worry and exhaustion. Rook took her arm again and guided her out of the house and into the waiting car. Zoey didn't protest when she pulled a blanket from behind the seat and tucked it around her. It wasn't until Rook told George to take them back to her place that Zoey came alive.

"I need to go to the office," she said, her eyes wide and darting.

Rook put a hand on her leg. Zoey might be used to seeing the carnage of battle, but this death, so out of context, seemed to have taken her completely off guard. "You've suffered a bit of a shock. Let me take you back to my place and get you warmed up and then we can sort out the best plan."

"There is no best plan. I need to prepare a report." She gripped Rook's hand. "Did you get a copy of the letter? They're going to want to see it."

Rook stared into Zoey's eyes. She detected fear, but she also saw a strong sense of determination. Zoey was driven by duty, but if she let a blind allegiance to authority guide her, there was a strong likelihood she would place herself in danger. The backseat of the car was no place for this conversation, so she needed to stall. "The... uh, police need to catalog everything. I asked them to hurry. They should be finished soon so why don't you wait with me? I need to check in with Julia and she's probably going to want to talk to you too. We can make the call from my place and then do whatever we need to do after together. Okay?"

Zoey seemed relieved at the suggestion she didn't have to face whoever with whatever the letter meant on her own. She nodded and sank back against the seat, pulling the blanket tight around her. In that moment, Rook was filled with a strong desire to protect Zoey from whatever came next, whether it was threats from Mitchell or repercussions for not reporting Mitchell's death to her commanders. Rook only hoped Zoey would forgive her when she learned their investigation had turned in a whole new direction and Zoey was no longer in charge.

Chapter Fourteen

W ould you like me to park the car and help you in?"
Rook looked out the window at the sound of George's
soft-pitched question, surprised to see they were already in front of
her townhouse. She glanced over at Zoey. Her eyes were closed and
her head was resting against her shoulder. She hated to bother her,
but they couldn't just sit out in the car. "If you don't mind getting
the front door, I think I can handle the rest."

She kept an arm around Zoey until they were inside where she
eased her onto the couch, the blanket still wrapped around her. Rook
smoothed out the blanket and murmured softly to ease her back to
rest. "Wait here. I'll be right back." Zoey's eyes were closed again,
and Rook dropped a quick kiss on her forehead before she strode off
toward her study.

She should make this call from the office where she knew the
phones were secure, but she wasn't about to leave Zoey alone so she
decided to risk it. Julia answered on the first ring.

"What the hell, Rook? I thought one of your signatures was
discretion. What did you say to this guy that had him eating his own
gun hours later? This isn't going to stay quiet for long."

Rook took a deep breath. Julia was right. No matter what steps
they took, the human element meant someone was going to talk
about what had happened tonight at the Mitchells' house. The wife,
the kids, possibly a neighbor who'd overheard the sound of the shot
that tore through Mitchell's brain. Who would blab wasn't the issue,

but it was only a matter of time before someone burst from the strain of keeping a juicy secret. "You're right. The story will break soon, so we need to work fast. He didn't leave a suicide note per se, but he did leave a letter. It's vague, but loaded with clues, and I'm working on it."

"Clues? Are you saying this wasn't really a suicide?"

"Blake says there's no question he fired the shot."

"She should know," Julia said, echoing Rook's thoughts. Blake had seen enough brutal killings in her capacity as a CIA operative to know how to read a crime scene. "Okay," Julia said. "So, this guy was on your witness list and he offed himself. Any chance he was depressed about something else? Wife? Girlfriend? Boyfriend?"

"Remember I mentioned the clues?" Rook started at the sound of a loud clatter from the other room and she rushed to get off the line. "I've said as much as I can say right now, but there's more to all of this than we originally thought. I'll keep you posted." She hung up before Julia could respond and dashed back toward the living room, but Zoey wasn't there. She tried the kitchen next after matching the sound of the clatter with the sound of dishes and found Zoey standing by the sink.

"I'm sorry," she said, her voice quiet and still. "I knocked over a plate when I was trying to get a glass out of the cabinet." She held up a small blue melamine dish. "Luckily, not breakable."

Her lopsided smile tore at Rook's heart and she stepped closer until they were only inches apart. She placed her hand over Zoey's, eased the dish from her hand, and placed it on the counter. "Why don't you go sit back down and I'll get you something to drink?"

"I got it."

"Seriously. It's been a crazy long day. Let me help you out."

"I don't need your help."

The strain in her voice belied the words and Rook reached for her arm. "Come on. I got this."

Zoey jerked away. "I can get my own damn drink." She started pacing. "And I can make my own decisions about who to call and what to report. I don't appreciate you managing me. Is it because you hate the Army or is it just me you don't trust?"

Warning bells sounded in Rook's brain, and she cast about for ways to deescalate the situation. "I trust you. If I didn't trust you, I wouldn't have brought you to Mitchell's house tonight. For that matter, I wouldn't have you here in my house."

Zoey shook her head. "It's not your call whether I get to go to the house of a fellow service member." She ticked off her points. "He was on *my* witness list. *I* was one of the last people he talked to. He left a note to *me*. He is *my* responsibility."

Rook wished she could turn back time and give Julia a big fat no instead of agreeing to work on this case. What in the hell had she been thinking? She had other clients, from large corporations to well-heeled celebrities and politicians who provided a steady run of work. It could only be hubris that made her cast aside her disdain for the military on an ask from the president. Did she honestly think getting involved with a case from the White House was going to be the pinnacle of her career? All it was going to do was crater her practice and drive a wedge between her and Zoey.

That last realization left her a little stunned. Why did she care about distance between her and Zoey? Zoey epitomized everything she didn't like about the military from blind allegiance to orders to absolute faith in a system designed to fail from the sheer weight of covering its own tracks. Sure, Zoey had bucked the system a bit and become a whistleblower, but even that had been done through military channels. She wasn't set up to see the bigger picture or relate to civilians in any way.

"Nothing about this investigation is yours," Rook said. She heard the growl of frustration in her voice but didn't care to hide it. "The military is an arm of the government, not the government itself. You don't get to pick and choose who you investigate and who you don't." She stepped closer until they were inches apart. "You say it's not my call? Well, it's not your call either."

"Maybe you should drop this case. Surely you have better things to do like prop up cheating husbands and drunk drivers?"

The words stung. Rook balked at Zoey's barb, but she couldn't deny the truth in her words. A large part of what she did seemed frivolous to some. She'd rationalized her work was important because she was there to help people in the midst of crisis when they were most vulnerable, but was her role as a savior diminished if the crisis was of their own doing? If so this case was no different. No one had made Bloomfield's son risk his father's future by purchasing the services of a call girl, but she'd shown up to help just the same. If Zoey couldn't see the similarities between the cases Rook usually handled and this one, then they would never bridge the differences between them.

They stared at each other for what seemed like forever until Zoey broke the silence. "I'm sorry. I shouldn't have…" Her face flushed and she rushed the words. "I shouldn't have come back here with you."

Rook filled in the blank she'd left unsaid. They shouldn't have kissed. She'd brought Zoey back here, partly because they needed to talk about the letter Mitchell had left, and partly because she had been worried about Zoey's physical state after witnessing the scene at Mitchell's house, but there was a completely separate part of her that had hoped they might fall back into the easy intimacy they'd shared before Julia called to tell her about Mitchell's suicide.

She'd been wrong to hope. Zoey's anger was natural, and it was pretty clear she didn't need Rook to hold her hand, but they still needed to talk about Mitchell's letter, to debrief about exactly what Zoey had said to Mitchell yesterday that had prompted him to kill himself and leave his final words for a woman who'd only met him once.

But Rook didn't want to do any of that. She just wanted to hold Zoey and tell her everything was going to be all right. Not the way she comforted clients in trouble, but like a lover, soothing away the trouble of her partner. But Zoey would never fill that role, and she wasn't even sure why she wanted her to.

❖

Zoey fumbled to put the key in the lock and then waved at George as she walked inside her dark and empty house. On the drive over she wondered what he thought of her, spending so much time with his employer and in her personal space. Did he often drive women home from Rook's townhouse, late in the evening or was she an exception to the rule? Rook had insisted that he drive her home and she'd been too tired to argue. Now that she was here, stepping over boxes, she wished she'd checked into a hotel for the night.

The first thing she did was change clothes. Even though she hadn't touched Mitchell's body, she felt as though she reeked from the scene of his demise. She shuddered at the memory of his body on the ground, bits of brain splattered across the floor. Who commits such a gruesome act when they know their family will find them? He'd either been desperate, apathetic, or both.

She walked into the kitchen and rummaged through boxes, looking for a glass and the one nice bottle of whiskey she kept around for special occasions. It didn't measure up to anything Rook had in her fancy liquor cabinet, but then again she was merely a public servant, not a high-powered fixer paid big bucks to ensure outcomes.

Okay, that was a little unfair. Rook had had opportunities she hadn't and made choices that had never been available to her. Who was she to say that her life might have taken a very different path if she hadn't relied on her connection to the service to get her out of Imperial, Texas, and the chains that bound her there.

As if on cue, her phone rang. She pounced on it, but it wasn't Rook. "Good evening, General Sharp. I was just about to call you," she lied, projecting assurance into her voice.

"Figured you would've called me a helluva lot earlier, Major."

"I'm sorry, sir. I—"

"I don't want to hear it tonight. Report to General Bloomfield's office at oh seven hundred, sharp."

He clicked off the line before she could respond, and she was both relieved and frustrated at the call. Now she had all night to come up with a reason for not calling him from Mitchell's house—something besides "Rook Daniels told me not to," because that would go over like a ton of rocks.

Resigned to a sleepless night, she dug through boxes until she found a juice glass, one of a mismatched set she'd collected over the years, and a bottle of eighteen-year-old Balvenie her last CO had purchased directly from the distillery on a family trip to Scotland. He'd given it to her on the occasion of her promotion to major and she'd rationed it over time. She poured the amber gold into a glass, doubling her usual dose. Was Rook enjoying a similar indulgence right about now, like the one they'd had before their kiss?

The kiss. As she sipped her Scotch, she relived every detail of their touch, from the soft, yet forceful press of Rook's lips against hers to the way she teased with her tongue. She'd wanted more and had been prepared to ignore the cautionary voice in her head warning against getting involved with Rook, but the call from Julia had waylaid her plans. Considering how the evening wound up, the interruption was a godsend, but in the moment, she'd felt robbed, and now she was missing the connection.

The realization struck her. She'd lived her life with so little real connection to anyone else that the instant pull to Rook surprised her. Yet from the very moment she'd seen her at the airport, Zoey had been drawn to her. Cool, confident, effortlessly charming, Rook had won her from the start.

What had changed? Rook was still the same person who'd thoughtfully arranged a personal tour of the monuments along with a private picnic in a beautiful park. Nothing about that night had seemed designed to impress, only to please. And tonight, even after her burst of anger at finding out Zoey had spoken with Mitchell without telling her, Rook had come around to comfort her after the shock of seeing her name mentioned in Mitchell's suicide note.

Maybe she was the jerk, not Rook. Maybe her lack of connection wasn't a factor of time and place, but because she didn't want to get too involved in the messiness of being a part of other people's lives. If that was the case, Rook was better off without her. But the real question was, was she better off without Rook?

All signs pointed to no.

CHAPTER FIFTEEN

The next morning, Zoey found Lieutenant Louden lurking outside her office. "They're waiting for you in General Bloomfield's office."

Zoey held back a curse. She'd arrived an hour early, hoping to have a few minutes to make a list of bullet points about what she'd seen at Mitchell's place before she had to face what was certain to be a dressing down. "How pissed off are they?"

"Hard to tell. I heard loud voices, but I couldn't make out if it was both of them or just one. Care to share what happened?"

Zoey briefly considered whether the details of Mitchell's death were something she should keep private, but decided Louden, in his capacity as Sharp's assistant, would see every report that was filed anyway. "I guess you know by now, Colonel Mitchell committed suicide." Louden nodded and she continued. "He came by to see me day before yesterday. He was pissed off and he tried to get me to agree to leave him out of our investigation."

"Ballsy."

"I guess," Zoey said, although she thought desperate was a better descriptor. "He left a note for me in his study where he…you know…Anyway, it was very cryptic and I'm not sure what to make of it."

Louden nodded. "I'm sure you'll sort it out. Do you have the note? I bet the general is going to want to see it."

"I left it at the scene." She started to say with the men in suits and Rook's team but then realized how that would sound to two generals who were used to running their own operations. The full extent of how much trouble she was in settled squarely on her shoulders. Not wanting Louden to witness her meltdown, she said, "I hate to say this, but do you mind showing me the way to Bloomfield's office? I swear I'll learn my way around at some point, but it's only my first week and there's been a lot going on."

The walk to Bloomfield's office took about ten minutes—enough time for Zoey to sort through the events of the last two days. The volume of activity—the initial review of the case file, the trip to the White House, the interviews both here and at McNair, and her confrontation with Mitchell and his suicide—had been overwhelming even before she added the push and pull with Rook. She wondered what Rook was doing right now. Was she getting an earful from Julia about the status of the investigation? Had sharing the story of her brother's death exposed emotions she'd preferred to have left buried? Did Rook regret their kiss or did the memory still linger, despite the brewing conflicts between them?

"Come in," Bloomfield barked when Louden rapped on his office door. With a look of sympathy, Louden peeled off and left her to enter the lion's den on her own.

Zoey drew in a breath and shoved all other thoughts to the corners of her mind where they belonged. "Good morning, General."

"Not as good as it could be," he said. "Major, is there some reason you decided to traipse all over Colonel Mitchell's house without contacting anyone in your chain of command?"

Zoey stood in front of his desk and glanced around the room to see if she could get a boost from Sharp, but he was seated across the room with his arms folded over his chest and a blank expression. She had no desire to tell either of these men that she'd arrived at the scene with Rook, but she had to find a way to explain how she'd found out about the shooting and why she'd ceded authority to Rook once they'd arrived at Mitchell's house.

"I was told we were to work directly with the White House on anything related to this investigation." She cast about for a tactful way to say what was on her mind. "Respectfully, sir, we should keep you out of this as much as possible to avoid even the appearance of impropriety."

"Are you telling me Mitchell is wrapped up in this stupid situation out of McNair?"

"I have a feeling even answering that is a minefield you don't want me to cross."

Bloomfield turned to Sharp. "You were right about this one. She doesn't hesitate to speak her mind."

Zoey couldn't quite tell from his tone whether he considered that a good thing, but she was beginning not to care. If they didn't want her in this position, the solution was easy—send her back to Fort Bragg where she could work on arm wrestling her CO into assigning her another deployment. Of course that would probably mean her promotion would be stalled indefinitely. And they'd have to assign someone else to work with Rook Daniels or leave Dixon in charge. She was confident Rook would hate that, but would Rook miss her if she were reassigned?

Ugh. What was she thinking? She'd never considered her career in terms of another person. One kiss and she was losing all sense of practicality. But it had been one very hot, addictive kiss.

Zoey shook off the memory of Rook's lips on hers and focused on the generals who held her future in their hands. "Respectfully, sirs, you put me in this position because I speak my mind. I'm as good as any other soldier when it comes to following orders, but when it comes to righting a wrong, I can't help but speak out, and if that's a problem, I'm not the right person for the job."

Bloomfield's laugh was a loud roar. He punched Sharp in the arm and pointed at Zoey. "Oh, you're the right person for the job. When this mess is all cleared up, I want there to be no doubt that every stone was turned to make sure I wasn't involved in any wrongdoing. My son never should have gotten involved in this mess, but I'll be damned if that boy is going to muck up my career when he can't even handle his own, no matter how many opportunities are handed to him." He raised his hands in the air. "That's all I have to say on the subject. Go with General Sharp and talk about the rest out of my presence. Fair enough?"

"Yes, sir." Zoey saluted him and followed Sharp from the room. Despite the early hour, she spotted plenty of people in the halls and wondered how many of them had been called in to deal with a crisis of their own. Sharp walked briskly, without talking until they were back at his office. They passed Louden. Did he ever go home? He shot her an encouraging smile, and she filed it away for comfort as Sharp closed his office door behind them.

"I heard Rook Daniels was at the scene," he said without preamble. "Is that how you knew about Mitchell eating his gun?"

"Yes, sir." No sense lying since he probably already knew the answer. "She and I were going over interview notes when she got the call." Partly true since they'd intended to do just that. She prayed he didn't ask for more details, certain she wouldn't be able to conceal her whirling mix of emotions where Rook was concerned.

"Who called?"

Again, she hesitated and felt silly for it. "Julia Scott from the White House."

"Tell me what you saw at Mitchell's."

Zoey thought fast, but couldn't come up with an excuse not to tell him what he likely already knew. She relayed the details in a sharp and concise manner. Mitchell's wife and kids escorted from the house. No signs of foul play. Mitchell shot with his own gun.

"Did he leave a note?"

And just like that, her matter-of-fact recollection stalled. There was no practical reason not to tell him about the note, but it felt like a betrayal somehow. Mitchell had told her to trust no one, but he'd meant the people directly involved with the case. Right? Telling herself she just wanted to find out more details before mentioning the note, she settled on a half-truth. "The agents on scene were still investigating when we left. I've requested a full report of their findings."

"Agents? What agency? Were the DC Police there?"

"I don't know and no." She dreaded saying the next part. "I assumed the agents at the scene were either FBI or Secret Service, but I don't know for sure. It was pretty clear they'd been notified by the White House." She stopped talking since all she had to offer were suppositions, and at this point Sharp was shaking his head.

"I'm not telling you how to run this thing, but this is not a situation like Nine Tech. Innocent people aren't getting ripped off. Some soldiers couldn't be bothered to keep a lid on their libidos and they embarrassed the service. Not only that, but their stupidity could cost a good man from achieving a post that could benefit the mission of this administration and the Joint Chiefs. I think you know what needs to be done, so I'm leaving it to you to take care of things and get this wrapped up pronto. Are we clear?"

They were as far from clear as they could possibly be, but Zoey knew she'd exhausted the tolerance of her commander and there was only one correct answer. "Yes, sir."

Louden stopped her on the way out of Sharp's office. "Everything okay?"

She looked back at Sharp's door. "It will be. Did you ever get hold of Colonel Mitchell's personnel file?"

He shook his head. "No. It's still showing restricted, and I'm pretty sure that's not going to change anytime soon."

"Of course." She should've known there would be a hold on the file until the circumstances regarding his death were officially certified. "Thanks for checking." She started to walk away, but a thought popped into her head. "Do you happen to know if Colonel Mitchell was a Ranger?"

Louden raised his eyebrows and she quickly added, "Strange question, I know. It's just…" She faltered for a moment, not wanting to share the contents of the note with him when she hadn't yet told Sharp. "I'd heard somewhere that he was and I may have had a friend who served with him." Lame response, but it was all she could come up with on the fly.

"I have no idea," Louden said. "I didn't know him, but maybe you could ask General Bloomfield's son. He was enrolled in one of Mitchell's classes at McNair."

Zoey filed that information away as she made her way back to her office. The reference to the US Army Ranger's motto in

Mitchell's letter—Rangers lead the way—had been scratching at the edge of her mind since she'd read the words. It was such an odd way to sign off any kind of letter, let alone a final missive, and she wondered if Mitchell had been trying to send her some sort of message with those last words.

She did plan to talk to Donny Bloomfield again, but she didn't want to ask him questions about Mitchell's suicide with Dixon sitting next to her. Sharp had said Dixon was assigned to help her find her way around, but that she was in charge. After her whirlwind start, she knew her way around well enough. It might be time to ditch Dixon and do the interviews with just Rook.

No, not a good idea. She needed to figure out the meaning of Mitchell's message on her own. She rummaged in her desk for a pen and paper to make some notes and she uncovered a business card. Major John "Jack" Riley, Intelligence. She remembered his words from her first day, which seemed so long ago. *This place can be a little crazy to get used to when you've been out in the world.* Understatement of the universe.

Zoey stared at the phone and considered her options. Her first instinct was to call Rook and talk to her about what they should do next, but she couldn't decide if she was letting desire eclipse duty. Rook didn't trust the military, and Sharp had made it abundantly clear he didn't trust Rook. Zoey glanced again at Jack's card and, before she could change her mind, picked up the phone and dialed.

Rook started at the sound of a door opening, and it took her a moment to figure out she was in her office and she'd been fast asleep with her head on her desk.

"You look like hell," Lacy said as she shut the door behind her.

"What time is it? And please tell me that's coffee in your hand."

"It's eight a.m. and this is indeed coffee. I'll give it to you if you tell me why you worked here all night."

"I didn't work all night," Rook said, reaching for the mug. "I just got here very early."

"Are you doing solo work on the side?"

Rook had the good sense to look sheepish. She'd worked hard to foster a team approach on the cases that came into the firm, but aside from calling them out to Mitchell's house last night, she hadn't shared much on this one. "I guess it's time to have a meeting."

"Already on it. Drink your coffee and take a shower. They'll be in the conference room in thirty minutes." Lacy shut the door behind her when she left, and Rook reached for the coffee. It would have to do double duty today because she was exhausted. She'd spent the balance of the night after Zoey left sorting through everything she knew about the McNair case, including the preliminary findings from Mitchell's house, but so far she hadn't been able to make sense of Mitchell's death. It was time to brainstorm, and there was no better group to do it with than her team.

When she walked into the conference room she found Harry, Blake, and Eric already assembled, reviewing the information gathered at Mitchell's house, she briefly considered calling Zoey and inviting her to join them. Another brain could only help, right?

She dismissed the thought as fast as it came. The White House had hired her to make sure this scandal was contained. Zoey had failed to tell her about her encounter with Mitchell, and if she'd gotten wind of Mitchell's death first, she probably would've alerted the local police and her superiors, no doubt letting the ambiguous letter Mitchell had left behind leak into the public domain before they'd had a chance to decipher its meaning. Zoey wasn't part of her team; she was the arm of a bureaucracy Rook had been hired to work around. The searing kiss they'd shared last night was proof she had become a distraction.

Pushing all thoughts of Zoey aside, Rook took her seat at the head of the table and pointed at Blake. "Tell me everything you have."

Blake consulted one of the tiny Moleskine notebooks she always carried. Rook used to give her crap for using pen and paper to keep case notes when she'd come from the high-tech CIA, but Blake insisted she'd be the only one with any good intel in the event of a terrorist attack on the power grid or a simple power outage.

"Not much to tell. Gun was registered to him. We found an aging box of the same caliber ammo in his desk missing only one bullet. His were the only prints on the gun and the angle of the shot was consistent with a self-inflicted wound."

"And the note?"

"I'll take this one," Harry said. "I showed it, along with some confirmed samples of his handwriting, to an analyst I know. Best in her field. She says he wrote the note. There are a few letters and words that are shaky, but that's to be expected considering the circumstances."

"Okay, we know two things for sure," Rook said. "He shot himself and he left a note. Here are the things I want to know: what does the note mean and what was his involvement with the Lorraine Darcy Agency?"

Eric raised his hand. "My turn. I examined the computers at the house. The one in the main study appears to be for family use and it was clean, but the one in his study was a treasure trove of inappropriate material."

"Let me guess. He used that computer to hook up with 'escorts' from the Darcy Agency?"

"More than that."

"Really? You're telling me he had even deeper secrets?"

"The deepest, for a high ranking military officer." Eric punched a button and the images from his laptop were projected onto the built-in screen at the front of the room. The display showed a cascading series of emails, but many of the sentences contained in the messages had words redacted. Rook squinted at the strings of incomplete sentences and tried to make sense of them.

"What are we looking at?" Blake asked.

Eric set his cursor on the first sentence and pointed at the blacked-out spaces. "I haven't had a lot of time to analyze this, but at first glance it looked familiar so I started working on a theory." He divided the information on the screen into two sections. "Over here," he said, pointing to the left side of the screen. "There are three emails Mitchell exchanged with the Darcy Agency. Notice the dates."

"Two years ago."

"Yes. Just FYI, I found some chatter online saying that was the same time the Darcy Agency started renting space at the address you and Major Granger visited yesterday."

Had it only been yesterday? "Okay," Rook said. "So, he's like a charter member of Escorts-R-Us. I'm not getting where you're going with this."

"Read the text of these three emails and give me your first impression."

Rook started to tell Eric to blurt it out or she was moving on, but she held her tongue in the face of his earnest expression. She'd indulge him for five more minutes, but then she was pulling the plug on this little detour. She shifted her attention back to the screen and started reading. "The language is stiff, broken. Like the author is not a native English speaker."

"Exactly."

"So what you're saying is the escorts at Lorraine Darcy might be well skilled in other areas, but drafting emails in English, not so much."

"I'm saying way more than that." He pointed again at the redacted words. "There's a pattern here with the missing words. I've seen something like this before." He started banging on the keyboard. "Hang on." More typing. "Here it is. Take a look at this."

Rook stared at the screen, the right side of the screen showing the emails from Mitchell's computer and the left a letter on some official looking letterhead with a scattered series of small redactions. The pattern didn't make sense to her, but it was eerily similar. "What is this?"

"Bear with me because this is going to sound crazy." Eric pushed his laptop to the side and faced them. "It's code."

"I've seen something like this before too," Blake said, her eyes trained on the screen.

"I bet you have," Eric replied. "I heard the CIA still trains their operatives in old-style Soviet coding systems, you know, for historical perspective. Betcha didn't know they were still using it."

Harry struck his knuckles on the table. "Hold up. Are you two trying to say Mitchell was working for the Russians?"

Rook kept staring at the screen while the rest of her team started talking all at once. If Eric and Blake were right and they'd uncovered messages utilizing a Russian coding system, then this case had suddenly mushroomed into way more than her firm was equipped to handle. She let them talk for a few more minutes then held up a hand to signal it was time for her to talk. "Eric, can you break the code?"

"Yes."

"How long would it take?"

"I can write a program—a few hours, tops. But if you want me to do that, I should get an air-gapped computer."

"I have no idea what that means."

"It's a computer that's never been connected to the Internet. That way we can be sure that no one will get access to the information once the code is broken unless they have physical possession of the computer."

Rook paused, her mind spinning through a list of options. She could call Julia right now, set up a meeting and tell her what Eric had found. They'd turn over the emails and NSA hackers could break the code and let the White House know if there really was some kind of Russian meddling with the Pentagon. And the Daniels Agency would be free to go back to dealing with Senator Newman's public relations nightmare and whatever new scandal was due to hit the evening news.

That's what she should do. But once she turned the information over, she'd never know what the messages were or what they meant. Her other option was to have Eric break the code here at the office. Once they knew what the messages were, they could notify Julia and assist with managing the fallout. The practical choice was option A. *But then you might never know if Zoey was involved or in danger.*

Did Zoey know about any of this? Why had Mitchell mentioned her specifically in his suicide note? Rook didn't think she could let this go until she had more answers, but depending on what this information was, hanging on to it could constitute a federal offense.

She looked at the three faces staring at her and made a snap decision. "I want to know what these messages say, but I have a feeling our client would prefer that we turn over the information we've got so far and let them sort it out. Whatever decision I make impacts all of us, so let's take a vote. All in favor of stopping now and handing this off to whatever agency the White House wants to involve, raise your hand."

She waited, but every one of them—the hacker, the lawyer, and the former CIA agent—sat perfectly still, hands flat on the table. "Okay, then." She pointed to Eric. "Someone go buy this man a new computer."

Chapter Sixteen

Zoey sat at her desk with her eyes trained on the door, wishing she'd arranged to meet Major Riley somewhere else. She'd managed to avoid Dixon most of the day, but he could show up any minute and she wasn't interested in discussing her theories about Mitchell's death with him.

Not that she had any workable theory. Mostly all she had was a hunch that Mitchell had left a clue in the letter he'd left behind. A clue meant for her and she was determined to sort it out, hopefully, with Major Jack Riley's help. Like she'd conjured him, he poked his head in the partially open door. "Major Granger?"

"Come in, please. And it's Zoey." She motioned for him to sit. "Thanks for coming by."

"Happy to." He stepped into the room and pointed at the door. "You want this open or shut?"

"Closed is good."

He shut the door and settled into the chair in front of her desk. "I would have invited you to my corner of the building, but there are a lot of gatekeepers. It's definitely easier this way."

Zoey cast a quick look at his card that she had positioned on the corner of her desk and read the single word under his name. "Intelligence, like if you tell me what you really do, you have to kill me?"

He assumed a super serious expression. "Absolutely, but I don't think I was even supposed to tell you that much." He broke into a smile. "To be honest, most of what I do is pretty boring. Analyst stuff."

She wondered if that was really true, but played along. "Quite a change for you."

"It's definitely been an adjustment from running ops in the field, but I'm not as young as I used to be."

Zoey wanted to ask him about his experience running a Delta Force unit, but she suspected like most soldiers who'd worked in Special Forces, he wasn't big on sharing. Besides, as interested as she was in his service, she'd asked to meet with him for another reason entirely. Before she could get to the reason for their meeting, she was interrupted by a knock on the door.

"Come in," she called out, scrambling for an excuse to get rid of Dixon. But it wasn't Dixon. Lieutenant Louden strode in and started walking toward her desk, but he stopped abruptly when he saw Major Riley.

"I'm sorry," Louden said. "I didn't realize you were in a meeting."

"It's okay. Major Riley, this is Lieutenant Louden, General Sharp's assistant."

Jack reached his hand out to Louden who stared at it for a moment before accepting the handshake. "I know Major Riley," Louden said. "Nice to see you, sir."

"Of course you do," Zoey said, remembering Sharp was Jack Riley's godfather and probably knew most of the general's staff. "I forget everyone around here is connected in some way. Lieutenant, how long have you worked for General Sharp?"

Louden shuffled in place as if he was uncomfortable to be in the spotlight. "For a while now, ma'am. The general and I have developed quite a productive working arrangement."

Odd way to phrase it, but Zoey understood what he meant. It wasn't unusual for an officer moving his way up the ranks, like Sharp had, to single out other soldiers to be part of his inner circle and support them along the way. If she'd been more interested in setting down roots than seeing the world, she imagined she would have been by Sharp's side all along as well. As it was, she'd benefitted plenty from Sharp's at-a-distance assistance over the years in the form of several below the zone promotions.

"I brought the files you requested," Louden said, handing over a sealed envelope. "Are you going to want the conference room again this afternoon?"

"No, not today." Zoey knew she should schedule interviews with the higher ranking officers who'd used the Darcy Agency, not to mention set up a re-interview of Donny Bloomfield as soon as possible, especially in view of Sharp's admonition to bring this matter to a close, but she wasn't up for spending the afternoon sitting across from Rook, acting as if nothing had happened between them. Not yet.

Louden looked at the door. "If you don't need anything else then."

Zoey dismissed him and waited until the door was firmly shut before she resumed her discussion with Jack.

"He seems like a nice guy," Jack said. "Has he been helping you find your way around?"

"He's been great. This place is so big I forget what a small world it can be. Louden worked with the general all these years, you and your sister are both Sharp's godchildren. Did I hear correctly that your father served with General Sharp?"

"You did. They were both part of the Ranger unit that led the invasion of Grenada. General Sharp received the Medal of Honor for saving my dad, along with the rest of their unit when they were ambushed by the resistance forces."

"Wow, I had no idea. I mean I've seen the medal, but he doesn't talk about it. Grenada, huh? That was a long time ago." She marveled at the fact she'd never heard the story of Sharp's heroism. There were a lot of soldiers who would've traded on the telling, but he had never breathed a word of it as far as she knew.

"Yep. My dad was barely out of West Point and had just finished Ranger training. It was his first assignment and he wound up dropped in a hot mess, pinned down between resistance fighters. Sharp risked his life to draw enemy fire and saved all but one man from a certain death. Dad and the rest of the guys who served with him still call him Mr. Hero whenever they get together. Sharp hates it."

Zoey filed the story away, determined to look up the details at some point as a way of gaining further insight into her mentor, but for now she seized on the mention of the Rangers to turn the conversation back to her original purpose. "Thanks for telling me about this. I don't want to keep you longer, but I had a question about the Rangers I was hoping you could help me answer. Do you happen to know Colonel Nicholas Mitchell?"

"Isn't he an instructor at McNair?"

"He was." Zoey hesitated before blurting out, "He committed suicide last night."

"You're kidding. That's horrible."

Zoey nodded, as the memory of seeing Mitchell's body in a pool of blood and brains came flooding back. Words couldn't convey how horrible it truly was, so she only nodded in agreement. "This is going to sound like a strange question, but do you know if Colonel Mitchell was ever part of a Ranger unit?"

If Jack thought the question was odd, his expression didn't show it. "I don't think so. I mean I don't pretend to know everyone who is, but I do know of him and I think I'd know if he'd been a Ranger. Are you investigating his death? Have you looked at his file?"

She didn't know the answer to the first question. Did investigating Mitchell's death fall under her mandate to sort out the Darcy Agency mess? If it did, surely she had the right to talk to anyone she thought might have valuable information and share information she had. She wasn't entirely convinced that was the case, but Sharp hadn't given her much guidance other than she needed to "wrap it up."

"His file is on restricted status," she said. "And it has been for at least the last few days, but he left a note. I'd show it to you, but I don't have a copy." She took a breath before plunging ahead. "It was addressed to me." She reeled off a summary of the points in Mitchell's letter, ending with, "He signed off with the motto, 'Rangers lead the way.' I checked his public profile, but I don't see anything about having served as a Ranger. Even if he was a Ranger, it seems a bit odd, but if he wasn't, then I think he was trying to tell us something."

"Like a coded message?"

"Exactly, but I'm not equipped to figure it out. I thought if he was a Ranger, then at least I'd have somewhere to start."

"Where is the letter?"

"I don't know." The last time Zoey had seen it, the tall, leggy blonde on Rook's team had been slipping it into an evidence envelope. Several times that morning, Zoey had contemplated texting Rook to see if she could get a copy so she could study it some more, but reaching out to Rook now after she walked out on her last night felt weird.

But Jack knew Rook. Zoey remembered the way the two of them had kidded around at Addison's party. Maybe he could get the letter from her.

But this wasn't his case. He had his own work to do, but the voice in her head prompted Zoey to blurt out, "I think Rook Daniels has a copy, but I can't ask her." At his questioning look, she said, "Long story. But if you asked her, maybe she'd give you a copy." A few beats of silence passed and she had a feeling she was losing him. "That letter is the key to his death and…"

This was it. Time to decide if she was going to tell him everything or just enough bits and pieces to get him to acquire a copy of Mitchell's letter. The letter would be valuable sure, but if she told him the rest, he might be able to help her sort through the information she and Rook had gathered so far and determine what to do next. Since Rook wasn't around to be her sounding board, she needed someone and he was in intelligence after all. She took a moment to organize her thoughts and then started to tell him the story of the late night call to the police from the Ivy Hotel. She told him everything, from how much Dixon's annoying presence bothered her to her dissatisfaction with the lack of guidance she'd received.

When she finished, she stared at him and waited for a reaction. She didn't have to wait long. His drawn expression told her he believed some, if not all, of what she'd told him, but she could tell he was also conflicted.

"And you've been talking to witnesses?" he asked.

"Yes, but we've only scratched the surface. I could use your help. I know you have your own work, but if there's any way you could help me get a little of the information I need to put this to bed, I would appreciate it."

"Don't you have a team assigned to work on this?"

Zoey thought about her "team." Dixon, who she'd planned to ditch as soon as possible. And Rook. Rook had a team, but they reported to Rook, not her, and so far, she wasn't getting any information from Rook's team. "It's just me. Look, I know you probably have better things to do, more important things, but I sure could use the help. If you'll just point me in the right direction and sit in when I re-interview Donny Bloomfield, that'll do. Okay?"

Jack looked at the stack of files on her desk and raised his eyebrows in question. "Yes," she said. "That's part of it. Go ahead, take a look."

He pulled the files toward him and flipped the first one open. His expression didn't change, but she detected a subtle increase in the pace of his breathing as he flipped through the pages. "Are these officers who used the agency?"

"Yes. Those are the repeat customers." She pointed at another stack. "The one-offs are over in this pile."

"Some of these officers are very powerful people. Are you sure you want to do this?"

"Want to? No, but I don't see that I have a choice."

"There's always a choice."

He was right. She could disobey Sharp's orders and refuse to work on the case, a move that would send her career tanking. Of course, confronting some of the people on this list might have the same effect, but at least she'd have answers. Mitchell had been in trouble, and she'd ignored his cry for help. Now he was dead and if she didn't follow the lead he'd left, his death would be on her conscience for the rest of her life.

❖

Rook paced her office, unable to concentrate on anything else while she waited for Eric to crack the code he'd found in Mitchell's letters.

"You're wearing a hole in the carpet," Lacy called out from the doorway.

"He said a few hours and it's been four."

"It's been less than three hours total and we had to get the computer, that was one. He'll be done any minute. Genius takes time." Lacy picked up the coffee mug from the edge of her desk. "No more of this stuff until we have some answers."

Rook started to protest, but Lacy was right. She was so amped up on caffeine and adrenaline she was due for a crash any moment. She needed something to keep her mind busy until Eric was done. "Can you try to reach Major Granger again?"

"I've called twice, but she's been in meetings. Have you tried sending her a text?"

Rook sighed. She'd called Zoey several times since she'd insisted on leaving last night, but all she got was the canned outgoing voice mail message that came standard with every phone, and her texts had gone unanswered. She'd resorted to having Lacy try to reach her, but apparently that was a dead end too. Zoey was either cutting her out of the investigation or cutting her off personally or both—neither of which were good. She started to insist Lacy try her one more time, but the sound of Lacy's desk phone ringing cut her off. "Maybe that's her."

"Hang on." Lacy picked up the call from Rook's desk. "Daniels Agency. How may I direct your call?" A few beats of silence passed and Lacy shook her head in Rook's direction. "Yes, Senator. She's right here. One moment." Lacy punched the hold button and held out the phone. "Senator Newman. His office has just been informed that a grand jury has been convened in Columbus to look into the death of Sheila Edgar."

"Talk about bad timing. He needs a lawyer."

Lacy shook the handset. "Uh, last I checked you were a lawyer."

"A real lawyer. You know, the kind that actually goes to court and does lawyer things."

"Dammit, Rook, he needs you. Even if he's looking at criminal charges, make that especially if he's looking at criminal charges. He's going to need you to handle the fallout."

Rook shot a look at the office door. "I can't leave right now. What if Eric finds something or Zoey—Major Granger calls?"

"It's an hour flight. I'll book you a private plane. You'll be there in no time, hold his hand, and fly back in the morning or tonight if you can stay awake that long. Take Harry and then Harry can stay over and babysit."

Rook took the phone. She barely got two words out before Newman's panic took over. What if an arrest warrant was issued? What if the sheriff showed up at his office or, God forbid, one of the many functions he had scheduled with his constituents this week?

She let him ramble on for a few minutes, but cut him off when she couldn't take it any longer. Lacy was right. It would be much easier to calm him down and control the damage in person. As much as she trusted Eric's expertise, she also believed he'd exaggerated a bit when he said he could write a program and crack a code in a few hours. Taking care of Newman might be the perfect solution to her growing impatience at not having answers and not hearing from Zoey. Decision made, she injected her voice with calm and said, "Senator, I don't think you have anything to worry about, but I'm going to fly out to help you through this. I'll be there in a couple of hours."

By the time Rook combed her hair, brushed her teeth, and squirted eye drops in her eyes, George was waiting to take her and Harry to the airport. On the drive, she tried one last text to Zoey, abandoning all pretense that she was trying to get in touch with her for professional reasons.

I'll be out of touch for a while. Miss you. I have no regrets. Hope you don't either. Talk to you soon.

She spent the rest of the ride to the airport pretending she wasn't waiting for a response, which was just as well since none came. It was for the best. She needed to focus on Senator Newman's problems and then clear her head for whatever Eric found. The next few days were going to be busy and she needed to be at her top form, not mooning over some infuriating woman, even if that woman was super attractive, captivating, and one of the best kissers she'd ever met.

Chapter Seventeen

I can't believe you made me come all the way out here."

Zoey resisted the urge to roll her eyes at Donny Bloomfield's sulking disposition. He'd started grousing that morning when she'd called him to say they were doing follow-up interviews and his presence was ordered at the Pentagon this afternoon. She was actually surprised he hadn't ratted her out to his daddy, but at this point she cared more about answers than diplomacy, which was why she'd demanded the meeting on her time and her turf.

Funny how she already considered the Pentagon her turf. It wasn't really. She'd been here only a few days and didn't at all know her way around, but she had an office here and, in addition to the helpful Lieutenant Louden, she now had a friend in Major Jack Riley. She thought back to her first day when she'd tried to fake knowing her way around to keep from looking foolish in front of Rook.

Where was Rook now? Was she working her own angles on this case? Zoey could hardly blame Rook if she was working without her since she'd ignored Rook's texts and calls since she'd stormed out last night. Kicking herself for cutting Rook out, she itched to call her now, to see if they could connect, but she'd have to wait. Donny Bloomfield was in the hot seat, and Jack was waiting for her to take the lead.

After looking through all the files earlier, Jack had excused himself from her office and cleared his schedule. She didn't know what he was working on, but she did know that he had autonomy because he'd told her that much. He'd escorted Lieutenant Bloomfield to the conference room, and she could tell that Donny was a little intimidated by the buff and handsome major who didn't look like he took shit from anyone. All it took was one fierce glare from Jack and Donny quit his whining.

"Tell me everything you know about your professor, Colonel Mitchell," Zoey commanded.

"You're barking up the wrong tree there. I don't know anything about him."

Zoey held his gaze long enough for him to start squirming in his seat before she pressed on. "That's funny. We have information that he was a customer of the Darcy Agency. With that in common, you would think you might have some other details about his personal life."

Donny shrugged. "News to me. I may not like him, but I'm not going to lie to get him in trouble."

"Why don't you like him?" Jack asked, his tone deceptively light and friendly.

An oh-shit expression crossed Donny's face as he realized he'd revealed too much. "He's a hard-ass. Treats us like plebes instead of officers. The guy never lets up."

Zoey reflected about Donny's continued use of the present tense to refer to Mitchell. She supposed it was possible Donny didn't know about Mitchell's death, but she'd be surprised if word hadn't made it around among his students. She decided to wait on revealing the truth to see how this interaction played out. "He says you don't take this program seriously. That you and your friends think your time at McNair is a pass to party and he's only pushing you to be better."

"That's bullshit."

"I agree." She let the statement settle for a moment and then pressed on. "I mean the guy is married and he's paying prostitutes for sex? Who's he to lecture you?"

Donny's eyes gleamed. "Exactly. Especially since he's the one who hooked us up in the first place."

Now it was Zoey's turn to be surprised. She glanced at Jack, but his face was stone. Not sure what else to do, she played along. "We thought that might be the case. What do you think was up with that?"

"I have no idea. Like I said, I don't know jack about the guy. Maybe he was getting a kickback or a little something something on the side." He punctuated his remark with a lewd gesture. "All I know is he slipped us the number for the hookers with our last exam. At the time I thought he was cool, but then when we got busted at that hotel, he went bat-shit crazy. I guess he figured he was going to get in trouble for hooking us up in the first place."

Zoey stared at him, focused on keeping her expression neutral which was pretty damn hard considering the bombshell he'd just dropped. Mitchell, who'd stormed into her office, pissed off that he'd been swept up into this investigation, had turned his students on to prostitutes? But why?

"Is he?"

"What?" Zoey asked, confused by the question.

"Is Mitchell going to get in trouble?" Donny asked, his tone sounding sincere for the first time. "Are we? My dad's already pissed off enough. I don't need a disciplinary action in my jacket to fuel his fire."

Angry that all he cared about was his record, Zoey growled, "I don't know what's going to happen to you, but Colonel Mitchell ate his gun last night, so you don't need to worry about him anymore."

❖

"I don't understand why you can't represent me," Newman said for the tenth time.

Rook groaned inwardly. She'd been in Ohio for three hours and she couldn't wait to leave. Since the senator's driver had picked her up from the airport, she'd been answering the same questions about his future with a lot of "I don't knows" and "it depends." After their car slowly nudged through the crowd of reporters blocking his street and delivered them safely to the house, Newman switched to asking her to represent him before the grand jury, and she was growing weary of repeating the same answer, over and over.

She injected her voice with all the patience she could muster. "You need a lawyer that specializes in this kind of case. That's not me, but I'll help you find someone. Whoever it is needs to be local, not some big DC firm. This case involves someone who died here in Columbus, so the outcome will be more about relationships with local officials than about how much they bill per hour. In fact, the bigger the show you put on, the more likely walls will start closing in around you. Having me here is pushing it. The Franklin County prosecuting attorney isn't going to be impressed when a bunch of lawyers show up in suits that cost more than he makes in several months."

"If you say so."

"You have to trust me on this," Rook said. "Have you talked to Jeanine?"

"I would if you hadn't sent her to New York."

She ignored the edge in his voice, thankful he was following her instructions by not talking about the case on the phone to anyone but her. "Lacy has already booked her flight back. She'll board a plane right after her speech at the conference and she'll be here later tonight."

This was the perfect time to bring up her planned departure. Harry was up to speed on everything he needed to know to shepherd Newman through the next couple of days. She'd already come up with a list of local attorneys and scheduled meetings for the next day. She only had to convince Newman he would be in capable hands with her gone.

Her phone buzzed with a text and she took it as a perfect opportunity to slip out of the room and let Harry take point. "I'll be right back," she said, not waiting for a reply before walking out of the senator's study.

The text was from Zoey and it was short and simple. *Sorry about last night. Developments here. Signal sucks in the building— Call me on the landline and I'll fill you in.* A few seconds passed and another text came in. *Miss you too.* She glanced back at the study door, but decided to wait to call Zoey until she was on her way to the airport where she'd have some privacy. She started to tuck her phone back in her pocket, but it rang. A quick look at the screen showed only the words unknown caller.

"Where are you?" Julia barked.

"Don't you people watch the news? On *West Wing*, there's like a million television sets crowded into your offices and everyone's always staring at them."

"In case you haven't noticed, this is not a TV show, it's a real White House and I need a real update. I heard you're in Ohio, but I find it hard to believe you would traipse across the country while you have an active case pending here. Any updates for me?"

Rook resisted pointing out that Ohio was hardly across the country. No need to make Julia madder than she already was. Instead she settled on a half-truth. "There's been a development, but we should talk in person." She looked at her watch. Even if she left now and met with Zoey as soon as she landed, it would still be late. "I'm flying back tonight. Let's meet in the morning. Okay?"

"Seven thirty a.m. Just you—I want to get a full update without anyone from the Pentagon looking over our shoulders trying to distract us."

Rook clicked off the line and stared at the phone, rereading the text from Zoey, trying hard not to be distracted and failing miserably. A second later, her phone rang again, but this time it was Eric. "Grand Central Station," she answered.

"Rook?"

She laughed. "Sorry, it's me. It's been a little crazy here."

"Got it. When are you coming back?"

"Tonight. I'm meeting Major Granger—apparently there have been some developments. You have news for me?"

"Yes. I was able to crack the code. Our guy was heavily involved with the agency, but he was reporting to someone else. I'm convinced there was more to the agency's business enterprise than providing entertainment."

Rook appreciated Eric's attempt to be vague because they were talking on an unsecured line, but what she really wanted were straight answers, and she needed to get out of Ohio and back to DC if she was going to get any. "Have Blake drop the laptop off at my place and I'll review the files."

Twenty minutes later, she was in the car on the way to the airport for her private flight back to DC. She risked a quick call to Zoey on the ride.

"Granger."

"You sound tired," Rook said. "Have they got you working around the clock?"

"Pretty much. I'm glad you called."

"Me too." Rook settled into the familiar rhythm of their conversation. "I'm sorry about last night too. I'm used to handling things my way without much input from anyone else."

"I'll take fifty percent of the blame. I know you were just doing your job, which is important, even if you are a civilian."

Rook heard the smile behind Zoey's pseudo-jab and laughed. "Duly noted. So are we okay?"

"Yes. Now, are you going to come back and work with me? I had to drag in other resources to help in your absence."

Rook's senses went on alert. "Other resources?"

"Jack Riley. He helped me re-interview Donny Bloomfield. Good thing too since Bloomfield dropped a couple of bombshells and no one would believe me if Jack hadn't heard it too."

Suddenly conscious they shouldn't be having this conversation on a cell phone, Rook stopped her. "Hey, I want to hear all about it, but I'm about to get on the plane. I'll call you when I land and we can meet. Okay?"

"Sounds perfect."

Minutes later, the car pulled up to the private hangars at the John Glenn Airport, and Rook thanked the universe for charter planes and the ability to afford them. She'd land in DC, meet Zoey, learn about the new developments, review the files Eric had sent, and prepare for her meeting with Julia. With any luck, she'd get the work part done in time for a do-over of last night's dinner with Zoey.

Chapter Eighteen

Zoey idled her car near the hangar, pretending to read messages on her phone while casting surreptitious glances at the runway to her left. She checked her watch for the umpteenth time. Nine o'clock. George had said Rook was due to land at eight and Zoey had been waiting since then. If Rook didn't show up soon, the security guard she'd seen looping the building was going to have her tossed out.

This was a stupid idea. Talking George into letting her pick Rook up at the airport was likely to get him in trouble and annoy Rook. Besides, her little sports car was hardly a plush town car full of Rook's creature comforts, and her attempt to re-create part of their very first meeting was a foolish sentiment. Since when had she become sentimental? *You're going soft, Granger.*

Nope. She had solid plans to focus on business. She needed to bring Rook up to speed on her meeting with Donny Bloomfield, and picking her up at the airport was a practical and efficient way to have their conversation in private. She tapped the steering wheel, pounding out her nerves, and decided to wait ten more minutes before she bailed on Mission Surprise Rook at the Airport.

Seconds before her self-imposed deadline ran out, a G6 roared to a stop on the runway, and Zoey's gut clenched, certain this was Rook's plane. She stared at the door, willing it to open, and finally released her breath when she spotted Rook descending the steps. Her stride was sure and easy, like she descended from expensive private planes on a daily basis. Maybe she did. Zoey remembered waving to Rook as she'd ascended in a chartered helicopter the day they met, and she thought again how their worlds were miles apart. The first time she had the realization, it hadn't mattered much, mostly because she didn't think she'd ever see Rook again, but now the gap between them was more of a challenge, and bridging it was a mission she wanted to accomplish.

Rook scanned the parking lot with a perplexed frown. As much as she enjoyed watching her, Zoey figured she better send a signal or Rook was likely to call George and ask him where the hell he was. Zoey stepped out of her car and leaned against the door. As she waved in Rook's direction, she felt a shiver down her spine spurring her to admit she hadn't come here to expedite business. She'd come because she hadn't wanted to wait the extra hour or so it would've taken Rook to drive into the city and the time it would've taken to arrange a place to meet. The past day with no contact had seemed much longer, and Zoey wished she could go back in time to before they'd learned of Mitchell's death, to the intimacy of Rook's living room, to the kiss they'd shared.

"Hey," Rook said, as she drew closer. "You're not George."

"No one could be George but George. He's amazing. I was thinking of stealing him from you."

Rook made a show of looking around. "Looks like you already have."

Zoey jingled her keys in the air. "Any chance I can take you where you need to go?"

Rook smiled broadly. "That depends." She leaned in close, her whisper leaving a trail of heat along Zoey's neck. "I'm supposed to meet up with this amazing woman. She's beautiful and smart and I need to see her in person to apologize for being a controlling ass last time we were together. Any chance you could help me out with that?"

Zoey turned slightly and met Rook's eyes. Her gaze was questioning, and despite her flirty manner, Zoey could tell Rook was the tiniest bit insecure about where things stood between them. She started to offer reassurance, but the heat between them sucked up all the air, and instead she raised her hand and tucked an errant curl behind Rook's ear. Big mistake because once she'd touched her she didn't want to let go. But they had work to do and they had to do that first or they would never get to it. Reluctantly, she dropped her hand slowly away, allowing her fingertips to linger against the skin of Rook's neck as she gently pulled back. "I think I can get you what you need," she said, pointing to the car. "Shall we?"

Rook's body shuddered as she released a long, slow breath. "Sure," she said, her voice low and husky.

They climbed into the car and Zoey drove out of the parking lot, turning onto the road before she realized this was as far as her plan went. She knew they needed to work, but the minute she'd seen Rook walk off the plane, thoughts of work had flown from her mind. Left to her own devices, she would check into the nearest hotel, so she said, "Where should we go?"

"That's a good question. Are you hungry? I figured out Senator Newman keeps his trim, athletic figure because he doesn't believe in eating. The last thing I had to eat was a fat-free, gluten-free protein bar that tasted like flavored cardboard. Maybe we could talk about the case over dinner?"

"I'm starving," Zoey said. She wasn't really, not for food anyway, but after the long travel day Rook had had, it was the considerate thing to say. And of course Rook would want to get right to work. Zoey fast-forwarded to them sitting at a crowded DC restaurant where politicians and other notables stopped by the table every few minutes to say hi to Rook. She could think of no more miserable way to spend the evening.

"Great. I hate to ask this, but do you mind if we work at my place? My office is full of half-done projects and we can get pretty much anything delivered in Dupont Circle." Rook grinned. "We can even have burgers again if you insist."

Zoey flashed to her earlier memory of Rook's couch. "Your place is perfect. And why don't you pick the food? I'll eat anything you want." She hoped the dark of the car hid the blush she felt fanning across her face at the double entendre. She had only the length of the drive to get her libido under control and she started by changing the subject. "Everything okay in Columbus?"

"It will be. I left Harry behind to handle things."

Zoey took the turn that Rook pointed out to her. "Would you rather have stayed yourself?"

"Once upon a time I thought I was the only one who could handle a case from beginning to end."

Rook paused and Zoey injected, "Control freak much?"

"Big time. But then I realized I couldn't handle more than one or two big cases without some substantial help. If I was going to grow my firm, I needed to start trusting someone else to help with the work and the best way to learn is by doing. Harry's been watching me for a while now. He'll have his own style, which is how it should be, but he'll cover all the bases just like I would."

"How did you start doing this kind of work?"

"Lucked into it. A few years out of law school, I got a job at the White House counsel's office, which turned out to be more about problem-solving than the law. I developed a talent for making lemonade out of lemons, and when that particular administration's term ended, I opened my own shop."

"Have you ever thought about doing anything else?"

"Have you?"

Zoey caught the slight edge and wished she hadn't ventured down this road. She reached out a hand and took Rook's in hers. "Sorry, that came out wrong. I didn't mean to imply there was anything wrong with what you do. I was only curious."

"It's okay. I'm tired and possibly cranky. Babysitting can do that to a person."

Of course. Rook had been going nonstop all day. Zoey felt foolish for imagining this evening would be about anything other than bringing Rook up to speed. "You've had a long day." Zoey glanced over at Rook who was opening her mouth to interrupt, but Zoey plowed ahead. "Why don't I fill you in and then drop you off at your place? We can go over anything else tomorrow. Okay?"

Rook slid her hand onto Zoey's thigh and gave her a light squeeze. Not overtly sexual, but loaded with possibility. "Not okay. I am tired and cranky, but seeing you waiting for me at the airport made me forget about everything else and now I'm really looking forward to spending the evening with you. Please?"

Zoey heard an undercurrent of desire in Rook's simple plea that reflected her own. She couldn't possibly say no, and the realization both scared and thrilled her at the same time.

❖

Rook watched from the kitchen as Zoey settled onto the couch and hugged one of the pillows to her chest, wishing she were that pillow. "Would you like something to drink?" she asked. "I'm having coffee, but I have a full bar and there's still some of that beer from last night." Had it really only been last night since they'd been here and she'd been sharing the details of Rory's death?

"Coffee sounds good."

Rook poured them each a cup, grabbed a stack of menus, and walked into the living room. Zoey leaned lengthwise against the arm of the couch with her feet crossed at the ankles, careful to keep her black leather boots from the upholstery. She'd shed the matching leather jacket, but she still looked sleek and sexy in her slim dark jeans and curve-hugging black T-shirt.

"Is that coffee for me?" Zoey asked with a sly grin, sitting up and pointing at one of the cups in Rook's hand.

Rook handed it over and settled onto the couch beside Zoey. "Sorry, I got a little distracted by the whole biker chick look." She nodded. "It suits you."

"You sound surprised."

"I am, a little. I mean you seem so all about the rules and regulations, but I'm thinking when you get out on the open road you break sound barriers in that car."

"Maybe." Zoey sipped her coffee. "Maybe everything isn't how it appears on the surface."

Truth, Rook thought, but it was time to change the subject because she was way too close to testing the boundaries between them. She handed over the menus. "I know it's old school, but I'd much rather flip through a paper menu than try to read descriptions on the tiny screen of my phone. What are you in the mood for?"

Zoey brushed through them quickly and then handed them back. "Everything sounds great. I trust you to pick something good."

Their fingers touched when Rook reached to take the menus back. There was that heat again—Rook didn't want to let go, and food was now the last thing on her mind. "How about this? Why don't you fill me in about your meeting with Donny Bloomfield and then we'll relax and order dinner?"

"That sounds perfect," Zoey said. "He came to the office today, and I interviewed him with Jack Riley. At first, Donny acted like he had nothing to say, but after we pushed, he started talking. Apparently, he and his friends don't like Mitchell much, but it was Mitchell who turned them on to the Darcy Agency. Slipped a note with the contact information into one of their exams. He never mentioned another word about it, but according to Donny, after the incident at the Ivy, Mitchell went off on them." Zoey shook her head. "I guess I could've told you all that in the car."

Rook reached for her hand. "If you'd told me everything before we got here, I have a feeling I wouldn't have been able to get you to come in."

"Maybe. Maybe not."

Zoey laced her fingers through Rook's, and Rook prayed for the strength to stay focused. "Did Donny say anything else?" she asked.

"No, but I think after the way Jack Riley stared him down, he would've told us if he knew anything else."

"Makes sense." Rook tread carefully with her next question, not wanting to break their connection by seeming to challenge Zoey's decisions. "How did Jack end up being there?"

"He was doing me a favor. I'd just cut Dixon out, but I wasn't smart enough to find a replacement first. I'd called him because I wanted to know if he knew anything about Mitchell having served as a Ranger."

Rook raised her eyebrows.

"You know because of the way he signed off his letter, suicide note, whatever you want to call it," Zoey said. "'Rangers lead the way'—it's the Army Rangers' official motto."

"What did he say?" Rook asked, not really following Zoey's train of thought, probably because she was way more interested in the press of her hand than business.

"Jack didn't know him. Maybe I'm making too much out of that part of the note. Anyway, since I'd already involved him, I asked him to help me out with Donny. Jack was the perfect fit, plus I got to find out the story behind how Sharp came to be his and Addison's godfather. Did you know that Jack's dad and General Sharp were part of the same rapid deployment force that invaded Grenada?"

"I had no idea."

"According to Jack, that's where Sharp got his Medal of Honor. Sharp never talks about it, but Jack says his father often tells the story of how Sharp saved their entire squad. Apparently, they all started calling him Mr. Hero after that. I bet he hates that."

Rook nodded, but her thoughts were back on Mitchell and Donny Bloomfield's story about Mitchell. "How did you leave things with Bloomfield?"

"We told him we'd be back in touch soon, but I'm not sure he's going to be any help. He strikes me as kind of dumb, and I bet he got into McNair by trading on his name, not his grades."

"I bet you're right," Rook said, "but I think we should re-interview the other students who were at the Ivy that night. I don't believe for a second that none of them knew about Mitchell's involvement." She started to mention the coded emails Eric had found on Mitchell's laptop, but decided to wait until she'd had a chance to look at them first. Right now she wanted to look at Zoey, not a bunch of emails. She looked down at their hands and then back up at Zoey who was watching her with a steady gaze. "Do you think we could take a little break? Maybe talk about something other than work—just for a little while?"

Zoey smiled and inched closer. "You do that? Take breaks?"

"Sometimes."

"Did you have something in particular you'd like to talk about?" Zoey asked, tracing Rook's thigh with her free hand. "Or maybe you'd like to go ahead and order dinner? We can do whatever you want."

Rook's entire body hummed with anticipation as Zoey's hand moved farther up her leg. She couldn't talk, she couldn't eat, she couldn't concentrate on anything except the white-hot heat coursing through her. She took Zoey at her word, pulled her close, and claimed her with hungry lips.

❖

Zoey pressed her lips into Rook's—fierce, demanding, unable to get close enough. Their first kiss had been extraordinary, but the hours in between, waiting, imagining, and fantasizing a repeat performance had every nerve in her body on high alert. The result was mind-blowing. She teased her tongue along Rook's lips and groaned with pleasure.

"This," Rook murmured, her whispered voice rough with desire. "This is what I want."

Zoey placed a hand behind Rook's neck and drew her closer. She dipped back in for another kiss and then met Rook's eyes, summoning the courage to ask for more. "Just this?"

Rook answered by tugging at Zoey's shirt, pulling it up over her head, and gently removing her bra. Zoey sat perfectly still, letting Rook's gaze sweep over her naked chest. "You like?"

"More than like." Rook placed a hand behind her and lowered Zoey back to the couch. She leaned down and traced her tongue slowly across her breasts, her touch growing more urgent with each pass. "You are so beautiful," Rook said.

"You're making me crazy," Zoey said, arching into Rook's tongue and pressing against Rook's knee nestled between her legs. "Show some skin, Daniels, or I'm going to lose it."

Rook leaned back and grinned. "Is that an order, Major?"

"Yes," Zoey gasped as Rook slid a finger along her crotch causing her to twitch with excitement.

"I guess I can follow orders as long as they apply to both of us." Rook sat up and held out a hand, ignoring Zoey's plea for her to stay. "Come on, we need a bigger space for what I have planned."

Zoey took her hand and allowed Rook to pull her into her arms. They kissed again, and now it felt more like a prelude to a deeper connection rather than a once in a lifetime experience they had to grab before it vanished. When they broke for air, Rook led her through the house and up the stairs, pausing at the threshold to a doorway.

"Change your mind?" Zoey asked, praying that wasn't the case.

"Not even," Rook said. "Just checking the situation. When I left here last, I didn't plan on having guests."

Zoey smiled and pushed past her, gawking at the size of the room. "I'm not sure how you'd know if something was out of place. Your bedroom is bigger than my entire house." She spun around to take it all in. "But if you need a minute to look for some other woman's lingerie…" She watched as Rook's face fell and she wished she'd never started the sentence.

Rook ducked her head. "I'm no virgin, but my home is my sanctuary. Very few people have ever been inside the front door, and none in this room."

Zoey stepped closer and lifted Rook's chin. "I only care about right now." She waved her hand between them. "I want this. Do you want this?"

"I can't remember ever wanting anything more," Rook said, pulling Zoey into her embrace. Her hand grazed the zipper of Zoey's jeans. "Weren't we talking about skin?"

"Why yes. Yes, we were." Zoey started unbuttoning Rook's shirt, which required extra concentration since Rook was unzipping her fly at the same time. She slid Rook's shirt off and kissed her shoulder while Rook slipped her hand into her briefs.

"You're so wet," Rook murmured.

"I bet you are too." Zoey took Rook's free hand and led her to a king-sized platform bed. She pushed Rook back gently onto the comforter and while Rook watched, she shucked off her boots and jeans and crawled between Rook's legs to unfasten her trousers. "Clothes are so overrated," she said, pulling at Rook's pants, her hands trembling.

"I completely agree," Rook said in a breathy voice as she lifted her hips to help her along. Zoey dropped Rook's pants to the floor and slowly stretched out over her, aching with want as her breasts brushed Rook's tight, smooth skin, and her thigh touched Rook's slick wet center. Rook hooked a leg over hers, pinning her closer and whispered, "Tell me what you want."

"I want you to touch me," Zoey placed her hand over Rook's, unable and unwilling to prolong the wait, "everywhere."

Rook answered with a slow, lingering drag of her fingers between her legs and then she flipped Zoey gently onto her back, bent down, and took one of her nipples into her mouth. Zoey shook with arousal as Rook's tongue teased while her fingers played with her throbbing folds, slipping in and out in a steady, building rhythm. "That feels amazing," Zoey said, her breath ragged.

Rook looked up and smiled. "Yes, it does." She held Zoey's gaze as she trailed her tongue down her chest to her abdomen. When Rook's tongue circled her aching clit, Zoey threw her head back and moaned. Rook drew her closer and closer to climax with long, slow strokes, taking her almost to the brink before pulling back to begin again, each pass making Zoey crazy with desire. When she couldn't stand it any longer, Zoey pulled Rook back up until they were lying face-to-face, and she dipped her fingers into Rook's swollen sex, loving the way Rook arched into her touch.

As she stroked Rook, Rook reached for her again. Zoey tried to slow her own reaction, to give Rook her full attention, but she was so close, so ready to come. She twisted the comforter in her fist, torn between holding the pleasure tight or letting it consume her, but within moments, she let go and bucked against Rook's hand, urging her to take whatever she wanted and offering it freely. As the waves of arousal crested over her, she threw her head back and cried out, feeling a level of freedom and release like she'd never known before.

Chapter Nineteen

Rook woke before her alarm and took advantage of the extra time by allowing herself a few minutes to linger next to the warm, naked body beside her. Slowly opening her eyes, she absorbed the reality of someone else in her bed.

Zoey's head was resting on her shoulder and the rest of her body was tucked up against Rook's side. Her eyes were closed and her face was relaxed and peaceful, which Rook took as a sign of satisfaction after the hours they'd spent in the throes of passion the night before.

She'd been satisfied too, more than, but seeing Zoey this morning had her longing for more, wishing she had nowhere else to be but right here, in her bed with Zoey in her arms. The feeling was new and strange and she wasn't sure what to do with it. Never before had she wanted to shut the rest of the world out. Usually, she invited it in as a welcome distraction from her bedmate's desire or demands for more intimacy, but last night with Zoey left her in a different place. Now she was the one craving intimacy, against her natural instinct to pull back once her physical needs were satisfied.

For the first time in her life, Rook realized she'd drawn all of her passion from her work, but work could only give so much. Ironic since work would have kept her from Zoey if she'd followed her steadfast rule not to get involved with clients. But she'd broken the rule and the sky hadn't fallen, and now she wanted to push the boundaries even further.

The vibration of her phone broke into her musings. She reached over and shut it off, but try as she might, she wasn't able to resist checking the screen to see who'd called. Relieved that she didn't recognize the number, she started to set it down, but noticed the time. Six a.m. She quickly calculated how long it would take to get ready and get to the White House for her meeting with Julia and thought she might be able to steal a little bit longer with Zoey, but then she remembered the files Eric had sent. Damn. She needed to review those before her meeting in case she needed to provide Julia with an update.

She glanced over at Zoey again and cursed the timing. She'd have to save more boundary-pushing for later. She brushed a soft kiss against Zoey's hair, gently extracted her arm, and rolled out of bed.

By six forty-five, Rook was showered and dressed. She'd packed the laptop with Eric's files to read in the car and penned a note for the still sleeping Zoey. She yawned as she wrote, but the exhaustion was the good kind, leaving her feeling slightly euphoric and like she could conquer the world if it weren't such a happy place that it didn't need conquering.

When Rook walked outside, she spotted George sitting in the car with his window rolled down, talking to a woman carrying a steaming Starbucks cup. As Rook strode over to the sedan, she heard the woman call out "thanks for the directions" and wave as she walked away. Rook smiled as the woman passed her and resisted the urge to grab the coffee and gulp some much needed caffeine before she opened the door and climbed in. "Good morning, George. I hope you enjoyed your evening off."

"I certainly did." If he felt bad about letting Zoey take over his chauffeuring duties the night before, it wasn't evident from the grin he flashed in the rearview mirror. "How about you?" he asked. "Did you enjoy your evening?"

She returned his smile. "Matter of fact, I did. Thank you."

"My pleasure," he said. As he pulled away from the curb, Rook stared back at the house, conflicted about whether she should have woken Zoey before she left, but she hadn't had the heart to disturb her. She closed her eyes for a moment and imagined a time in the future when, having been together longer, they found it natural to wake each other before they left for their respective jobs, but then her eyes popped open and she pushed aside the fantasy. *One night together and you're acting like a love-struck teenager. Get it together, Daniels.*

Rook fished the laptop from her briefcase and flipped through the files Eric had compiled, hoping the work would divert her attention from the distraction that was Zoey Granger. She needn't have worried. Eric had provided extensive annotations, showing how the code the Darcy Agency had been using worked, but she sped through that to get to the meat of his findings. Eric had found several iterations of agency files attached to Mitchell's emails and provided her with a breakdown of the information they contained, including references to their clients' ranks and security clearances and notes about their pleasure preferences listed right along with their other vulnerabilities, including past misdeeds and family connections. He'd concluded that the escorts at the Darcy Agency weren't offering prostitutes for pleasure, but rather as spies for an elaborate scheme of intelligence gathering and blackmail across the entire military structure.

Holy shit. Rook's gut clenched as she considered the implications. If these files were accurate, this scandal could rock the entire military, and as much as she dreaded having to deliver the news to Julia, she dove back into the files to make sure she was as prepared as she could be for their meeting.

Much of the code was in Russian, and Eric had included a table of those words and their English translations. Two words in particular jumped out at Rook—hero and ranger—sparking a memory. Wishing she'd paid more attention to what Zoey had said last night instead of concentrating on getting her into bed, Rook thought back over Zoey's recounting of her interview with Donny Bloomfield. No, that wasn't it. Zoey had used the words when she'd described her conversation with Jack Riley, and the story he'd relayed about General Sharp. What had she said? Something about Sharp having won a medal and his squad dubbing him a hero.

Another memory sparked, and she typed Sharp's full name into a Google search to confirm her hunch. As she scrolled through the results, she did some mental calculations. Before he'd been assigned to Fort Bragg, where he'd been Zoey's commander, Sharp had served in the 75th Ranger Regiment. Wikipedia gave her a quick rundown of the regiment's history, but it was the Ranger motto, located in the center of the page that sprang out at her as if it were surrounded by blinking lights. *Rangers lead the way.*

Mitchell had signed off his letter to Zoey with the exact same words. Zoey had mentioned something about it last night, and now Rook wished she'd listened more closely, but she'd heard enough to know that Sharp was not only a Ranger but also a hero. Was it a coincidence the corresponding words in Russian were popping up in Mitchell's emails? Was Mitchell's final letter a coded message to Zoey that Sharp was involved in what was turning out to be a spy ring posing as an escort service? She needed answers and she needed them now.

They were only about ten minutes from the White House. Rook pulled out her cell and called Eric, launching in the moment he picked up the phone, letting urgency override security concerns about discussing the case on an unsecured phone. "The files you sent me, is there any chance there was someone above Mitchell's pay grade directing the show?"

To his credit, Eric didn't act offended at her curt manner. "Absolutely. Mitchell received orders, but wasn't giving any of them. Someone else was definitely calling the shots."

"Any way to find out who?"

"I've tried to back trace the emails, but I can't locate the ISP they were sent from. Your pals at the White House may need to get NSA involved."

"I'm on my way there now, but in the meantime, I have another project for you." She reeled off everything she knew about General Sharp. "Put together whatever you can find on him, and I'll take a look at it when I get back to the office."

"Do you think he's involved in this?"

"I don't know, but I'm working on a hunch. Go as far back as you can on his service record and whatever personal information you can find."

"Got it. Anything else?"

Rook looked up to see George had just pulled into a line of cars near the guard gate. An image of Zoey, peacefully asleep, flashed in her mind. If Sharp, her mentor, was involved with a Russian spy ring, was Zoey involved as well? She squashed the thought as quickly as it had come. The Zoey she'd come to know was forthright and honest and there was absolutely no way she'd betray her country, but if she stumbled onto the same information Rook now had and chose to confront Sharp, she might be in danger.

She should warn her, but if Sharp was a spy, there was a better than even chance he or someone he was working with might have access to Zoey's calls, texts, and emails, and Rook couldn't afford to tip him off.

"Rook, are you still there?" Eric asked.

"Sorry. Yes, let me talk to Blake if she's in."

A moment later, Blake was on the line. "Rook?"

"Hey, Blake, I only have a minute. I need you to go to my place right now and deliver the following note to Zoey Granger." She gave Blake a second to find a pen and paper and then dictated her message to Zoey. "I'll explain later, but she needs this information before she goes into work today. Got it?"

"Got it."

Rook gave her a few more instructions, and by the time she hung up, they were inside the gate and George was parking the car. In a few minutes, she'd be expected to provide a full accounting of everything she'd learned so far, but all she could think about was Zoey and the night of lovemaking they'd shared. For the first time in Rook's life, work wasn't claiming most of her headspace, and her heart definitely longed to be back with Zoey. Maybe when this case was over, she'd take a break, do something fun. She couldn't remember the last time she'd taken a vacation that didn't involve hand-holding one of her clients. Her mind played pictures of her and Zoey, stretched out on the beautiful white sands of Seychelles—no phones, no clients, no responsibilities—and the only hand-holding would be the kind between lovers as they explored the island together. Before she climbed out of the car, she offered up a silent vow to bring this fantasy to life.

❖

Zoey padded her way downstairs to Rook's kitchen, having searched the rest of the house for her without success. The kitchen was empty, but she spotted a tented piece of paper sitting by the coffeemaker.

Coffee's ready. All you have to do is push the button. Had to make an early meeting, but I'll call you when I'm done. Last night was amazing. Rook

Zoey turned on the coffeemaker and reread the note, wondering what time Rook had left and how she'd managed to get ready for work without waking her. *Because you were sleeping the deep sleep of someone who just had multiple orgasms.* She smiled at the memory, the many memories they'd created across the expanse of Rook's bed last night. They'd both been insatiable and, as tired as she was, if Rook had woken her this morning, they would still be in bed, immune to the call of duty.

The coffeemaker dinged and Zoey broke out of her daydream and glanced at the clock. Seven thirty. She couldn't remember the last time she'd slept this late. She'd have to hurry to make it to the office before Sharp started looking for her. Surprisingly, the prospect of being late didn't make her anxious. In fact, she felt incredibly relaxed like she could handle anything the world threw her way. Was this the post-sex haze she'd heard about, but never experienced? Normally, she spent the hours after a sexual encounter thinking of ways to extricate herself from the other woman's bed and expectations of something more, unless she'd been lucky enough to find a like-minded woman who was only interested in a casual hookup, no repeat performance required.

She poured a cup of coffee in a to-go mug she'd found in the cabinet and was looking for her phone when she heard the sound of a key in the front door. Excited at the prospect of seeing Rook again before she had to tackle the drudge of work, she strode over to the door and threw it wide open, but instead of Rook on the other side, it was the blonde that had been collecting evidence at Colonel Mitchell's house the night he committed suicide.

The woman stuck out her hand. "Major Granger, I don't know if you remember me. I'm Blake Wyatt. I work with Rook Daniels."

Zoey looked down at the hand and gave it a quick shake. Who could forget such a gorgeous woman, but what was she doing here so early in the morning? And why did she have her own key? "Rook's not here."

"I know." Blake looked away. "Uh, would you like to change and then we can talk?"

"What?" Zoey asked before looking down and realizing she was dressed in only the T-shirt she'd had on last night that she'd plucked from the floor this morning. Shit. She didn't see much point in changing now since Blake had already gotten an eyeful. She shut the door and motioned for Blake to join her in the kitchen. "Is Rook okay?"

Blake looked puzzled. "Sure, she's fine, but she asked me to give you this." She handed over a note.

Zoey took the note, placed it on the counter, and looked back at Blake who showed no signs of leaving. "Anything else?"

"She wanted me to wait while you read it and then take you wherever you wanted to go."

The nerve of this chick, acting like she was in charge. Zoey stood tall and assumed as powerful a stance as she could while dressed in only a T-shirt. "Actually, I'm good. I'll call Rook when I've had a chance to read it."

"If she wanted me to stick around, she had a good reason."

Wow, she was going to have to be really direct. In her most commanding voice, Zoey said, "I'll be happy to tell Rook you did her bidding and were a great messenger, but right now I want to drink this coffee, get dressed, and go to work. The faster you leave, the faster I can accomplish those goals. Understood?"

Blake held up her hands in surrender and started backing toward the door. "Understood. But promise me you'll read the note before you talk to anyone else today."

"Sure, fine, whatever." Zoey waved her off. Blake set the key on the counter next to the note and strolled out like she was completely unaffected by Zoey's display of authority. When the door closed behind her, Zoey tossed her coffee down the sink. Blake's surprise visit had woken her up way faster than any caffeine could. She slowly unfolded the paper Blake had left behind and scanned the contents. It wasn't the same handwriting as the note Rook had left with the coffee, so if this message was from Rook, she'd dictated it to someone else.

Headed into meeting at White House. Found new evidence on Mitchell's computer that the Darcy Agency was a front for a Russian spy ring and have reason to believe Sharp may be involved. Try to avoid him until we can come up with a plan. I'll call you as soon as I'm done with this meeting.

Zoey read the note several times before she tossed it back onto the counter and picked up her phone. She punched the buttons for Rook's number and waited impatiently through the rings, hoping she wasn't in her meeting yet. When Rook's voice came on the line, it wasn't live but the outgoing message on her voice mail, and Zoey hung up without leaving a message.

Russian spy ring? Was this some kind of joke? The questions kept coming. Why was Rook meeting at the White House without her? Surely all these new developments hadn't happened while she was sleeping. Why hadn't Rook told her what was going on? Setting all that aside, what was this bullshit about General Sharp?

She picked up her phone and dialed Rook's number again with the same result. Frustrated, she stabbed out a text. *Got your message. WTF? Hoping this isn't some kind of sick joke. Then again, hoping it is. You better have a good explanation for cutting me out. CALL ME.*

She read it again before hitting send, debating over the all caps at the end but decided there was no sense hiding her anger, so she left them in place. Ten minutes later, Zoey was dressed in her clothes from the night before and walking to her car. When she'd woken up in Rook's bed less than an hour ago, she'd imagined a very different scenario, one that involved lingering touches and a slow, easy reentry to the real world. Everywhere she looked, people were rushing off to work, engaging in their normal routine, oblivious to the fact her world was crashing in around her.

Chapter Twenty

D o you think there's any chance you could stop pacing so we can figure this out?" Rook asked as Julia marched by her once again. She'd spent the last hour filling Julia in on everything Eric had found on Mitchell's network and she'd topped it off by tossing in her theory about Sharp.

"You're not allowed to come in here, ruin my day, and then tell me how I should react," Julia barked.

Rook didn't take the reaction personally. Every client was different, and her many years of friendship with Julia allowed her to be as frank as the situation demanded, so she barked back, "Dammit, Julia, sit down. We'll figure this out."

"Where's Major Granger and that other one, the guy, Donald? Davis?"

"Dixon," Rook supplied, stalling because she didn't want to admit she'd last seen Zoey tangled in her bed sheets. "I didn't include anyone from the Pentagon because you specifically asked me not to, remember?" She held up a hand as Julia started to speak. "And for the record, I don't think Major Granger is involved at all, but if we drag her in then Sharp may start to suspect she knows something."

"How can you be sure she's not involved?"

Rook scrambled for an answer, but it was easier than she thought. "Well, first off, she's been stationed overseas, which isn't definitive, I know, but it doesn't make sense with the pattern we're seeing. This agency targeted officers at the Pentagon. Their only deviation that we can see was the students from McNair, but I have a theory about that as well."

"Spill."

"Mitchell may have been instructed to compromise Donny Bloomfield to taint his father's nomination or gather blackmail material. Any chance you have Sharp on a backup list of nominees?"

"Great, so now the Russians are trying to pick our nominee for the Joint Chiefs?"

"I could be wrong about the McNair thing, but I'm certain I'm not wrong about Zoey."

Rook caught the slip the moment it fell from her lips, and she could tell by the sly smile on Julia's face that she did too. "Zoey, huh?"

"Don't even." Rook shook her head. "We've become...close. Trust me, Julia, she's not on the inside of this, and I haven't even shared my theory with her."

"I do trust you, but in a minute we're headed to the Oval to explain to the president and the head of the NSA what's going on. They're the ones who need to trust you because if you're right, all hell's about to break loose."

"Give me five minutes to check in with my team," Rook said, "and then I'll be ready to answer any questions you or anyone else has."

"Take the room. I'm going to do my pacing in the hall. The operator will connect you."

Rook called her office, and Lacy connected her directly to Eric. "Any luck on the email tracing?"

"No. It's going to take someone with a lot more infrastructure to break this chain."

"Well, I'm about to meet with the man in charge of the biggest spy network in the country. He should be able to help. Once we get the all clear, I'll put you in touch with his people and you can put your heads together." Without waiting for his response, she asked, "Is Blake back at the office?"

"Just walked in."

"Put her on." Rook did some pacing of her own, as much as the phone cord would allow, while she waited for Blake to come on the line.

"Hey, Rook"

"Did you find her?"

"Oh, I found her all right. Not in a very good mood, that one."

Alarm bells sound in Rook's head. "Care to elaborate?"

"She was still at your place, but I got the impression she misunderstood me showing up and letting myself in. Of course, she might just have been embarrassed that she was half-dressed when I walked in the door."

"Jeez, Blake, did you ever think of knocking?" Rook tried not to imagine what Zoey must have thought when Blake walked in like she owned the place.

"Sorry. I gave her the note, but she wouldn't read it while I was there. She refused a ride and she practically shoved me out the door. I hung around outside and picked up her tail."

"I asked you to deliver a note and offer her a ride, not spy on her." She took a breath and hated herself for her next question. "Where did she go?"

If Blake caught the incongruity of her question, she didn't let on. "She drove to a house in Vienna and about fifteen minutes later, she was in uniform and drove to the Pentagon. Once I saw her go past the guard gate, I headed back here."

More detail than she needed, but Rook was happy for it. Now if she only knew whether Zoey had read her note and would heed her warning about Sharp. When she hung up from Blake she stared at the phone. She could call Zoey and check in, but she didn't know anything about the phone system at the Pentagon and whether whoever answered the phone could stay on the line and listen in. A vague text would be better than an overheard call. She pulled her cell out of her pocket and cued up her text app to see she had a new text from Zoey. She read *WTF* and knew she was in for trouble, but by the last few words, she realized things were spinning out of control. She should have expected the fallout. After all, Sharp was Zoey's mentor. Springing the news the way she had had been thoughtless.

A text wasn't going to do. She needed to call Zoey and risk whatever happened. She picked up Julia's phone and had the operator connect her with the Pentagon. After a few connections, she finally reached a Lieutenant Louden who informed her that Major Granger wasn't in. She declined his invitation to leave a message as her mind sifted through possibilities for where Zoey could be since Blake had last seen her.

Before she could give it any further thought, Julia came back in. "Change of plans," she said.

"What's up?" Rook asked.

"Can't tell you, but President Garrett and I have to get to the situation room."

Rook went on high alert. "Related to this?"

"Something completely different." Julia pointed at the door. "One of the deputies from the NSA is coming in and you and your hacker are going to fill him in on everything you told me. He'll want copies of all the files you have, and when this is over, someone over there is getting fired because they didn't catch this before your guy did."

"Don't even think about trying to hire Eric." Rook had an idea. "I know you want me running point on this, but Eric really is better equipped to explain and it would be easier if the tech geeks talked one-on-one."

"You have somewhere you need to be?"

Rook considered a little white lie, but Julia had been her friend way longer than she'd been the White House chief of staff. "I'm a little worried about Major Granger—Zoey. Sharp has been a mentor to her, and I kind of sprung the information about his potential involvement abruptly. I need to go see her. Plus I want to make sure she doesn't talk to him until we figure out what to do next."

Julia cocked her head. "You really like this one, don't you?"

"It's not about that," Rook lied, hoping the warm blush curling up her neck wasn't showing.

"Right."

"Don't you have to be somewhere?"

Julia started back toward the door, but stopped before she left. "You know, I used to think I couldn't have it all, but look at me now. I'm in a relationship with the most amazing woman in the world, and I manage to make it work while running the country at the same time." She grinned. "A slacker like you should have it easy."

Julia was gone before Rook could shoot off a retort, leaving Rook to reflect before the NSA showed up. She knew Julia was kidding about the slacker part, but she'd been sincere about the rest of it. The short daydream Rook had had earlier about lying on a beach with Zoey came roaring back, but Rook realized for the first time she didn't want to share only fun and sun. She wanted to wake up in the same bed, discuss the day ahead over coffee at the kitchen table, share a ride to work—the little building blocks relationships were made of, and she wanted to share all of those things and more with Zoey.

❖

Zoey walked into her office and switched on the light. Only yesterday she'd let herself imagine this job was permanent, that she'd finally found a place to settle down—things that weeks ago she didn't even realize she wanted.

And then last night with Rook, the possibilities broadened further, opening the door to fantasies about making a home, having someone to share it with, being in love.

She'd been foolish. Foolish to believe her assignment here would be different from any other. Temporary and transient—those were the hallmarks of her existence, with her career the central core. Now even that was starting to fail her.

She'd read Rook's note a dozen times and still it didn't make sense. When had Rook uncovered this so-called information and why hadn't she shared it? And was Zoey really supposed to believe General Sharp was involved in a Russian spy ring? That was laughable. Rook was so used to representing reprehensible people, she'd either let her imagination run wild or she'd allowed her loathing for the military to bleed over into her work. Whatever the case, Zoey wasn't going to sit around and wait for something to happen. The best way to get to the bottom of a problem was to confront it head on. She left her office and headed for Sharp's.

The corridors still confused her, but she managed to shave some minutes off her usual time. When she arrived at the office suite, she practically ran into a captain who was rushing out the door. "The staff's all at Colonel Duncan's retirement breakfast," he called over his shoulder as his brisk strides carried him down the hall.

Zoey stood in the center of the quiet office space and contemplated her next move. Louden wasn't at his desk and Sharp's door was closed. For a brief moment, she considered backing away, but she decided to press on and risk interrupting, just in case Sharp was in. She raised her hand to knock on the door but stopped when she heard the raised voices within.

"She knows. It's only a matter of time before your cover is blown."

"If I go down, you go with me. Besides, you don't know the full extent of what she knows. It was your name on the recording, not mine."

A loud slam. "We can only hear half of what they're saying thanks to your slipshod listening device."

"We were lucky to get any information at all. The driver almost never leaves his car. Our agent only had a moment to place the device, and she had to do it with him watching her."

"Whatever. Your carelessness is going to get both of us arrested."

The last voice was Sharp's. Zoey was certain of that, and she was pretty sure the other voice was Louden's. Zoey leaned closer, careful not to make any noise. The conversation was riveting and strange and private, and she couldn't walk away without hearing more. She didn't have to wait long.

"What are you doing?" Sharp asked.

"I'm going to call her in, and you'll talk to her. She might not have talked to Daniels yet, but I want you to find out what she knows, and then we'll figure out what to do from there. Understood?"

Zoey played the words over in her mind until they tumbled into place, and she realized Louden was talking about her. She was the one they wanted to talk to and find out what she knew, and he was probably headed to his desk to call her. She stepped to the side just as the door opened and assumed what she hoped was a nonchalant expression, which wasn't easy considering her insides were frozen with fear. "Lieutenant," she said with a nod.

A flicker of surprise crossed his face before it molded into an icy stare. "Major Granger. Have you been waiting long?"

"Not too long," she answered. She needed to call someone and let them know what she'd just heard. Not just someone—Rook. She wished she could reach back through the data lines and grab back the text she'd sent this morning and replace it with another. One that said she trusted Rook and her judgment, trusted that the woman who'd spent the night making tender love to her wouldn't steer her wrong. She'd spent so much of her life relying on a team in her profession, but only on herself when it came to personal matters that she no longer knew when to draw a line and when to cross it. Determined to remedy that right now, she took a step toward the door. "It's not important. I have a meeting. I'll come back later."

She made it one more step before an iron fist clenched her arm. "You do have a meeting, Major. The general is inside waiting to see you. Please go on in."

Zoey contemplated her options, none of which were good. She could run for the door to the suite, but Louden's grip on her arm told her she wouldn't get far, or she could walk into the general's office and confront the man who she'd thought was her mentor. Rook was investigating Sharp. At some point, if Rook had hard evidence, she was going to tell someone else what was going on, and if they believed her, they might send someone to talk to Sharp. A lot of "ifs," but Zoey decided if she talked to Sharp now, it might buy Rook some time.

She walked into the office and found Sharp sitting behind his desk, but instead of his usual ruddy complexion and smile, she spotted worry lines crisscrossing his ashen face. "You wanted to see me, General?"

"Yes, Major. Have a seat." Zoey caught the two of them exchanging eye signals, which she assumed were meant to warn Sharp that she'd been lurking outside. Louden then abruptly announced he had to make a call and shut the door behind them.

"Do you have anything new to report?" Sharp asked.

Zoey stared at him, incredulous. Was he really going to pretend like she didn't know what was going on? "You're kidding, right?"

"Watch your tone, soldier."

She took a breath. She didn't care about obeying his orders, but she'd be more likely to get information out of him if she wasn't an ass about it. "Sorry, General. I do have a few questions." She had more than a few, starting with why a general was kowtowing to a lieutenant, but she started with something more subtle. "What do you know about Colonel Mitchell's background?"

Before he could answer, Louden burst back into the room and strode over to Sharp's desk where they engaged in a whispered conversation. Zoey eyed the door, but decided to stick with her original plan to stay and gather as much information as she could. She felt in her pocket for her cell phone and pulled it out far enough to see the screen. She set it to record and started to slide it back into her pocket, but stopped and opened the text app instead. She typed the words with one thumb, while stealing glances at Sharp and Louden. *In Sharps off. U were rt.* After she hit send, her thumb hovered above the keyboard. Having no idea where things would lead from here, she took a giant leap and she typed a new text—*luv u*—and hit send.

❖

Rook shouldered her way to the security window in the Pentagon lobby, ignoring the annoyed looks of people she'd pushed past. Eric had called while she was on the way here to tell her that the NSA had found additional information to implicate Sharp and they were in the process of "exploring their options," which probably meant getting a FISA warrant to pick him up and interrogate him on possible charges of espionage. Certain that if he was tipped off, he might do something desperate, she'd tried to call Zoey several times from outside the building, but she kept getting put through to voice mail.

"Major Granger isn't answering," the officer at the window announced. "Are you sure your appointment was for today, ma'am?"

Rather than explain she didn't actually have an appointment, Rook took a different tack. "Try Major Dixon." She fumbled through her wallet for his card and handed it to him. She tapped her foot while the officer dialed the line, and sighed with relief when she heard him talking to someone on the other end.

"She says she's supposed to meet Major Granger, but we can't reach her...Okay, I'll tell her. Hang on." The officer tapped on the window. "Major Dixon says he doesn't have an appointment with you either."

Rook stifled a nasty retort and reached through the opening. "I think there's been a misunderstanding. Let me talk to him."

"Can't do it, but I'll be happy to pass along a message."

"Tell him there's been a significant development in the case and I need to brief him. Tell him I just came from the White House." She listened to the officer convey her message, certain the message about the White House would pique Dixon's interest.

"Strike two. He said he's been reassigned, and you should get in touch with Major Granger."

Rook shook her head and started to walk away, but the officer's choice of words gave her an idea. "I get one more strike, right?" She grinned to try and win him over. "Try Major Jack Riley, Intelligence."

Her third swing was a hit and the officer handed her a badge and told her Major Riley would be down to get her shortly. Now that he was on his way, Rook had to think fast about how she was going to explain to Jack that his godfather might be committing treason.

He showed up quickly—not enough time for her to come up with a plausible cover. "Rook Daniels," he called out with a smile. "Last time I saw you, you were sipping ancient Scotch with my sister."

She managed to return his smile. "Pretty sure you were right there with us."

"What can I do for you?"

"I need to find Major Zoey Granger and she's not answering her phone."

"Maybe she's not here?"

"She is." Rook felt a growing sense of urgency and she knew her explanation—I know she's here because my ex-CIA operative employee followed her here—wasn't likely to garner his assistance. "It's imperative that I see her. It's a matter of national security," she said, knowing that last statement was just slightly less crazy than the other explanation.

He stared at her, puzzled, and then shook his head. "All right then, let's go find her."

Ten minutes later, they were standing in the doorway of Zoey's empty office. Jack walked in and looked around, picking up a cup of coffee on her desk, and placing his hands around it. "It's still warm, so she probably hasn't gone far."

"I think I know where she is, but before we go looking, I need to tell you something."

"Sounds ominous."

"It is." Rook motioned for him to take a seat, dreading what she was about to say, but focused on getting it out as quickly as possible. She started with the review of Mitchell's coded emails and ended with the news she'd just received about the NSA investigation, taking the time to answer his careful, pointed questions. When she told him everything she knew, she finished with, "I know he's your godfather and maybe this is all a big mistake, but if it is, then the faster we can clear it up the better, right?"

"Julia knows all about this?"

"Yes. She's briefed the president and the director of the NSA. To tell you the truth, this is probably all code-word clearance now and neither one of us should know about it, but I need your help to find Zoey." She started to correct that to Major Granger, but decided she no longer cared about pretending her relationship with Zoey wasn't personal. "Will you help me?"

She watched a parade of emotions cross his face, but ultimately it was stoic expression of the dedicated soldier that won out. "Yes."

Sharp's office suite was a brisk five-minute walk away, and when they entered, a sense of dread settled over Rook. No one was seated at the desk outside the door to Sharp's office, but they could hear raised voices from within. She and Jack lined up on either side of the door and she heard a male voice she didn't recognize saying, "She's trying to send a text. Why didn't you take her phone?" followed by Zoey's voice shouting, "Give that back to me, right now!"

Rook reached for the door handle, but Jack pushed her back, placing a finger over his lips. She nodded that she understood, but willed him to hurry up, and when he jerked the door open and burst into the room, she was right on his heels.

"Jack!" Sharp called out. "What are you doing here?"

While he was focused on Jack, Rook surveyed the room. Sharp was seated at his desk, and the other guy, the lieutenant, who'd escorted her to Zoey's office the first day they'd worked together, was standing beside Zoey who was seated in a chair across from Sharp's desk. If they hadn't heard the loud voices, the tableau would seem perfectly innocent, and Rook wondered if she'd overreacted. "Zoey, are you okay?"

Zoey grabbed her phone out of the lieutenant's hand and nearly toppled the chair to get away from him. "I am now. We need to get DCIS in here right now."

"Major Granger is under a great deal of stress," Sharp said in a commanding tone to no one in particular. "We were just discussing ways to make things easier on her. It was too much to ask her to work on this McNair thing so soon after the Nine Tech debacle. I'm thinking a short leave is in order, right, Major?"

Rook watched Zoey for her reaction and Zoey looked her directly in the eyes. "I think Major Granger might be taking a leave," Rook said, "But only because she deserves it for her act of heroism in uncovering your act of treason. The NSA should be here shortly." She reached for Zoey's hand and pulled her to the door. "I need to make some calls. Jack, you got this?"

"Yes, ma'am," he replied, pulling up a chair right next to Sharp.

Rook and Zoey were standing in the doorway when Zoey whipped her head around. "Where's Louden?"

Rook looked around. "I didn't see him leave. Is he part of this?"

"Yes," Zoey said. "I don't know the specifics, but he's definitely involved."

"On it," Jack called out. He picked up the phone on Sharp's desk. "This is General Sharp's office. We need to initiate a lockdown. General Sharp's assistant, Lieutenant Louden, has gone AWOL. Presume that he's armed and dangerous, but he needs to be apprehended alive. Send DCIS to Sharp's office pronto."

Satisfied Jack had the general under control, Rook led Zoey from the room, determined to put some distance between her and her traitorous boss. Rook tucked her arm around Zoey. "I guess we can't leave the building right now. Do you want to wait here or back in your office?"

"I don't know. I'm sorry, Rook. I should've listened to you."

Rook placed a finger on her lips. "It's okay. I shouldn't have sent Blake to give you the bad news. Are you sure you're okay?"

"I will be. There's probably going to be a shit storm to wade through first."

"You're probably right about that." Rook motioned for Zoey to have a seat at Louden's desk, and she took a deep breath as Julia's words from earlier echoed through her head. *You really like this one.* Not quite accurate. Maybe it was the knowledge that Zoey had been in danger or the rising emotion from this whole situation, but Rook was certain what she felt for Zoey was way past like, and she wanted to bring to life her fantasies about sharing everyday moments with her. This wasn't the time or the place, but they had a few minutes alone and she had to know if Zoey felt the same way. "We need to talk."

"We will, but not now." Zoey hung her head. "Sharp was like a father to me and he's been spying for the Russians for God knows how long. How could I be so stupid?" Her voice shook. "I'm not cut out for this."

Rook wanted to ask if "this" included her, but she was scared of the answer. Zoey was grieving a loss, and she had to let her be no matter how much she wanted to discuss things between them. Before she could form a suitable reply, her phone buzzed with the sound of an incoming text. She checked the screen and saw a text from Zoey. *In Sharps off. U were rt.* She laughed and held her phone where Zoey could see. "If I'd gotten this message earlier, I would've known for sure you were in trouble. Abbreviated words, barely any punctuation—so unlike you."

Zoey smiled. "You try texting under duress without looking at the screen and see what happens. To be honest, I didn't think there was a chance it would go through, but I had to try."

Rook reached over and squeezed her hand. "I'm glad you're okay. I don't know what I would've done if—" Her phone buzzed again, saving her from speaking out loud the unthinkable, that Zoey might not have been rescued. She took it as an omen, and rather than finishing her sentence, she looked at the phone which was sitting on the desk between them.

"Oh, Rook," Zoey's voice was strained and low. "About that…"

Her words trailed off, but it didn't matter because Rook was no longer listening, her entire focus trained on the second text Zoey had sent. Two simple words—*Luv u*—and at the sight of them, Rook's heart pounded, her chest tightened, and heat surged through her.

This. This was the tipping point. The signal that her growing feelings for Zoey were mutual, and it was up to her to make the next move. But Zoey's hesitancy, the edge in her voice, and the fact she'd pulled her hand away, forced Rook to recalculate.

She studied the message. The spelling was casual, juvenile even, but by her own admission, Zoey had been under duress. But she'd taken the time to send the message. It had to be true, right? Or had duress, not love, been her sole motivator? Rook knew better than most that people said all kinds of things in the heat of the moment, not all of them true.

She looked up into Zoey's eyes, knowing she'd find answers there, and she wasn't wrong. Reflected back at her was true affection, but it was mixed with a healthy dose of regret, which didn't bode well as building blocks for the future.

A loud crash startled them both, and Rook jerked her head around, looking for the source of the sound. Louden lurched out from behind a file cabinet, heading toward them. She stared, unable to move, and Zoey grabbed her, pulled her out of the way, and ran toward Louden. Rook yelled for her to stop, but Zoey's arm was already in motion and she landed a punch square on Louden's face, knocking him to the ground.

Rook ran to her side. "Are you okay?" But Zoey didn't answer, instead pointing to where Louden lay, his face red and his body wracking with uncontrollable seizures. As Louden thrashed on the floor in front of them, the door to the corridor flew open and armed soldiers burst in yelling for them all to hit the deck.

Chapter Twenty-one

Zoey heard the call to attention and stood ramrod straight waiting for the rest of the ceremony to begin. There was a time, when she was a young soldier, that standing in this position for any length of time had been an almost intolerable burden, every thought a distraction, every fluttering breeze a tickle designed to make her feel like she was coming out of her skin, but she'd learned to welcome the peace and serenity of having nothing more to do than stand still. In the calm she was able to dig deep and push out all distractions. She used to joke that standing at attention was like military yoga.

Not today. Today, a week after she'd watched Lieutenant Louden, a Soviet agent, take his own life with a cyanide pill after she'd confronted his asset, she was acutely conscious of her surroundings.

Normally, a promotion ceremony would be conducted on base and the full company would be in attendance. But today she would receive her silver leaf in the Rose Garden at the White House, in the presence of less than a dozen people, and the person doing the pinning wouldn't be her mentor, but a man she'd only met a few weeks ago.

When General Bloomfield called her name, she broke her formation of one and walked toward him. Then and only then did she glance into the audience, seeking out the one face she truly wanted to see. Rook was behind and to the left of the general, looking as dashing as she had the first time Zoey had seen her. Dressed in a jet-black suit with a royal blue shirt, Rook sat with her legs crossed, leaning back in her chair, looking completely at ease here in the center of power.

They'd had only casual contact over the past week. Both of them had been debriefed extensively by several federal agencies, and Rook had traveled to New York for Farah Hamil's mayoral candidacy kickoff event. When she and Rook had spoken, they'd both danced around the subject of anything more than the next conversation, the next meal, and they certainly hadn't talked about their uncomfortable scene outside of Sharp's office.

Zoey knew the lack of connection was mostly her fault, if fault was even the right word. Sharp had been right about one thing. She was suffering from a bit of trauma and was still reeling from the one-two punch of having to turn in peers for fraud, and then finding out her mentor was a kept asset of the KGB and had been for years. The system she'd spent her life to support had failed her miserably, and she wasn't sure of her place in it anymore. If she wasn't sure about the rest of her life, she knew for certain she had no business making promises to Rook she didn't know if she could keep.

The reception following the ceremony seemed elaborate, considering Zoey was the only officer who'd been promoted, but she supposed the general's presence was a key reason the White House was putting on a show. Bloomfield had announced his retirement the day before and pledged to help the president find an unimpeachable candidate to serve as Head of the Joint Chiefs. Although nothing about the investigation so far implicated Bloomfield in the scandal, he felt responsible for not knowing his deputy was engaged in espionage and, according to Julia, he'd stated his oversight as the reason for his retirement. Zoey was sad to see him go, but she respected him for his decision.

"I haven't been to many of these, but usually the person being promoted looks happier," Rook said, handing her a glass of champagne.

Zoey reached for the glass and let her fingers linger over Rook's for a moment, wondering if the heat between them would ever fade.

She met Rook's hopeful expression and wished she could return it with one of her own, but she was leaving and Rook's life was here with the clients whose controversies demanded her attention. If she couldn't have Rook, Zoey wanted a mission, a 24/7 distraction from the outside world, preferably in a desolate foreign country where there was no possibility she would be in the public eye. "Sorry, I am happy for the promotion, but conflicted about what's next."

"What *is* next? Although before you answer, you should know there's a rule that if you save someone's life, you have to spend the rest of your life at their side to protect them from further harm."

Zoey smiled. "I'm pretty sure that's just in the movies, but even so, I didn't save your life. Louden must've bitten down on the cyanide pill the minute he left Sharp's office. The poison takes a few minutes to take effect."

Rook waved a hand in the air. "Don't confuse the issue with science. Seriously, you charged that guy and punched him in the face. Pretty damn impressive. I heard Bloomfield is making sure you get whatever assignment you want." She lowered her voice to a whisper. "So what is next for you, Colonel?"

"I asked for deployment." Zoey blurted out the words, hoping rushing the news would make it less painful for both of them. "I can do the most good when I'm in the field."

Rook's smile vanished. "How many times have you been deployed? Don't you think it's someone else's turn to risk their lives for their country?"

Zoey uttered a silent curse for her insensitivity. Of course Rook was thinking about Rory. She injected her voice with what she hoped was a soft, comforting tone. "I'm in logistics, not combat. No real danger there."

"You're smart enough to know there's always danger."

"Maybe, but it's the kind I can handle, not the back-biting controversies that swirl around in this town."

"Sounds like it's me and my work you want to get away from."

"Look over there." Zoey pointed across the room at the press corps lining up waiting to catch photos. "I'm supposed to talk to them later so they can all write stories about the fresh faced soldier, new to the Pentagon who punched out a Soviet spy, while helping blow the lid off a major scandal. The headlines won't be accurate, the stories will only contain the most sensational details, and they will all gloss over the careers that were compromised along the way. That's what I want to get away from."

"What about the text you sent me from Sharp's office?" Rook said, her voice shaking. "You said you love me."

"I did. I do, but when I sent that…" Zoey grappled for the right words to explain she'd sent the message in the heat of the moment, without considering the consequences. She certainly hadn't factored in the poor cell signal that caused the message to show up after the danger had passed. "I didn't think, I didn't know…"

Rook finished for her. "You didn't know if you'd ever see me again. So it was like a good-bye."

"I guess so. Yes." Zoey sagged with relief that Rook understood, but at the same time sadness washed over her at the thought of saying good-bye to Rook. Nevertheless, she had to do it. She couldn't straddle Rook's world and hers. "Please tell me you understand."

"I can't, but I don't suppose that matters." Rook raised her glass and her smile was forced. "It was a pleasure knowing you, Colonel Granger."

She touched her glass to Zoey's, took a drink, and walked away. Zoey stood, torn between chasing after Rook, and standing her ground. Before she could decide, General Bloomfield appeared at her side.

"Colonel, may I have a word with you?" he asked, effectively making the choice for her.

Duty called and she'd pledged her life to it. Someday Rook would understand or maybe she'd just forget her. Zoey wasn't sure which one she wanted most.

❖

Rook sat across from Julia's desk and pretended to listen to her fill in the final details of the investigation into General David Sharp, but she was distracted by thoughts of when Julia had first called her here and she'd learned she'd be working the case with Zoey.

"Are you listening to a word I'm saying?" Julia asked, her raised voice cutting through Rook's thoughts.

"I heard you. Sharp was a Russian spy. I thought you'd already figured that part out."

"Yes, but we didn't know why. Contel," she said, referring to the attorney general, "agreed to offer Sharp a life sentence in exchange for a full accounting of all the leaks he's been responsible for over the years. Aren't you the slightest bit interested?"

"Sure." She wasn't, but she knew Julia didn't want to hear that. Rook hadn't been interested in much of anything since she and Zoey had parted at the reception following Zoey's promotion ceremony over a week ago. Since then she'd started, but hadn't sent, over a dozen texts to implore Zoey to reconsider her decision to go overseas, but every time she was paralyzed by doubt.

Maybe she just needed to focus on something else to take her mind off wondering about Zoey. "Tell me everything."

"Turns out the alleged act of heroism that got Sharp the Medal of Honor was the same thing that got him caught up with the Russians," Julia said. "The KGB had officers in Grenada at the time of the US invasion, and one of them witnessed what really happened when Sharp's squad was attacked. Sharp threw an injured man, one of his own, into the line of fire to avoid being hit himself. He may have actually saved them all in the end, but only because he sacrificed one of them to save himself. Hardly a hero."

"So what, the Russians blackmailed him?"

"Exactly. They waited until after he received the medal and then started sending him messages. They had photos seized from local journalists and alleged witness accounts that they threatened to release if he didn't work with them. Who knows if they really had any evidence, but apparently, he believed they did and that was enough. A better man would have faced the consequences of his actions, but he worked with them over the years, providing mostly small bits of intel to various Soviet spies. They were careful to keep it small until lately when he was poised to either be the right hand of the Head of the Joint Chiefs or be the nominee himself."

"And Louden?" Rook asked. "How did he fit in?"

"We may never know everything, but it appears he was a sleeper agent, activated to work Sharp as an asset once Sharp was assigned to the Pentagon."

"Unbelievable. And most of this information will never see the light of day, correct?" Rook asked.

"Not for a long time. The files have been ordered classified. The *Post* is no longer interested in the McNair sex scandal since Bloomfield is retiring, so we dodged a bullet there."

"Is this the part where you try to get out of paying me because you don't need me to spin the story?"

Julia leaned forward. "Actually, this is the part where we play let's make a deal. Would you like to collect your fee for this case or see what's behind door number two?"

Rook felt a surge of anticipation at the prospect of a new case, but her excitement was tempered with apprehension. But she quickly realized she was being silly. What were the chances whatever Julia was proposing involved another beautiful woman in uniform who'd steal her heart? Still, she proceeded with caution. "I'm willing to hear you out. That's the best I can do."

"Fine. I want you to come work with me."

"Didn't we just do that?"

"I'm thinking of something a little more permanent. We've been rocking along without a communications director since Timmons retired. The president hasn't been happy with any of the names I've floated for consideration until I happened to mention yours. You'd be doing me a big favor."

Rook's mind started spinning in a dozen different directions. "A few things come to mind starting with, working for you would hardly be permanent since you only have a few more years left until you're all out of here."

"Exactly my point." Julia started talking faster. "When you're done here you can go back to fixing things for regular people, but in the meantime, your team can handle your current clients. Turn the firm over to them and come work with us. You'll be in charge of crafting the official White House message for everything from climate change to the economy to civil rights. When we're done, you can start another firm or whatever else you want. You'll be able to write your own ticket."

"Stop." Rook played back Julia's pitch in her head and examined every crazy word of her proposal. But was it really that crazy? She had been grooming her team to take the lead on her cases and she was growing weary of pulling people out of the holes they'd dug with their own stupidity. Granted, the White House had its share of those, but this second-term, well-liked president had an aggressive, progressive agenda, and the job Julia was offering meant she'd have the opportunity to be a part of some major change-making. "You don't need to sell it anymore, but you do need to give me time to think about it."

"Fair enough," Julia said, raising her hands in surrender. "I promise not to call you until tomorrow."

Rook stood. "Then I'm getting out of here now so I can have some peace between now and then."

"Wait, there's something else." Julia reached into her desk and pulled out a folder. She slid it across the desk, but kept a hand on it. "The president declassified this report this morning. The official declassification won't go into effect for a few weeks, but counsel said we could provide you, as a family member, with an advance copy."

Rook's hand shook as she reached for the file. "Is this what I think it is?"

"It's the full report regarding your brother's death. I'm warning you that shit may hit the fan when the news comes out because a certain pro athlete who left a lucrative NBA contract to enlist was involved. Of course, there's also a chance no one else will think to request it." She placed her hand over Rook's. "I'm truly sorry that the circumstances were kept from you."

"Why now?" Rook paused, trying to figure out what was bugging her. "And how did you know?"

"You can thank Colonel Granger. She contacted me specifically to ask."

"I would thank her, but I don't know where she is." Rook had considered several times using Eric's skills to find out, but a stubborn part of her said that if Zoey had wanted her to know she would've told her, and at this point a text or phone call seemed so hollow and possibly pointless if Zoey was already overseas.

She'd even gone so far as to have George drive her to Zoey's house in Vienna. When Zoey didn't answer, she'd peered through the front window only to see stacks of boxes sitting in a room with no furniture. Clearly, Zoey had already deployed or she was getting ready to, and either way, she'd moved on.

"She's at McNair," Julia said.

"What?" Rook was certain she'd misunderstood.

"She took a teaching position at the college. She started this week."

Rook reeled at the news. Zoey was working in DC, not at a base overseas. A permanent job only miles away. "Okay then."

"What's that supposed to mean?"

"I don't know."

"A minute ago when I said she was at McNair, your whole face lit up, but now you look like someone stole a client from you," Julia said. "I thought you liked this one."

"Like doesn't begin to cover it."

"Then what's the problem?"

What was the problem? Rook circled through all the possible responses. Zoey hated the work she did. Zoey was still in the military. There was more, but most rang hollow. "She told me she loved me, but then she took it back." Not entirely true, but close.

Julia sighed. "You sound like a twelve-year-old. What did you do when she told you? Did you say it back?"

Rook started to explain that when Zoey said it, she'd been in the middle of a high stress situation, that by the time she received the text she was no longer sure Zoey still meant the words.

But if she loved Zoey, why hadn't she taken the time to tell her how she felt? She'd had plenty of opportunities during the days after Sharp had been arrested. She could've said the words at the reception when she'd asked Zoey to stay.

Julia was right. She was acting like a child—insecure about admitting her feelings until she knew they'd be returned. When Zoey had made it clear she was leaving, Rook had crawled back into her comfortable world of no personal commitments. But it wasn't comfortable anymore, and it never would be again now that she'd had a glimpse of what could be. If she'd had the courage to tell Zoey the depth of her feelings, would Zoey have given them a chance?

There was only one way to find out. Rook grabbed the file from Julia's desk and headed for the door. "I'll let you know what I decide," she called out as she left, but she already knew exactly what she had planned, and for the first time in her life, it had nothing to do with work.

❖

Zoey reminded the class about the reading assignment and dismissed them exactly on the hour. When the last student left the room, she sat behind her desk and drank in the quiet, finding she liked it much more than she could have ever imagined.

The professorship had been General Bloomfield's suggestion after he politely denied her request for a deployment. "You've done your part," he'd said, echoing the words Rook had spoken at the reception after her promotion ceremony. "Now share what you've learned with other officers."

He'd insisted, and she'd agreed. The fact was, the idea of going back to a base—even one overseas—after her face had been in every paper and cable news channel was distasteful. And there was no way she was working in the Pentagon again. Her early career dreams of moving up the ranks were the product of naiveté, and she'd been clueless about the collateral consequences advancement would have on her psyche.

So now she taught the logistics she'd learned in the field, along with ethics, to officers at a war college. They'd go on to apply the lessons she'd learned and she would have the space and time to explore having a personal life. Once she got over Rook Daniels—not an easy feat since Rook's face showed up in the news almost daily. She'd considered calling several times, but nothing had really changed. Classroom or not, she was still a soldier and Rook still thrived on the kind of public controversy Zoey struggled to avoid.

"You look good behind that desk."

Zoey stared at the doorway, unable to believe her eyes. "I was just thinking about you." The honest words tumbled out.

Rook stepped into the room. "Word is you've abandoned the front lines for the classroom."

"It's true. I might have been strong-armed a little, but I'm kind of liking it."

"I'm glad."

Rook's voice was soft and low, and Zoey wanted to wrap up in its warmth. The distance she'd placed between them dissolved. Seeing Rook standing here, close enough to touch, made the wall she'd erected between them seem like a stepping stone. She stood and walked toward her. "I'm glad you're here."

Rook smiled. "There's a lot of glad between us." She shifted in place. "Julia gave me a copy of Rory's file this morning. She tells me I have you to thank."

"I knew it was important to you."

"It is, but I'm learning that I don't always know what's most important to me until I've let it slip away."

Zoey reached for Rook's hand and laced their fingers. "I walked away, not you."

"You didn't walk very far."

"I know." Zoey willed Rook to hear the subtle acknowledgement of hope in her voice.

"But I let you and maybe that's what you wanted," Rook said. "Maybe it's what you still want, but I had to come here and tell you that I love you. I love you and I want to see if we can make a life together. And if it means I need to change what I do for a living, then—"

Zoey leaned in and kissed Rook, brushing her lips softly at first, but then claiming her with hard strokes of her tongue to send a sure signal she no longer second-guessed the depth of her feelings. When they broke for air, the words came rushing out. "I love you too." Zoey jabbed a finger at Rook's heart. "You. And whatever you decide to do with your life won't change that as long as I can be by your side." She pulled Rook's hand and pointed to the door. "Now, let's go make a life together."

THE END

About the Author

Carsen Taite's goal as an author is to spin tales with plot lines as interesting as the cases she encountered in her career as a criminal defense lawyer. She is the award-winning author of numerous novels of romance and romantic intrigue, including the Luca Bennett Bounty Hunter series and the Lone Star Law series.

Books Available from Bold Strokes Books

Change in Time by Robyn Nyx. Working in the past is hell on your future. The Extractor series: Book Two. (978-1-62639-880-1)

Love After Hours by Radclyffe. When Gina Antonelli agrees to renovate Carrie Longmire's new house, she doesn't welcome Carrie's overtures at friendship or her own unexpected attraction. A Rivers Community Novel. (978-1-63555-090-0)

Nantucket Rose by CF Frizzell. Maggie Jordan can't wait to convert an historic Nantucket home into a B&B, but doesn't expect to fall for mariner Ellis Chilton, who has more claim to the house than Maggie realizes. (978-1-63555-056-6)

Picture Perfect by Lisa Moreau. Falling in love wasn't supposed to be part of the stakes for Olive and Gabby, rival photographers in the competition of a lifetime. (978-1-62639-975-4)

Set the Stage by Karis Walsh. Actress Emilie Danvers takes the stage again in Ashland, Oregon, little realizing that landscaper Arden Philips is about to offer her a very personal romantic lead role. (978-1-63555-087-0)

Strike a Match by Fiona Riley. When their attempts at matchmaking fizzle out, firefighter Sasha and reluctant millionairess Abby find themselves turning to each other to strike a perfect match. (978-1-62639-999-0)

The Price of Cash by Ashley Bartlett. Cash Braddock is doing her best to keep her business afloat, stay out of jail, and avoid Detective Kallen. It's not working. (978-1-62639-708-8)

Under Her Wing by Ronica Black. At Angel's Wings Rescue, dogs are usually the ones saved, but when quiet Kassandra Haden meets outspoken owner Jayden Beaumont, the two stubborn women just might end up saving each other. (978-1-63555-077-1)

Underwater Vibes by Mickey Brent. When Hélène, a translator in Brussels, Belgium, meets Sylvie, a young Greek photographer and swim coach, unsettling feelings hijack Hélène's mind and body—even her poems. (978-1-63555-002-3)

A More Perfect Union by Carsen Taite. Major Zoey Granger and DC fixer Rook Daniels risk their reputations for a chance at true love while dealing with a scandal that threatens to rock the military. (978-1-62639-754-5)

Arrival by Gun Brooke. The spaceship *Pathfinder* reaches its passengers' new homeworld where danger lurks in the shadows while Pamas Seclan disembarks and finds unexpected love in young science genius Darmiya Do Voy. (978-1-62639-859-7)

Captain's Choice by VK Powell. Architect Kerstin Anthony's life is going to plan until Bennett Carlyle, the first girl she ever kissed, is assigned to her latest and most important project, a police district substation. (978-1-62639-997-6)

Falling Into Her by Erin Zak. Pam Phillips, widow at the age of forty, meets Kathryn Hawthorne, local Chicago celebrity, and it changes her life forever—in ways she hadn't even considered possible. (978-1-63555-092-4)

Hookin' Up by MJ Williamz. Will Leah get what she needs from casual hookups or will she see the love she desires right in front of her? (978-1-63555-051-1)

King of Thieves by Shea Godfrey. When art thief Casey Marinos meets bounty hunter Finnegan Starkweather, the crimes of the past just might set the stage for a payoff worth more than she ever dreamed possible. (978-1-63555-007-8)

Lucy's Chance by Jackie D. As a serial killer haunts the streets, Lucy tries to stitch up old wounds with her first love in the wake of a small town's rapid descent into chaos. (978-1-63555-027-6)

Right Here, Right Now by Georgia Beers. When Alicia Wright moves into the office next door to Lacey Chamberlain's accounting firm, Lacey is about to find out that sometimes the last person you want is exactly the person you need. (978-1-63555-154-9)

Strictly Need to Know by MB Austin. Covert operator Maji Rios will do whatever she must to complete her mission, but saving a gorgeous stranger from Russian mobsters was not in her plans. (978-1-63555-114-3)

Tailor-Made by Yolanda Wallace. Tailor Grace Henderson doesn't date clients, but when she meets gender-bending model Dakota Lane, she's tempted to throw all the rules out the window. (978-1-63555-081-8)

Time Will Tell by M. Ullrich. With the ability to time travel, Eva Caldwell will have to decide between having it all and erasing it all. (978-1-63555-088-7)

A Date to Die by Anne Laughlin. Someone is killing people close to Detective Kay Adler, who must look to her own troubled past for a suspect. There she finds more than one person seeking revenge against her. (978-1-63555-023-8)

Captured Soul by Laydin Michaels. Can Kadence Munroe save the woman she loves from a twisted killer, or will she lose her to a collector of souls? (978-1-62639-915-0)

Dawn's New Day by TJ Thomas. Can Dawn Oliver and Cam Cooper, two women who have loved and lost, open their hearts to love again? (978-1-63555-072-6)

Definite Possibility by Maggie Cummings. Sam Miller is just out for good times, but Lucy Weston makes her realize happily ever after is a definite possibility. (978-1-62639-909-9)

Eyes Like Those by Melissa Brayden. Isabel Chase and Taylor Andrews struggle between love and ambition from the writers' room on one of Hollywood's hottest TV shows. (978-1-63555-012-2)

Heart's Orders by Jaycie Morrison. Helen Tucker and Tee Owens escape hardscrabble lives to careers in the Women's Army Corps, but more than their hearts are at risk as friendship blossoms into love. (978-1-63555-073-3)

Hiding Out by Kay Bigelow. Treat Dandridge is unaware that her life is in danger from the murderer who is hunting the woman she's falling in love with, Mickey Heiden. (978-1-62639-983-9)

Omnipotence Enough by Sophia Kell Hagin. Can the tiny tool that abducted war veteran Jamie Gwynmorgan accidentally acquires help her escape an unknown enemy to reclaim her stolen life and the woman she deeply loves? (978-1-63555-037-5)

Summer's Cove by Aurora Rey. Emerson Lange moved to Provincetown to live in the moment, but when she meets Darcy Belo and her son Liam, her quest for summer romance becomes a family affair. (978-1-62639-971-6)

The Road to Wings by Julie Tizard. Lieutenant Casey Tompkins, air force student pilot, has to fly with the toughest instructor, Captain Kathryn "Hard Ass" Hardesty, fly a supersonic jet, and deal with a growing forbidden attraction. (978-1-62639-988-4)

Beauty and the Boss by Ali Vali. Ellis Renois is at the top of the fashion world, but she never expects her summer assistant Charlotte Hamner to tear her heart and her business apart like sharp scissors through cheap material. (978-1-62639-919-8)

Fury's Choice by Brey Willows. When gods walk amongst humans, can two women find a balance between love and faith? (978-1-62639-869-6)

Lessons in Desire by MJ Williamz. Can a summer love stand a four-month hiatus and still burn hot? (978-1-63555-019-1)

Lightning Chasers by Cass Sellars. For Sydney and Parker, being a couple was never what they had planned. Now they have to fight corruption, murder, and enemies hiding in plain sight just to hold on to each other. Lightning Series, Book Two. (978-1-62639-965-5)

Summer Fling by Jean Copeland. Still jaded from a breakup years earlier, Kate struggles to trust falling in love again when a summer fling with sexy young singer Jordan rocks her off her feet. (978-1-62639-981-5)

Take Me There by Julie Cannon. Adrienne and Sloan know it would be career suicide to mix business with pleasure, however tempting it is. But what's the harm? They're both consenting adults. Who would know? (978-1-62639-917-4)

The Girl Who Wasn't Dead by Samantha Boyette. A year ago, someone tried to kill Jenny Lewis. Tonight she's ready to find out who it was. (978-1-62639-950-1)

Unchained Memories by Dena Blake. Can a woman give herself completely when she's left a piece of herself behind? (978-1-62639-993-8)

Walking Through Shadows by Sheri Lewis Wohl. All Molly wanted to do was go backpacking…in her own century. (978-1-62639-968-6)

A Lamentation of Swans by Valerie Bronwen. Ariel Montgomery returns to Sea Oats to try to save her broken marriage but soon finds herself also fighting to save her own life and catch a murderer. (978-1-62639-828-3)

Freedom to Love by Ronica Black. What happens when the woman who spent her lifetime worrying about caring for her family, finally finds the freedom to love without borders? (978-1-63555-001-6)

House of Fate by Barbara Ann Wright. Two women must throw off the lives they've known as a guardian and an assassin and save two rival houses before their secrets tear the galaxy apart. (978-1-62639-780-4)

Planning for Love by Erin Dutton. Could true love be the one thing that wedding coordinator Faith McKenna didn't plan for? (978-1-62639-954-9)

Sidebar by Carsen Taite. Judge Camille Avery and her clerk, attorney West Fallon, agree on little except their mutual attraction, but can their relationship and their careers survive a headline-grabbing case? (978-1-62639-752-1)

Sweet Boy and Wild One by T. L. Hayes. When Rachel Cole meets soulful singer Bobby Layton at an open mic, she is immediately in thrall. What she soon discovers will rock her world in ways she never imagined. (978-1-62639-963-1)

To Be Determined by Mardi Alexander and Laurie Eichler. Charlie Dickerson escapes her life in the US to rescue Australian wildlife with Pip Atkins, but can they save each other? (978-1-62639-946-4)

True Colors by Yolanda Wallace. Blogger Robby Rawlins plans to use First Daughter Taylor Crenshaw to get ahead, but she never planned on falling in love with her in the process. (978-1-62639-927-3)

Unexpected by Jenny Frame. When Dale McGuire falls for Rebecca Harper, the mother of the son she never knew she had, will Rebecca's troubled past stop them from making the family they both truly crave? (978-1-62639-942-6)